# ON THE

## *Way*

## TO

## *You*

# KANDI STEINER

Published by Kandi Steiner
Edited by Elaine York/Allusion Graphics, LLC/ Publishing & Book Formatting, www.allusiongraphics.com
Cover Photography by Perrywinkle Photography
Cover Design by Kandi Steiner
Formatting by Elaine York/Allusion Graphics, LLC/ Publishing & Book Formatting, www.allusiongraphics.com

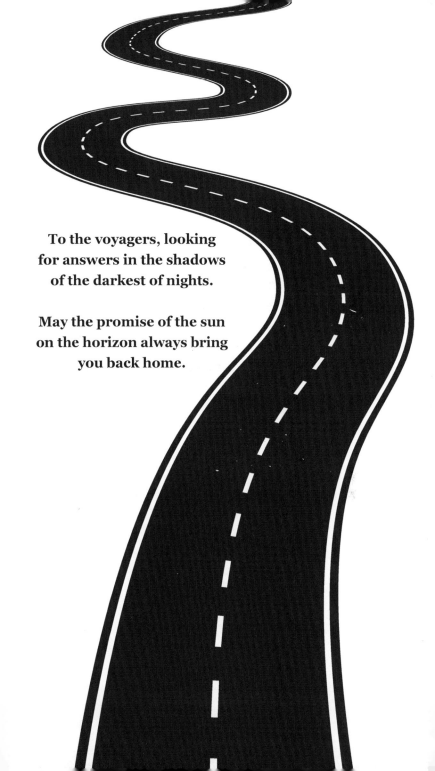

To the voyagers, looking
for answers in the shadows
of the darkest of nights.

May the promise of the sun
on the horizon always bring
you back home.

*What makes you happy?*

Those were the words he said to me the day I met him. He asked me a simple question, one I should have been able to answer easily. There were plenty of answers, after all.

My books made me happy, and my dog, Kalo, made me happy, too. Yoga made me happy. The way the sun always manages to come back, no matter how dark the storm, made me happy. I was the happiest girl in the world.

Or so I thought.

That day had started just like any other. I woke up with the sun, dragging my yoga mat out of my closet with a yawn to start my Friday. I fed Kalo and took her for a walk, ate breakfast alone, and checked to see if my parents were still alive. Referring to them as my "parents" is kind of a stretch, though, because that would imply they did some kind of parenting. In reality, I'd been taking care of myself since I was old enough to pour my own cereal. I was still amazed I'd managed to make it to see my twentieth birthday.

Daryl, my father, had made it to work by some miracle that Friday morning and was already gone by the time I was packing up my backpack to head to work. Cindy, my mother, was doped up but breathing, which was a win in my book. She was sprawled out on the old, dingy, sunken-in couch in the living room of our trailer, and I didn't say a word to wake her before I pushed through the creaky metal door and out into the fresh Alabama air.

Well, it *would* have been fresh, if we didn't live in the Longleaf Pine trailer park.

Still, I had a smile on my face as the morning dew settled on my skin. With one last wave at Kalo, who was looking at me through the hole in my bedroom blinds, I hopped on my bike and started the short ten-minute bike ride to Papa Wyatt's Diner, the restaurant I'd called home ever since I could remember, and my place of employment since I was sixteen.

"I hate Alabama," Tammy said as soon as I pushed my bike through the front door to a chime from the small bell above. Orange and black streamers hung from the door frame, each of them sticking to my forehead a bit as I passed by. Sweat was snaking its way from my damp hair down the back of my collared uniform shirt, finding a rather uncomfortable home where the sun doesn't shine, but it didn't matter.

Alabama was hot, but Papa Wyatt's Diner was exactly the same as it was every day. I found comfort in that, in the fact that I was able to work there at all, to get out of my house and do what I needed to do to make ends meet. I had plans to get out of Mobile, and I was so close to making it happen I could taste it.

"No, not you!" I joked with a feigned shock face as Tammy helped me situate my bike in the back storage closet. "I just can't imagine you hating *anything,* Tammy."

She glared at me, hands hanging on her hips. "It's Halloween and it still feels like the inside of a sweaty jock strap out there. Fall doesn't exist in this town."

"Well, I can't argue with that," I said, a longing sigh on my lips. "I'd kill for some sweater weather right now." I pulled my long blonde hair into a quick braid and let it hang over my left shoulder, retrieving the orange hair tie from my pocket to add a little holiday spirit. My thick, black-framed glasses had slid down my nose in the Alabama heat, and I used one finger to push them back into place.

I craved a true fall season, too, and I knew I'd find it in Seattle. It used to be *if* I made it, but now I knew it was *when*. I'd been saving for years, even after having to help my parents with the bills. I could have already been out of that town if I would have told them to shove off when they asked for rent or grocery money, but the truth was that I needed a place to live, too — and food to eat.

Lily, my best friend, used to let me stay at her house all the time. Her mom didn't even bat an eye if I was there when Lily wasn't, because they knew my home situation. But Lily went to college right after we graduated, just like everyone else, and I stayed back, attending our local community college and saving for my dream school.

If it weren't for Tammy letting me crash on her couch on the nights when my parents' fighting got really intense, I probably wouldn't have had enough sanity left to joke with her every morning.

"Yeah, well, at least you'll get it soon. At *Bastyr*." Tammy smiled, punching her log-in into the register as I prepped the coffee machines. "But for now, you get summer in October." She glanced over my shoulder at the front door. "And weirdos who still want hot coffee, anyway."

I didn't even need to turn to know Mr. Korbe was standing on the other side of the glass, hands resting easily in the pockets of his worn, brown dress slacks and what little hair he had left swept over his freckled head. I threw him a wink and a wave before smiling back at Tammy.

"Just a few more months." The words came out airy and light, riding on a fantasy I'd had since I was twelve. My dream school was three thousand miles away on the Pacific Northwest coast, and after years of saving, I was almost to the point where I could make the move.

Almost.

"Did you get your acceptance letter yet?"

I swallowed, dusting off the front of my apron before heading for the door. "Not yet. But it'll come." I paused when I'd almost reached the lock, eying Tammy who was bouncing a little now, biting back a smile. "What? Why are you looking at me like that?"

"Something big is going to happen today. I feel it." Tammy was older than me by thirty-two years, the dark bun at the nape of her neck peppered with hints of gray. Her eyes creased with laugh lines as her smile widened.

"Uh-oh, did you read your tarot cards again this morning?"

"Nope, but you know my gut feelings. My intuition is never wrong."

I laughed, because as much as I wanted to argue with her, it was true — she always had a feeling when something was coming, good or bad. I'd believed in her psychic abilities ever since I was a thirteen-year-old dirty kid with my feet hanging from the barstools in front of the cash register. She used to buy me a grilled cheese and a slice of pie out of her own pocket, and when I turned sixteen, she got me a job so I wouldn't have to go hungry ever again.

"Well, then, maybe my letter will come today."

"There's my optimistic girl." She whistled, hollering into the back kitchen. "Door's opening!"

"Strippers locked away!" our cook, Ray, yelled back.

Tammy rolled her eyes and I chuckled, unlocking the door to welcome Mr. Korbe inside.

And so the morning went. I refilled coffee and served up plates of scrambled eggs and pancakes to the same faces I'd seen day in and day out for years. I took a picture with little Sammy Jones, who was dressed up as an "Army guy GI Joe," in his own words, and listened to Mr. and Mrs. Boone tell me about the new vegetables in their garden. I helped Tammy top off the ketchup and mustard when breakfast faded into lunch, and tried not to cringe when the old man known affectionally as Scooter checked out my ass as I passed his booth — it was hard to do, since I'd sat on his lap when he played Santa every year until I was ten.

Yep, it was a completely normal day.

Until it wasn't.

I heard the faint chime of the bell as I cashed out the Boones. "Welcome to Papa Wyatt's, just grab any open booth and I'll be right with you," I called without even looking up from the register. One finger pushed my glasses back up my nose as I popped the register closed and hurried back with the change, offering the Boones one last smile and letting them know I'd see them on Sunday. Which I would.

I always did.

My eyes were on my hands as I pulled the notepad from my apron pocket and the pencil from behind my ear, feet moving on autopilot to the newly occupied booth, but when I looked up at the person sitting in it, everything stopped.

Everything.

Time, my heart, the greeting that was two seconds from leaving my lips.

We had plenty of travelers stop in the diner on their way through town — hard to escape that when we were less than two minutes from I-10 — but those travelers usually fit a code. They were the spring break road trippers on their way to the beach, or lonely truck drivers with sad, weary eyes, or a family of four with kids bouncing in their seats and throwing apple sauce while the parents begged me for more coffee. None of them, and I do mean none of them, looked like *him*.

His sandy-blond hair was tussled, one hand absent-mindedly running through it as he looked over the menu. From the view I had of his profile, I noticed the deep dent of his cheeks, the smooth squareness of his jaw, the long slope of his nose, bent just a little at the top, like it'd been broken before. He was dressed like the men on the magazines lining the grocery store checkout lane, sporting a cerulean blue sweater over a button-up, plaid dress shirt, the sleeves of both shoved up to his elbows. My eyes followed the fabric down to where it gathered above the light brown belt around his hips. When he dropped the menu to the table, I snapped my attention back to his face.

Which was now angled straight up at me.

His eyes were deep honey pools, bright and intense where they lay sheltered by thick, dark eyebrows. And there were two, small, perfectly symmetrical lines creased between those eyebrows as he looked up at me, like he'd asked a question I hadn't heard, like he'd been asking questions his entire life without finding a single answer.

In a whoosh, reality sucked me back into the restaurant and I blinked in rapid fire, clearing my throat as I flipped to a new page in my notepad. "Can I start you off with a drink? Coffee, tea?"

I tried to keep my eyes on the notepad, waiting for his response, but he was still staring at me. I lifted my gaze to his, tracing those two creases right above his nose. He wasn't necessarily scowling, but he certainly wasn't smiling.

"Sir?"

He blinked, but his eyes never left mine. "Coffee. Black."

His voice was low and modulated, like a smooth pour of the drink he'd just ordered.

I nodded, rolling my lips together. "I'll give you a minute to look over the menu."

When I was back behind the counter bar, I refilled the two customers there before pouring a steaming cup for Mr. GQ, massaging my thigh as I did. It was more out of habit than pain, but Tammy eyed me with concern from where she was piling plates on her arm in the kitchen window.

"You okay, Coop?"

I was still in a fog, and I stopped pouring the coffee just before it tumbled over the lip of the small, white, porcelain mug. "Huh?"

Tammy nodded to my leg, and I looked down at my hand still massaging the muscle. It looked normal, under the corduroy black fabric of my work pants, but beneath it was the scar of my loss, the muscle weak and small in comparison to my other leg. Phantom pains still made themselves present from time to time, reminding me of what once was there — before the accident, before life as I knew and understood it had been altered beyond recognition.

"Oh." I stopped, smoothing the same hand over my apron before carefully balancing the saucer and cup, already heading back to the booth. "I'm fine. Phantom pains, I barely even notice them anymore."

She forced a smile. "Okay. By the way, what's the story on that tall glass of water in booth nine?"

I shrugged, pretending like I hadn't noticed how attractive he was, the blush crawling up my neck betraying me. "Dunno. He likes his coffee black, that's about as far as our conversation has gone."

"You should ask him where he's from."

"And you should deliver those pancakes."

She grinned. "You think he's cute."

"I think he's hungry."

"Mmm-hmm."

"Shut up."

She laughed as I slid past her and back onto the floor, hands shaking slightly as I checked in on my other booths before placing the full cup of coffee in front of my new customer. He wasn't looking at the menu anymore. He was simply staring out the large windows of the diner, eyes distant, brows still slightly pinched.

"Ready to order?" I asked, pulling out my notepad again. I didn't even need it. I hadn't written down an order in more than two years. But I needed something to look at, something other than him.

"What makes you happy?"

He was still staring out the windows, but when a few seconds passed without an answer from me, he turned his gaze to mine.

And I couldn't speak.

*My books, my dog, yoga, the way the sun always manages to come back, no matter how dark the storm.*

He didn't raise his brows or ask again, didn't tap his foot or wave his hand in front of my face. He just looked back at me, almost with understanding, as if he knew the question wasn't easy to answer. Maybe he didn't believe it had an answer at all.

But it did. I *had* answers — I had plenty. I was Miss Optimistic. I counted my blessings daily. I always looked at the bright side of my life, ignoring the shadows of it, choosing to focus my energy on whatever positives I could grasp.

Still, none of that mattered.

He asked me what made me happy, but that's not what he really asked.

What he really asked was — *are* you happy?

And I couldn't speak.

"I'll have the steak and eggs, please," he said after a moment, turning back to the window and reaching down for his coffee. He took a sip with me still staring at him until I finally tore my eyes away, pretending to write in my notepad.

"Coming right up."

I zipped back through the diner and into the kitchen, ignoring Mr. Hollenbeck as he raised his hand at me indicating he was ready to order, too. I couldn't take his order, not yet, not until I took a breath.

Ray quirked a brow at me when I blew through the swinging door, spreading my hands flat on the silver metal table next to the sink, eyes closed and head down as I forced an exhale.

"You okay, slick?"

"Steak and eggs, please."

I opened my eyes again, standing straight, and Ray saluted me with his spatula. "You got it."

*This is stupid*, I scolded myself. It was like I'd never talked to a boy before, or *seen* one for that matter. It was no secret that I wasn't exactly the most social girl when I was in school, especially after I lost my leg, but I had a few friends. I had conversations with boys — group projects, book clubs, customers. So why was I stunned speechless by *this* particular one?

Annoyed, I blew out a breath, rebraiding my hair over my shoulder before pushing back through the door. I immediately made my way to Mr. Hollenbeck, smiling and nodding as I took his order, all the while way too aware of booth number nine.

"So, where's he from?" Tammy asked when I rejoined her behind the counter.

"I didn't ask."

"You should."

I scribbled out the check for the trucker at the end of the bar, offering him a smile and telling him no rush as I slipped it over the counter to him. Turning back to Tammy, I leaned a hip against the bar.

"He asked me what made me happy."

She frowned. "What? That's weird."

"I know."

"What did you say?"

"That's the weirder part," I confessed. "I didn't have an answer. I just stared at him."

"Plenty of things make you happy," Tammy said, clearly as concerned as I was about my lack of response. "You're literally the happiest girl I know."

"I know. I can't explain it. He's... his presence is paralyzing."

Tammy eyed him over my shoulder just as Ray tapped the bell.

"Order up!"

I grabbed the plate of steak and eggs before Tammy could say anything else, making my way back to his booth.

"Here you go," I said, setting the plate in front of him. "Can I get you anything else right now?"

He looked up at me, and the faintest hint of a smile played at the corner of his lips. "No, this is great. Thank you."

I nodded. But I didn't move.

*Go back to the bar, Cooper.*

"So, where ya traveling from?"

He cut a corner off his steak, pausing to look up at me with it mounted on his fork. "Florida."

He popped the bite into his mouth.

"Ah," I said, as if it made sense or something. Nothing about him made sense. "Business or pleasure?"

He humphed the way one would when recalling an inside joke. "Neither."

I watched as he dug into his egg, spilling the yolk onto his plate. The man wanted to eat in peace, I was sure of it, but I couldn't move.

"Well, where are you heading?"

"Washington," he answered easily.

My stomach did a flip, tugging on the part of my heart tied so reverently to the dreams I'd had all my life. *Washington.* It was where I wanted to be, where I knew my life would really begin.

Up until that point, he'd only made me uncomfortable — in a curious, fascinating way.

Now, he'd made me jealous.

"Well, that's a long drive. Better eat up and get some energy." I forced a smile. "Let me know if you need anything."

My mind raced as I allowed my body to fall back into the motions, checking on customers and delivering orders, cashing out and calling out greetings and farewells as people came and went. It was the first time in my life that it bothered me — the fact that they were coming and going, and I was staying.

I was always staying.

I didn't realize I was avoiding his table until I saw he'd placed a twenty-dollar bill near the edge of it, a signal that he was ready to go. Because he would go, he would leave, and I would stay.

Just another normal day.

"I'll grab your change," I said, reaching for the twenty.

He shook his head. "Not necessary."

"Thank you," I said softly, smiling. "And, hey, have fun in Washington. It's… that's where I want to go. I'm saving up now. My dream school is there." I shrugged, not sure why I was telling him. I was one-hundred percent sure he didn't care. "Can't wait for an October where I don't sweat," I added with a chuckle.

I lifted my eyes to his, ready to walk back to the bar and leave him be, but he stopped me short.

"Want to come?"

I balked. "Excuse me?"

"To Washington. Do you want to come with me?"

For a moment, I just stared at him, the way I imagined I'd stare at a naked man running down the street or someone asking me to loan them a million dollars.

And then I laughed.

"Are you crazy? I can't just *go* with you," I said, shaking my head at the ridiculousness of it all. "You're a stranger. I don't even know your name. You could be a serial killer."

He watched me, those damn lines forming between his brows, and then he shrugged.

"Okay."

He wiped his mouth with his napkin before dropping it onto his plate as he stood. My heart was in my throat again, because when he wasn't sitting in a booth, he towered over me. He was at least six feet of lean muscle and hard edges, and he shoved the sleeves of his sweater up his arms a bit more, eyes catching mine as he stepped into my space.

"You never answered my question."

I swallowed, body trapped in a strange limbo, torn between leaning into him and running as far as I could in the opposite direction.

"What makes you happy?"

*My books, my dog, yoga, the way the sun always manages to come back, no matter how dark the storm.*

I opened my mouth, ready to answer this time, since I'd run over the responses a thousand times in my head at this point, but he turned before I could, leaving me standing there with a list of things that made me happy and a heart that whispered with every beat that the list was a lie.

I didn't move from the booth until the front door closed behind him, the echo of the little bell ringing in my ears as I silently opened the register and deposited his twenty, counting out the change and dropping it in the tip jar Tammy and I would split at the end of our shift.

"What was that about?" Tammy asked, dropping a pile of dirty dishes into the large bucket we took turns carrying into the back. "I saw him standing all close to you and then he walked away and you just stood there like you'd seen a ghost."

"He asked me to go with him."

"What?!"

I nodded, arms feeling foreign as I grabbed a wash cloth and wiped down the bar. "He's going to Washington. I told him that's where my dream school is. And he asked if I wanted to go with him."

"Oh, my God!"

"Yeah."

Tammy stood with her hands hooked on her hips, shaking her head frantically before she threw her arms up. "Well, you have to go! What are you still doing here?!"

I scoffed, rolling my eyes. "Oh, yeah, Tammy. Let me just go jump into a car with a random guy and let him drive me across the country."

"Um, yes. Do that. Go. Now." She stole the rag from my hands, shoving me toward the door.

"Tammy!" I wriggled out of her grasp. "That would be insane. And dangerous. He could kill me!"

"Oh, yeah, because he really looks like the murderer type."

"They don't exactly have a specific look," I deadpanned.

She sighed, gripping my arms in her weathered hands. "Listen to me, Cooper. You have been working at this diner since the day you turned sixteen, and saving to move to Washington since that very day, too. Now, here you are, twenty years old, still dying to get out of Mobile and still way too smart to waste your life 'saving' and never doing." Tammy paused, her eyes searching mine. "You're stuck, baby girl. And that's okay, we've all been stuck a time or two before. But this is it, your chance to pull your feet from the muck of Mobile and that awful place you've called home for way too long."

I frowned, my heart sinking with her words. It was true, I was stuck, but this wasn't a part of my plan. *He* wasn't a part of my plan.

"I... I don't have enough yet."

"Yes, you do," she said, reaching both fists into the tip jar and pulling every single dollar out of it. She wadded it up and shoved it in my front apron pocket. "This should help, and last week's paycheck hit our accounts this morning. If you run out of cash along the way or need help once you're in Seattle, just call me. I'm serious." She shook her head, a crazed smile on her face. "I mean, what do I honestly spend my money on anyway other than scratch-off tickets?"

My hands were clammy, and I wrung them together, still shaking my head. "I don't even know if I got in."

"You'll get in. If not this semester, then next, and you know it."

"What if he kidnaps me?!" I whisper-yelled.

At that, Tammy paused, like she'd just realized she was stuffing me into a car with a stranger. Her eyes shot up to the door before finding mine again. "Look, I know it's a little crazy. It's a little scary. In fact, I think this is why I never had kids because encouraging you to do this isn't very motherly or whatever. But, Cooper, remember what I said this morning?" Her eyes lit up again. "I could *feel* it. I knew something big was going to happen, and this is it."

"Me getting kidnapped by a strange boy was the *good feeling* you had?"

"You're not getting kidnapped, you're getting a free ride to a new life. Give me your phone."

I couldn't do anything in that moment but stare at her.

"Phone." She said with a snap of her fingers. She snatched the device from my hands as soon as I numbly pulled it from my pocket, and then she was tapping around on the screen. "There. I shared your location with both me and Lily. I'll keep an eye on you the whole time. And you call me every morning and every night to check in, okay?"

"What about Wyatt? I can't just leave him short-staffed."

"Don't worry about this place." She waved her hand. "We'll manage."

"And my parents—"

"Are awful people who have always treated you like a mistake and a regret instead of a human."

My throat was tight with the air I couldn't inhale fully, heart like a war drum under my ribs. "I can't... I can't do this. I—"

"Yes, you can. He has a car. He's *gorgeous,* in case you didn't notice. And he's a free ticket to the place you've always wanted to go. Cooper," she said my name to call my attention back to her, hands on my arms again as she leveled her face with mine. "You are *dying* in this town. Not your body, but your soul." Her eyes pleaded with mine like she knew from experience. "Life isn't supposed to be safe," she added with a laugh. "If it was, they wouldn't call it living. They'd just call it existing. And you've existed long enough, baby girl. It's time to *live.*"

My eyes darted back and forth between hers, brain warring with my soul.

*Be safe.*

*Take a chance.*

*This is crazy.*

*This could be fun.*

*You could die.*

*You could finally live.*

*You don't even know him.*

*You want to.*

*Leaving Alabama is scary.*

*Leaving Alabama is what you've always wanted.*

Tammy leaned in even closer, lowering her voice to a whisper. "Your worthless parents are going to suck you dry if you stay. Don't let them. This is it, Cooper. This is life calling." She shrugged. "Are you going to answer, or just let it ring?"

I think I went blind in those next few moments, because I hardly recall rounding the edge of the bar. I barely remember the feel of my heart in my throat and the sun on my face as I pushed through the front door just as he started backing out of the spot where he'd parked his convertible.

"Wait!" I called, the sound of my own voice breaking through the haze.

He stopped, sunglasses reflecting the front of the diner I never thought I'd leave as I struggled to catch my breath.

"I just need to grab my stuff."

# Chapter 2
## Mobile, Alabama

*This is insane. This is insane. This is insane.*

Those three words were on repeat in my head as I hastily shoved clothes and personal belongings into the one and only duffle bag I owned.

Kalo hopped around my ankles as I flew through my tiny bedroom, tossing items over my shoulder and onto the bed next to my open bag. She licked my face when I got close enough, turning in circles with the same excitement she got as soon as I said, *"Wanna go outside?"*

"We're going on a trip, Kalo," I said to her, scruffing up the soft fur on her head with one hand. She was an Australian shepherd mix, no more than twenty-five pounds with eyes that slightly crossed, which only made me love her more. "With a man. Who I just met." I paused, swimsuit clutched in my hand. "Whose name I don't even know."

Kalo cocked her head to the side, watching me, and I laughed, ditching the swim suit and rushing to my tiny bathroom to rummage through the necessities.

All my life, I'd dreamed of leaving Alabama. I'd dreamed of crossing the country, starting a new life, leaving my past behind. Now that the moment was here, I realized the first thing I should have done all those years ago was make a packing list.

Because nothing I was packing made any sense.

Yoga pants, three of my favorite paperbacks, including my very worn copy of *Catcher in the Rye*, jeans, the framed picture of Tammy and me on my eighteenth birthday, a dozen or so shirts and tank tops, hair ties, hair brush, razor, three random dog toys, and my eReader. I only owned two sweaters and one pair of boots, and I threw them in the bag, too, followed immediately by my extra liner and socks for my prosthetic leg.

I could still remember the day I could finally afford the extra supplies for my leg, after saving and saving on my own, insurance only covering one set of each once I was in my final leg. I'd gone through several growing up, but now that I was done growing, I had my permanent leg. I was lucky my dad even managed to have insurance at all, and I was pretty sure the only reason he did was because his place of employment took it out of his check before he could even see it.

I added a pair of athletic shorts, ones I only ever wore when I was alone and I figured would stay buried in my bag until we reached Seattle. My tiny Thai Buddha statue Tammy had purchased for me at a flea market was staring at me from the corner of my desk, begging me to bring him along, so I tucked him in the side pocket of my bag.

Then I stood in the middle of my room, looking around at the faded yellow walls, once white, tainted by cigarette smoke from my parents no matter how I'd tried to keep it out.

My room was small. The same twin bed I'd slept on since I was eight was sunken down in the middle, shoved against the far wall right under my enlightenment poster.

The springs creaked and groaned each time I applied even the slightest bit of pressure. The desk that sat next to it was old and tattered, too, the warped wood nicked in several places. Kalo's dog bed rested under the old box TV I'd watched cartoons on as a child and barely turned on at all as a teenager, and not a single movie sat on the shelf below that TV, the space occupied with books, instead.

My eyes caught on my copy of Emerson's prose and poetry, and I threw that in my bag, too.

The carpet was light brown and stained all over, the sheer curtain covering my window littered with moth bites. Standing in the middle of it all, hands on my hips, I knew I wouldn't miss a single thing, no matter what I left behind.

So, I zipped up my duffle bag without adding another single thing, slinging it over my shoulder before grabbing Kalo's bed under one arm and my yoga mat under the other. I took one last look at the room, the place that never felt like home, the prison, and then I turned my back on it forever.

"Cindy," I said louder than necessary, tapping my mother's shoulder where she lay on the couch. Sweat matted her ashy blonde hair to her forehead and she squinted, swatting her hand in the air to tell me to go away. "Cindy, I'm leaving."

"Okay?" she said gruffly, rolling over to face the back cushions of the couch. "What the fuck do you want, a going away party?"

I sighed. "Not for work. I'm leaving. I'm moving out."

"About time."

I stood beside the couch, eyes taking in the slight heap of bone and skin that was my mother. It was hard to believe I'd come from her, that I'd been built inside her, and yet the only thing we shared in common was our last name and DNA.

"I'm really leaving," I said again, voice low. "I'm getting in the car with a boy I just met and I'm driving away. And I'm never coming back to Alabama." I paused, letting that sink in — both for her and myself. "Never."

My mother was quiet save for the ragged breaths leaving her lungs, and for a moment I thought she'd fallen back to sleep, but then she spoke.

"Make sure he wears a condom."

I closed my eyes, not sure why somewhere deep in my heart I expected more, wanted more. She'd never given me anything, only taken, why should today be any different?

With a quick scribble, I left a note for my dad on the folding table where I'd eaten cereal every morning since I could remember, then I shoved through the front door of our trailer for the last time, leaving the smoke and the stink and the scars behind.

As soon as I expelled a long breath and lifted my eyes to where the boy from the diner stood leaning against his car, I halted.

He'd followed me as I rode my bike back to my house, and I'd ditched that same bike in my front yard before sprinting inside without another word. But here he was, waiting for me, and again, the same three words cycled through my head.

*This is insane.*

"I don't know if I packed the right stuff," I admitted, feet moving toward him and the car. "I wasn't sure what to pack, honestly. It's still hot here but I know it won't be in Washington. Then again, we'll be in the car, so I guess it doesn't really matter too much what the weather is like. We can just adjust the air. I mean you can, since it's your car. I won't touch the air. Or the radio. I promise. I'll be like a fly on the wall. Or, well, not a fly, because flies are annoying. I'll be like a butterfly. Like, the caterpillar in the cocoon before the butterfly actually happens." He was just looking at me with those same questioning eyes, though the corner of his mouth twitched at a smile. "I won't be a problem, that's what I'm trying to say."

"Good to know."

I nodded, adjusting the yoga mat under my arm. He was just leaned up against the car, which I realized now was not only a convertible, but a BMW, too. His hands were tucked easily into the pockets of his navy blue pants, one ankle crossed over the other as he watched me.

When he stood straight and opened the passenger side door, Kalo bolted from where she'd been sniffing the grass at my side and jumped right into the front seat, parking her little butt down and letting her tongue hang out as she panted up at us.

He eyed her, one brow cocked as he turned back to face me.

"Kalo. I rescued her when she was a pup." I shrugged. "Can't leave her behind."

He wet his lips, looking back down at Kalo with a curious stare. "Will you be like a butterfly, too?"

Kalo popped up, little paws pressing into his chest as she lapped at his face before jumping into the backseat.

He chuckled, wiping at the slobber on his chin before turning to me with an outstretched hand aimed at the bag over my shoulder. I handed it to him, mind still racing with all the reasons this was the dumbest idea ever as he loaded my bag into the trunk, taking my yoga mat next.

I dropped Kalo's bed into the back seat and she immediately climbed into it, turning in two circles before plopping down.

And then I had a panic attack.

"Wait!"

He paused mid-reach for the handle on the driver door, but he was still relaxed, a peaceful expression on his face as he did what I asked.

I couldn't catch a steady breath, ears ringing and fingers reaching blindly for my braid. I pulled it over my shoulder and picked at the ends of it, mind racing, questions burning through me.

"What's your name?"

"Emery."

"Emery what?"

"Emery Reed."

I nodded, over and over, still picking at my split ends. "Okay, Emery Reed, and have you ever been convicted of a crime?"

He laughed, just one quick, humored bark, the noise warm and comforting. "No. Have you?"

I wrinkled my nose. "Of course not."

"Okay."

"Okay," I agreed, looking up and down my street. One of my neighbors a few trailers down was sitting on their porch, watching me with curious eyes. "Are you dangerous?"

"If I was, I wouldn't tell you."

"But you're not, right?"

He shrugged. "Guess you'll find out."

I scoffed. "I'm serious. You're not like... crazy or anything, are you?"

At that he threw his head back and laughed again, eyes warm when they found mine. "Of course I am. Aren't you?"

A warm breeze blew between us then, the faint smell of pumpkin riding on its wings, giving me the first scent of fall I'd had all season.

"Can I get in now?" he asked, eyes not leaving mine.

I swallowed, and then with a quick nod, he opened his door as I slipped into the passenger seat, and we closed the doors at the same time, the quiet thunk of them solidifying my choice.

I was leaving Alabama.

I was going to Washington.

With a strange boy.

Whom I had just met.

Who admitted out loud that he's crazy.

He fired up the engine, the soft purr of it sparking a wave of chills up my arms. And there was no ceremonious goodbye, no rush of memories as he put it in drive and pulled away from my house that never was a home.

I'd nearly shredded the end of my braid, so I threw it behind me, right leg bouncing as I wrung my hands together in my lap.

"I'm Cooper," I finally said when we pulled out of the trailer park. "Cooper Owens."

"Nice to meet you, Cooper."

I nodded, leg still bouncing.

"So, why are you going to Washington?"

He shifted, switching hands on the steering wheel as those two familiar lines creased between his brows. "There's just something I need to see."

"Well, that's not vague or anything."

He didn't respond, pulling onto I-10 and picking up speed. The wind blowing through the car from the top being down whirled more now, picking up the stray strands of my hair and twirling them around me.

"How old are you?" I yelled over the wind, heart still thundering under my ribs, nervous system in a practical breakdown as it fired off all the warning signals.

*DON'T TALK TO STRANGERS.*

*DON'T GET IN CARS WITH STRANGERS.*

*DON'T TRAVEL ACROSS THE COUNTRY WITH STRANGERS.*

"Twenty-three."

"What do you do?"

He shook his head, as if my question disappointed him. "I drive."

"Like for a living?"

"No, like right now, in this moment, I drive."

"Well, that's not what I meant."

"What did you mean?" he challenged, glancing at me quickly before returning his gaze to the road.

I stammered, hands waving erratically around me. "I don't know, just like, who are you? Tell me something to help me freak out less about the decision I just made to get in the car with you."

He paused. "If I do kill you, I promise to take care of your dog."

I narrowed my eyes. "Funny."

He bit back a smile, and I lost my train of thought watching the slow spread of it on his face, the wind whipping through his sandy blond hair, the sun casting a warm glow over half of his face and cool shadows over the other.

"Wait, I know," I said with a snap of my fingers, pulling my cell phone from my back pocket. "Is your name Emery Reed on Facebook? I can just look through your profile and reassure myself that you're not a serial killer."

"I don't have a Facebook."

I balked, heart stopping in my chest before kicking back to life. "What do you *mean* you don't have a Facebook? Everyone has a Facebook." My nerves sparked to life again, head shaking of its own accord. "Oh, my God, you really are going to kill me, aren't you? Oh my God, oh my God."

Suddenly, the car veered to the right and a scream ripped through my throat, Emery riding the tail of a semi-truck and cutting off an old van before pulling off onto the shoulder, stopping us altogether with enough force to send me flying forward before I was jerked back against the seat again.

"We almost wrecked!" I panicked, checking the backseat to make sure Kalo was okay. She just stared up at me goofily from her bed like *I* was the crazy one.

"Hey," Emery said, calling my attention back to him. "Are we doing this?"

Cars and trucks zoomed by behind him, each one rocking our car with a *whoosh* as I tried to calm my racing heart. He wasn't annoyed, his face wasn't screwed up with impatience, his eyes weren't accusing or judging. He was simply watching me. He was simply waiting. I knew that look, because I'd been waiting my entire life.

"Are we doing this," he asked again, voice even steadier than before. "Or not?"

And in perhaps the most chaotic moment of my life, on the shoulder of I-10, with cars zipping by and a stranger waiting to drive me to my new life, I closed my eyes, pressed my head into the warm leather seat, and took my first breath.

"We're doing this," I whispered, eyes still closed.

"Okay," he said, and then I felt a hand on my knee.

My eyes shot open, heart back in my throat.

"Seatbelt," he said, squeezing my leg before reaching into the center console for his sunglasses. He slid the frames into place. "And I hope you like The Black Keys."

His hand reached for the knob, cranking up the volume, and then he pulled back onto the highway, effectively ending my freakout.

Kalo popped her head between our seats, nudging my elbow with her wet nose. I looked down at her, still in a daze, numbly petting her head to assure her I was okay.

Then, with one more deep inhale, I shook the negative thoughts from my mind, choosing instead to embrace the moment.

I was leaving Alabama.

I was going to Washington.

Everything I'd always wanted was finally happening, even if it wasn't exactly how I'd imagined it, and the next breath that left my lungs also left a sense of peace behind it, one that filled me from the inside out.

I think I knew, even then, that the greatest adventure of my life was about to begin.

I didn't know who I was, or who I'd become, or where I'd go when we got to Washington. I didn't know where we'd stop on the way, or how we'd get along, or how I'd feel when we hit our final destination, when we said goodbye and went our separate ways.

I didn't know any of that.

But I did know something about that day, and that boy, and that car felt right.

I knew as the sun warmed my skin and the wind blew through my hair that I was *never* coming back to Alabama.

And ten minutes later, when we crossed the state line, I smiled.

I smiled, and I didn't look back.

## Chapter 3

### Somewhere in Mississippi

My dad used to hit my mom.

I was nine years old the first time I saw it happen, though I couldn't be sure it was the first time it'd happened *ever* or just the first time I'd witnessed it. That memory was burned into my brain, the image of Daryl winding up and smacking Cindy square across the cheek, sending her flying back into the wall, where there's still a hole today.

I thought Daryl was evil then.

I thought Cindy and I would become closer, that we'd run away, but we didn't.

Because she was evil, too.

There were always drugs in our house — the bad kind. The kind that make craters in your face and dull the life in your eyes all at once. I remember that starting around the time I was nine, too. Maybe that was just the year I grew up.

I knew they wouldn't care the day I left, but part of me wondered if they'd argue, anyway. It was me, after all, who put groceries in our kitchen. It was me who paid half of our bills, since my dad was the only one working, and he spent most of his money on whiskey and lottery tickets. But it was after five now. Daryl was home, and he knew I was gone.

And still, my phone hadn't rang.

My body was in a sort of numb trance, with the car engine humming beneath me and the wind whipping through my hair. The music volume hadn't been touched again since we left Alabama, and I just watched out the window as Mississippi floated past. It reminded me of Alabama. I didn't really mind that we never stopped.

I didn't really mind that Emery didn't talk, either. Once we left Alabama, I slipped out of my freakout and into a strange awareness of being. My body was in the car, but my mind was on my yoga mat, opening itself to new possibilities. I knew it was a big moment in my life, one that would alter everything, and yet I was struggling to grasp it. I almost felt numb.

It wasn't until we crossed over into Louisiana and ran right into bumper-to-bumper traffic that Emery reached forward for the dial, the wind dying down right along with the music.

"Why do you think people deny the existence of aliens?"

His voice surprised me a little, and Kalo popped her head up in the back seat, looking at him with a cocked ear before laying back down with a sigh.

"Well, I suppose —"

"Do you think it's because we, as humans, just need to feel like our lives are worth more than they are?"

My mouth was still open, but I popped it shut, eyes on the South Carolina license plate in front of us.

"I mean there are *infinite* galaxies — we don't even know how many there are, and we've found a shit ton. The universe is just this... this *massive* plane of mass and matter and time and space and distance. And yet most of our population thinks we are the only intelligent lifeforms, that we're like God's only project or whatever."

"I take it you're not religious," I finally said.

"Are you?"

He asked the question the same way he'd asked what made me happy, in a way that made me question the answer before it left my lips.

"I am, but not in the way you think I am."

He laughed, switching hands on the steering wheel and leaning his elbow on the center console. "What other way is there? You either believe in a higher power or you don't."

I traced the lean lines of muscle in his forearm with my eyes, noting the comfortable way he gripped the wheel, the confidence that showed even through his dark sunglasses.

"I believe in the universe, and in things happening for a reason." I paused. "And, yes, I guess I do believe in a higher spirit."

"In God?"

"Not like the old white man with a beard and a staff but yes, I believe in God."

"Why?"

I laughed, the sound foreign as I shrugged my shoulders and tossed my hands up. "I don't know, what do you mean *why*? You're telling me you don't believe in anything greater than yourself?"

"I believe in science. And science has given me absolutely zero reason to believe there is anything or anyone watching over me, or dictating my destiny, or promising that life doesn't just end when this—" He thumped his chest with a fist. "Body stops working."

"I believe in science, too. But science only goes so far sometimes, and then something else takes over."

"*God,*" he mocked, the tiniest smirk on his lips as he glanced at me.

"Maybe," I defended.

Emery shifted his weight again, hand sliding down to grip the bottom of the steering wheel as the traffic began to clear. "I think religion, in any form, is just the result of fear. Fear of dying, fear of being alone. We all want to believe that we're special, that some man in the sky loves each and every one of us, even with our flaws." He shrugged. "But the truth is we're just humans. We're just animals. And when we die, we become food for the earth and the bugs. The circle of life."

"That's a little morbid."

"I think it's comforting."

I balked. "How in the world is that comforting to you?"

Emery looked at me then, and I only saw myself reflected in the lenses of his shades. "Because we're just a blip on the radar, Cooper. Just like every other animal before us. And no matter how much we take while we're here, we always have to give it back."

His eyes went back to the road and I heard the click of the turn signal before we rounded a semi, picking up speed. Emery reached for the music dial but I stopped him.

"Wait." My hand wrapped around his wrist and he looked to me, fingers still on the dial. My cheeks flushed with heat as I dropped my grip, clearing my throat. "We should play a game. A road trip game. How about twenty-one questions?"

"That's too many."

I laughed. "Okay, well, what's the magic number of questions you're okay with, Emery Reed?"

He didn't smile. "Zero is preferable."

"Oh, come on," I pleaded, turning in my seat a little so I could face him. I adjusted my seat belt over my shoulder and tucked my prosthetic under the opposite knee. His eyes hadn't fallen to my leg yet, hadn't inspected it, hadn't realized I was lacking. I wondered if they would, and if so — when. "Humor me. We're going to be stuck in this car together for who knows how long."

He still didn't answer.

"How about ten?"

"One."

"Five."

He huffed. "Fine."

I smiled in victory, fingers unwrapping my long braid just to rewind it again. "Okay. First question. Why are you on a road trip to Washington by yourself?"

"I'm not by myself."

"Well, you *were*," I deadpanned.

We slowed again, hitting another string of traffic. "I told you, I just have to see something."

"You know, this game doesn't work if you don't give me just a *little* more detail than that."

Emery's jaw tightened, and I watched his chest as it pushed a long exhale down. "My grandmother just passed away, and there's a place in Washington that was her favorite in the world. She made me promise I would go see it."

I swallowed. "Were you close with her?" I didn't want to say *I'm sorry.* No one ever did when death came up, though it seemed to be what we all went for automatically, anyway.

"That's two questions. I think it's my turn."

I threw my hands up. "You're right. Okay, your turn. Shoot."

"Why did you get in a car with a stranger to travel across the country?"

My jaw hung open. "Hey, that's not fair! You asked me to come!"

"I didn't say I didn't. I asked you why you got in the car." Emery raised one eyebrow, glancing at me for just a second before turning his attention back to the road.

"I don't know," I murmured. "I've been wanting to go to Washington, anyway. It was a free ride."

"Oh, come on," he chided, his voice mimicking mine as he repeated my words back to me. "You know, this game doesn't work if you don't give me just a *little* more detail than that."

I swallowed, eyes trying to catch on the little yellow lines as we zoomed through them. I wanted to give him a real answer, I just hadn't figured it out yet myself.

"I was dying in that town," I finally said, my voice low. I wondered if he could hear me over the wind. "And I don't want to die before I've even had the chance to live."

I was just as surprised by the words as Emery was, his sunglasses reflecting my face again as I watched the two creases form between his eyebrows.

"My turn," I said quickly. "Why did you ask me to come with you?"

"Oh, that's easy," he said with a smirk. "You're a girl. And you're hot."

My entire face burned like I'd opened an oven door and stuck my head inside. "I... um..."

"What?" he probed. "You don't think you're hot?"

I laughed, splitting another end off the tail of my braid.

"You really don't," he mused, watching me curiously. I couldn't look at him now. "I was just kidding, Cooper. Not about you being hot, because you are, but about why I asked you to come."

I still didn't turn to him, lip pinned between my teeth. "So, why then?"

It was silent, only the hum of his car and the oddly comforting sounds of traffic filling the space between us. He stalled long enough for me to glance over at him again, and when I did, he was watching the road, his jaw tight.

"Because I know what death from the inside looks like," he said.

I watched him, waiting for more. *And... what? You didn't want me to die? You wanted to save me? You thought I was too young to die?* But he didn't continue, so I pulled my leg from under the other, feet planted on the floorboard.

"You asked me in the diner what makes me happy," I said. "What about you? What makes you happy?"

Emery full-on smiled, and the brightness of that smile was enough to make me forget how to breathe. The wrinkles at the corners of his lips, his teeth in a straight white line, his sunglasses lifted on his cheeks — it was beautiful. "I know I said five questions, but you'll have to settle for two. We're here."

Kalo popped up in the back, tongue hanging out of her mouth as I took in the skyline in the distance, complete with the Saints football stadium. "New Orleans?"

Emery pulled his sunglasses off, dropping them into the center console. "Hope you like gumbo."

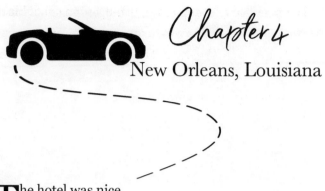

# Chapter 4

## New Orleans, Louisiana

The hotel was nice.
*Really* nice.

I sank down into the mattress of the bed closest to the door, stretching my legs out and rubbing Kalo's head as I looked around. We were right in the middle of the French Quarter, and the rich golds and deep reds of the bedding and curtains in our room made me feel like I'd stepped back in time. It was a small room, and the architecture was straight out of the twenties, the tall arches and intricate windows, but it was regal. And expensive, that I knew without asking.

Emery dropped his bag onto the opposite bed, eyes on his hands as he unzipped it and shifted through, pulling items out and plopping them onto the comforter. I was still looking around, stomach dropping at the thought of how much it cost to be in the center of the city, where everything was happening, in a hotel this beautiful.

"I can help pay for the room," I finally said, though my throat was dry with the offer. I had money saved, but I'd still planned on saving for a few more months. I needed to make what I had last, and that wasn't going to happen if we kept staying in places like this.

"Not necessary," Emery said, fishing out a small black toiletry bag. "I'm going to take a quick shower, if you want to do the same after I'm done. Then we can go grab dinner and explore a bit?"

My stomach flipped, and I hated it. "Sure."

I smiled, tucking my hands under my thighs, legs hanging off the edge of the bed. He eyed my feet, and in a second all the blood in my face washed away.

*Here it comes.*

I waited for him to ask, to point it out, to look at me with pity and sorrow.

But he didn't do any of that.

"You're short," he said, matter of factly. "Like, *really* short."

"I'm five foot," I defended with a chuckle. "It's not *that* short."

Emery quirked a brow. "I've seen taller fifth graders."

"Weren't you going to take a shower?"

He smirked, heading for the bathroom without another word. When the door clicked closed behind him, I breathed a sigh of relief, popping up from the bed to retrieve Kalo's food from my bag. The little food and water bowl I'd picked up from the gas station popped up like a kid's toy, making bowls from flat plates, and I poured the pebbles in before reaching for my water bottle and emptying the remaining contents into the opposite bowl.

"Dinner is served," I said to her, rubbing behind her ear as she hopped down from the bed and went to work devouring the food first. I stretched my arms over my head, walking to the window and opening the curtain.

The sun had already set, one of my least favorite parts of fall. The days were too short, the sunshine too brief, but nighttime in New Orleans looked a lot brighter than it did in Mobile. The lights twinkled from the street below, the crowd already large and loud, the night alive.

I sifted through the clothes I'd brought, realizing I had definitely not prepared for going out. Sitting in a car? I had clothes for that. But going out on the town with Emery Reed in New Orleans? Yeah, I had nothing.

I heard the shower kick on as I settled on a simple, thin black t-shirt that tied in a knot at the front and a pair of dark jeans. I set the clothes to the side, along with my own toiletries, and then I plopped down on the bed again, looking at Emery's stuff spread out on the other.

My eyes flicked across the heaps of clothing and came to land on a thick, leather-bound book with a thin ribbon of the same leather marking a page in the middle. I tilted my head, eyeing it curiously before crossing the small space between the beds and picking it up.

I knew it wasn't polite to touch his things, especially without asking, but that didn't stop my fingers from brushing across the worn cover, or tracing the frayed edges of the paper, or flipping it open to the first page and breathing a little shallower when my eyes found skinny, messy script inside.

*Grams wants me to start a journal.*
*She bought me this because she said it looked manly enough for me to maybe give it a shot. I still don't want to do it, but it's Grams, and she knows whatever she asks me to do, I will.*

*My therapist told me to start a journal a few months ago and I, politely, of course, told her to fuck off.*

*She wanted me to write about my feelings.*

*I told her I didn't have any.*

*But Grams said I should write out my thoughts, that I should write about the good days and the bad days to see what triggers each. She wants me to write about the dreams I'm having. I'm already annoyed just from writing this, so I doubt I'll stick to it.*

*I never stick to anything.*

I slammed the book shut, hand splayed on top of the front cover with my eyes bulging out of my head as I looked around like someone had seen me. Kalo was the only one, and she didn't seem to care as she lapped up the last of her water and jumped back onto the bed, circling the foot of it twice before flopping down.

*It's his journal.*

My heart beat loud in my ears as I looked back down at the leather, thumb tracing the stitching at the edge of it before I slowly flipped it back open.

*This is wrong. This is private. This isn't meant to be seen.*

A loud tropical beat sounded from across the room and I jumped, nearly flinging the journal across the room.

It was my phone, and I shook my head, making sure the journal was right where I found it before grabbing the ringing device from where I'd left it on my bed.

"Well, hello, best friend," I answered, flattening a palm over my racing heart as I sat on the edge of my bed.

"Don't 'hello, best friend' me," Lily snapped. "Why did I get a notification that you shared your location with me? And WHY ARE YOU IN NEW ORLEANS RIGHT NOW?"

My eyes skirted to the bathroom, the sound of the water running still filling the otherwise silent room. "Because I left Mobile."

"I can see that. It feels kind of creepy, actually, watching your little dot move across the map."

"For good."

She paused. "Wait... are you... is this it? Oh, my God, are you on your way to Seattle?!" Someone shushed her in the background. "Oh shut up, like you need complete silence to study for biology."

"Where are you?" I asked on a laugh.

"The library. It's where I live now that I'm in my core classes." Someone shushed her again. "Bite me!"

Lily was in her third year at the University of Illinois, slowly but steadily working toward her degree in speech therapy. She'd had the worst lisp when we were younger, and if it weren't for her own therapist, she'd likely still have it. She wanted to be just like the girl who'd worked with her, helping young kids work through speech impairments. As happy as I was for her when she finally overcame it, I was thankful she had that lisp. Our imperfections brought us together — her speech, my leg — and without her friendship, I wouldn't have made it through high school.

"Why don't you just text me?" I suggested, but my heart tightened, hoping she wouldn't hang up. We barely talked on the phone anymore, almost always texting, and I missed her. She was the closest thing I had to a sibling, and her family was the only reason I believed a house could really be a home, if the right people were inside it.

"As if," she answered quickly. "Wait, so did you get in? Did you rent a car? I'm so confused."

"I'm with a boy."

Lily paused, like she'd misheard me. If I was her, I'd have thought the same. I didn't talk to boys — that was always more her forte. "Um, do I know this boy?"

"No. I don't even know him."

"Wait. You got in a car with a stranger?"

"Hence why I shared my location," I reminded her. "Actually, Tammy shared it. I was too busy freaking out and listing all the reasons I shouldn't go."

"Well, I can add a few to the list!" she yelled. "Who is he? Are you safe? What if he's a *murderer?!*" She whispered the last word, as if he could hear her through my phone, or maybe she was finally being considerate to the other students in the library with her.

I laughed. "Look, I promise I've already freaked out enough for the both of us. But he's... nice. And he's not going to kill me," I added, scrunching my nose. "I don't think."

"Real comforting."

"At least, if he does, you'll know where to find the body."

"Still not helping."

I chuckled again. "I've got it under control," I promised her. "He's a good guy." I believed myself when I said it, even though I had no proof to back it up. Not yet. Not enough to feel as confident as I did when I said the words.

Lily scoffed. "Like I care if he's a *good guy*. Is he hot?"

I didn't get the chance to laugh before Lily rambled on, asking me question after question and listing off reasons why this was absolutely insane. But there was no way I could have responded to a single point she made, anyway, because the bathroom door swung open, and Emery walked out of the steam with only a towel wrapped low around his hips.

Suddenly, I couldn't hear Lily anymore. I couldn't feel my hands. I couldn't *not* stare at him.

His shaggy hair was damp, dripping water from the ends of it down his neck and over the lean muscles of his chest, his ribs, his abdomen, all the way down to the edge of the towel. He ran a hand through his hair, ruffling it slightly with his eyes on the phone in his hand. It was playing music and he paused it, not even looking up at me when he spoke.

"She's all yours."

His arms were so muscular.

His abs were so defined.

His waist was so lean.

His towel was so low.

I snapped my eyes shut, shaking my head. "Uh, I have to go, Lily. I'll call you later. Love you, bye."

"Wait—"

I ended the call, plugging my phone into the charger before grabbing the clothes I'd set aside and the small bag with my extra liner and socks, dipping into the bathroom without another look in Emery's direction.

I still wasn't breathing as I ran the bath water, peeling my diner uniform off and propping myself on the edge of the tub. I stared at the heap of cloth on the floor as I removed my prosthesis, realizing I would never be wearing that uniform again.

Even though I'd done it for more than eight years, taking off my leg was still just as strange to me as it was the first time I did it. My hands moved on autopilot now, though, where they used to stumble through the process, fussing with the pin that would release all the parts with a simple click. I watched my hands numbly as they removed the leg, sliding it off the thick socks that I wore beneath it. I peeled them off next, one by one, followed by my liner, and then I was face to face with my scar.

I took my time cleaning my stump before lowering myself completely into the water, sighing as the hot water rushed up to my neck. I let myself soak for a while before washing my hair and cleaning my liner, then I dried myself with one of the fluffy towels, switched to the new liner and socks, and slid my stump back into the prosthesis, standing to wiggle my knees until it clicked into place.

The bathroom mirror was fogged over, and I ran my hand over the glass, making a circle just big enough to see my face. I knew what my body looked like. I knew the petite frame of it — the barely there chest, the narrow hips, the tan, freckled skin. And I knew the left thigh was thinner than the right, and that it ended in an uneven, unnatural cut just below my knee. Even with my leg on, even with the socks thickening my thigh and knee, I never forgot what was missing. I never forgot what I'd never have again.

My long, wet hair stuck to my back as I dressed, and I smoothed a thick drop of keratin oil between my palms before brushing my fingers through the strands. I could barely see without my glasses on, which was fine by me, and I didn't push them back into place until I was fully dressed and pulling the bathroom door open.

Emery's eyes found me when I emerged from the bathroom, and I stood at the door with my rumpled uniform tucked under one arm and my toiletry bag hanging from my opposite hand. I planned on moving, on walking back over to my bed and sitting next to Kalo, but once his eyes found mine, they pinned me. They felt more like hands as they made a slow descent all the way to my Toms. The strong and steady way they took me in, how they wrapped around my arms, holding me in place, making it impossible to breathe, let alone move.

His eyes were darker in the hotel room light, and his hair was still damp as he ran a hand lazily through it. "I'm not that hungry yet, are you?"

"I could wait," I lied, my stomach growling in protest as my feet finally found the ability to move again. I tucked my dirty clothes into the side pocket of my duffle bag, slipping a new hair tie over my wrist as I turned back to face Emery.

"Cool. Let's hit a few bars before dinner, then."

"Okay."

He eyed me. "Don't look so scared."

"I'm not," I lied again. His journal peeked out from where he'd stuffed it back into his bag, and I ripped my eyes from it and back to him.

Emery stood. "First thing's first — we need costumes."

"Costumes?"

He crossed the room to me, stopping with less than five inches between us, his own body towering over mine as a barely there smile found his lips. "Well, it is Halloween, isn't it?"

My twenty-first birthday wasn't for another three months, so it shouldn't have been a surprise when I said I didn't drink. But it was. Every single time. Because even if it wasn't *legal* for me to have a beer yet, it was still *normal* for me to want one. Except I didn't. I never had.

I told Emery this as he picked random headbands off a street cart on Bourbon, placing one after the other on my head and tilting his head to the side as he watched me, trying to decide what I should be for the night. He had a pirate patch over his eye and a bandana tied over his hair, along with a fake gold earring clipped on his left ear. He completed the look with a pirate sword hooked into a brown leather belt at his waist.

For me, the choice was between a cat and a devil.

Neither made sense, since I was allergic to cats and my list of sins was five lines long, the worst of the offenses being that I stole a backpack from Mr. Harold's store when I was thirteen.

Still, Emery decided the devil horns suited me, and after I was equipped with a red plastic pitchfork and a tail that hung awkwardly from my tailbone, we were swallowed by the chaos that was Bourbon Street.

I couldn't open my eyes wide enough to take it all in. There were hundreds of people crowding the street, pouring in and out of bars, all of them dressed in costumes and their necks decorated with layers and layers of beads. It wasn't even Mardi Gras, but I learned quickly that it didn't need to be for everyone in that city to celebrate and show skin for plastic necklaces.

Emery grabbed my elbow and pulled me closer to him as we walked through a particularly crowded part of the street, his eyes on a bar in the distance.

"It's like you've never been to a block party before," he said, his mouth close to my ear.

I just laughed, my gaze not catching on one scene for too long before I was finding something else new. "I haven't. This is... insane. There are so many people, and it's so loud!"

"And smelly," he added, and I laughed again. He wasn't wrong.

Emery had to guide me the entire way until we got to the bar, especially since I was stopping at every street performer we passed along the way. There were saxophone players and flame throwers and magicians, voodoo doctors and bead vendors, and a group of religious protestors holding up signs that read, "Jesus Is Watching." There was so much to look at that it was impossible to see it all, but I still tried, eyes wide as I took in everything for the first time.

"You sure you don't want anything?" Emery yelled over the live music in the first bar we slid into. He had ordered a *grenade*, which made me fear for his life.

"I wouldn't mind a water."

His brows knitted together, a curious expression flashing on his face before he ordered me the water, taking the barstool next to the one I'd propped myself onto.

We turned in our seats, listening to the middle-aged man playing an acoustic guitar as he made jokes with a bachelorette party gathered around his tiny stage. It was curious that the bar was so packed and loud and yet felt so intimate and cozy at the same time. It was like we were all just a group of old friends, reunited for the evening.

I sipped on my water as the man on stage started his version of "Sweet Caroline." My free hand was absentmindedly rubbing my left thigh, but I pretended I was just tapping along to the beat when Emery's eyes would catch on my fingers. Sometimes it was phantom pains, other times it only felt like pins and needles, like my leg was asleep, and right now I had a combination of the two as my feet dangled from that barstool.

We weren't there for long before two things happened at once, almost so in sync I thought they were planned.

One, an adorable brunette more than a little blessed in the bust area propped herself right between Emery's legs, her chest directly in his line of sight as she leaned up to whisper something in his ear. I flushed red, tearing my eyes from the scene and back to the stage, but my view was blocked by a dark-haired, tattoo-covered man as he smirked down at me.

"Water, huh?" he said, appeasing my half-empty plastic cup. "I knew they went hard in NOLA, but no one warned me about girls like you."

My cheeks heated double-time, and a nervous laugh shot from my lips as I took another sip.

He seemed to be about my age, maybe a little older, and he leaned one elbow on the bar to my right, effectively separating me from Emery and the busty brunette from the bachelorette party.

"I'm Vinny," he said, reaching out a hand for mine. His entire forearm was covered in ink, and my eyes traced the lines of it as I slid my hand into his.

"Cooper."

He grinned, tapping one of my devil horns once he dropped my hand from his grip. "What'd you do to earn these, Satan?"

I swallowed down the rest of my water, abandoning the empty cup on the bar and immediately reaching for my hair. I gathered it at the back of my neck before pulling it over my shoulder, hands fussing with the ends of it as I tried to play cool.

"I stole a backpack once."

Vinny laughed. "I knew you were trouble."

He asked where I was from, and I answered just as the overwhelming sensation that I was being watched washed over me. Vinny started in on a story about the one time he spent a night in Mobile, but not a single word of it registered, because Emery still had that girl between his legs, her back to me, her lips whispering God knows what in his ear, but his eyes were like laser beams on me.

There was no emotion behind his stare, his expression as smooth as a pond at night. One hand rested on the waist of the brunette practically crawling into his lap, the other sat wrapped around his drink, but his eyes were on mine, asking me something I couldn't answer, or maybe telling me something I already knew.

I kept his gaze for just a second before snapping my attention back to Vinny, nodding and smiling as he continued his story. I could still feel Emery's eyes on me, could see him in my peripheral, and heat crawled up my neck as I tried to focus on what Vinny was saying.

"So, you just in town for the night?"

I nodded. "Yup. Just passing through."

Vinny leaned in a little closer, the distinct smell of whiskey on his breath. It reminded me of my dad, in the absolute worst way, and I fought against the urge to cringe. "What do you say we make the most of it, then?"

I swallowed, Vinny's eyes flicking to my lips as he leaned in, and my heart picked up speed.

He was cute, but did I want him to kiss me? Did I want to *make the most of the night* with him?

My fingers paused where they were braiding my hair, and I looked over Vinny's shoulder, seeking Emery, but he wasn't there.

"Hey."

I jumped a little at his voice, whipping around to look up at him. He towered over Vinny, standing at the front of my barstool now, not even acknowledging the man who stood to the right of it.

"You ready to grab a bite to eat?"

I nodded, relief washing over me as I turned my attention back to my new friend. "Sorry, the devil needs sustenance. Have a good night, Vinny."

"Yeah, have a good night, Vinny," Emery repeated, his jaw set like stone as he glared at the tattooed man.

Vinny stood straighter, putting distance between himself and the bar, eyes roaming over Emery, unimpressed, before finding mine again. He didn't say another word before grabbing his drink from the bar and making his way back to the crowded dance floor in front of the stage.

Emery watched him go, a scowl set on his face until his eyes found mine again. His expression smoothed, and he held out a hand, helping me down from the barstool.

"How's your luck, Cooper Owens?"

"So, you don't drink," Emery mused as I chowed down on the last of the Po-Boy sandwich dripping deliciousness over my hands. I didn't even care how unattractive I looked as I chewed the last bite, dropping the wrapper in the trashcan outside of Harrah's Casino before wiping at my hands with the stack of napkins I'd had shoved in my back pocket.

"Nope," I murmured around the mouthful, wiping at the edges of my lips and dropping the napkins into the trashcan, too. Emery watched me with an amused smile, hands tucked easily into his front pockets. He hadn't eaten anything, opting for another drink, instead, but it didn't stop me from grubbing down. "Never have."

"That because you're not twenty-one yet, or is there another reason?" he asked, pulling the large glass door open for me to walk through.

A symphony of ringing bells, cheers, and laughter hit me all at once, combining with a cloud of cigarette smoke that I squinted my eyes against as a man standing at the front door took my ID. It was the fake Tammy had purchased for me as a joke, and I'd never used it — never needed to — but it seemed to be legit enough to work because the man handed it back to me without so much as a second glance, taking a look at Emery's next.

I didn't even have time to be nervous about him checking it before it was back in my hand, and I slid it into my back pocket with wide eyes still looking around me. It was the first time I'd ever been in a casino and I scanned the bright lights of the machines, the crowds gathered around the tables in the back, the man's voice announcing over the intercom that someone had won fifteen-thousand dollars with their player's card.

"My parents drink," I answered when Emery was beside me again.

His brows furrowed as we walked the outer aisle toward the bar, my eyes still bouncing off the various machines. "And so you don't."

"Exactly."

He nodded, and though I hadn't told him anything, he seemed to understand everything I didn't want to say.

Emery ordered a Tom Collins at the bar, making sure he got me a water with it, before leading us right into the middle of the slot machines.

"Okay, pick your poison," he said, eyeing the machines as we walked.

I laughed. "I don't really gamble, either."

"Not for you," he said quickly. "For me. Pick a machine."

I chewed my lip, nose scrunched as I surveyed the options. I spotted a vacant one a few rows away with a big screen above it, all with boxes wrapped like birthday presents. There were streamers and party poppers and cartoon people dancing all over the screen, and I pointed to it with a shrug.

"That one looks fun."

He followed my finger until he found the machine I'd pointed out, then he nodded, guiding us toward it and pulling over a spare barstool so I could sit beside him. Emery slipped in a twenty-dollar bill and the machine sprang to life, a loud, goofy voice yelling out a welcome to us.

He pushed the button for max bet, eyes on the spinning lines of the screen. "You don't get along with your parents," he said, and the machine dinged with a prize half of what he'd bet. He hit the button again.

It wasn't a question, but I answered anyway. "They're not really parents, honestly. More like roommates."

"Were they pissed that you left?"

A dry laugh left my lips. "They didn't even notice."

He looked at me for a long moment, but I kept my eyes on the screen, watching as he won three dollars thanks to a line of party streamers. He tapped the button again, watching the screen with me.

"What about you," I asked. "Are you close with your parents?"

"No," he answered easily. "Not because they're bad people. They're actually pretty perfect," he admitted, like he hated that fact. "But I'm not really close with anyone."

"By choice or circumstance?"

"Both." The machine punctuated his sentence with a sad horn. He lost that bet. "I'm not exactly the easiest to get along with."

"So, there's no one you're close with, then?"

"Not anymore."

I waited for him to continue, to tell me what *not anymore* meant, but he just sipped on his drink, finger tapping at the max bet button again.

"That mean there used to be someone you were close with?"

Emery paused, eyes flicking over to mine before adjusting back on the screen. "My Grams."

I nodded, heart in my throat as the first page of his journal flashed in my memory, along with our conversation earlier in the car.

"What was she like?"

He smiled a little, even though the twenty he'd put in the machine was now down to six dollars and seventy-two cents. "She was quiet, and kind. She listened a lot, not just to people but to the world around her." He looked at me then. "You remind me of her."

"I do?"

Emery nodded. "This is it, last bet." He jerked his head toward the machine. "I think you should take the last spin."

He was changing the subject, and I let him, closing my eyes and sticking my tongue out as I popped the plastic button with a flat palm. "Big money, no whammies!" I yelled.

Emery bit back a smile, curious eyes watching me instead of the machine.

I shrugged. "I've always wanted to say that."

The lines lit up and the screen cleared, all of a sudden filled with rows of tiny presents like I'd seen before we sat down.

"Holy shit," Emery laughed the curse. "You got the bonus."

"I did?!"

"Pick a box."

I bounced in my seat, picking box after box, some of them doubling our prize or sending us into a new level of the bonus. Each time I picked a box that wasn't a dud we screamed, drawing a small crowd, all of them laughing and rooting us on. By the time it ended, the last three dollars we'd bet climbed up to five-hundred and twenty-two, and a few whistles rang out over the applause as the machine counted up our winnings.

"I can't believe that just happened!" I squealed, fingers twirling the ends of my hair over my shoulder.

Emery hit the *print ticket* button and stood, laughing.

"You really were lucky, like a penny heads up on the highway," he said. I cranked my neck to look up at him, the sharp edges of his jaw and cheek bones highlighted with shadows in the casino light. He looked a little intimidating.

He looked a little beautiful.

"Maybe I should call you Copper."

I grimaced. "Please, don't."

"Too late."

And then he laughed, and I did, too, and the stranger with the car didn't seem quite so scary anymore.

# Chapter 5

New Orleans, Louisiana

I woke to the gentle sound of my alarm the next morning, and my eyes shot open, hands scrambling for the device to shut it off before it woke Emery. When the room was silent again, I snuck a glance in his direction.

He was still just a rumple of body under the big comforter, the sides of it pulled free from where it had been tucked under the bed. One foot stuck out and hung over the side of the bed, and his hair peeked out from the opposite end, the only proof there was a human there at all.

Inhaling a deep breath and letting it go softly, I scrubbed a hand over my face, eyes focusing on the intricate designs that covered the all-white ceiling above. Kalo huffed next to me, laying her head on my hip, and I rubbed behind her ears until she was asleep again, my mind waking up slowly.

Last night had been fun, and the entire concept of road tripping across the country with someone I didn't know felt a little less insane now that the sun had risen on a new day, but I still wondered where the day would lead, where the trip would take us. I glanced over at Emery again, my gaze falling on where his journal lay face down on the bedside table, the pages flattened against the wood to mark where he'd been writing the night before. I'd pretended to fall asleep quickly, all the while listening to his scribbles over the page, wondering what it was he could be writing.

*You're not reading his journal,* I chastised myself, taking another deep inhale before reaching under the covers for my prosthesis. I never slept with it on, but I also didn't want to take it off in front of Emery... not yet. So, I'd waited until he clicked his light off, until his breathing intensified to a soft snore, and then I'd carefully removed it, tucking it under the sheets with me.

Once it was back in place, I sat up slowly, swinging my legs over the edge of the bed. I adjusted the prosthesis again before rolling the pant leg of my yoga pants down over it and standing, wiggling my knees until it locked into place.

As quietly as I could, I slipped on my shoes and tucked my yoga mat under my arm, making my way toward the door. The room was still mostly dark, the curtains pulled closed except for a tiny sliver in the middle which provided just enough light for me not to fall on my face.

"You can do that in here," Emery murmured, but his voice was so deep and loud in the otherwise silent room that I jumped.

Flattening a palm over my racing heart, I turned to face him, but he was still buried under the covers.

"It's okay," I finally said, voice a whisper, like I was still afraid to wake him. "I prefer to do it alone. I'll be back soon."

There was movement under the comforter and then an arm stuck out, one thumb raised in understanding before he pulled it back under the covers.

I smiled, letting myself out into the hallway.

The hotel gym was expansive, with top-of-the-line equipment lining all three walls, but luckily for me it was empty that morning. I laid my mat down in the free space lining the large windows overlooking the French Quarter, stretching my arms over my head as I looked out at the city slowly coming to life.

When I was ready, I lowered myself down into a seated position, once again taking my prosthetic leg off and setting it to the side. I unwrapped my socks and peeled off the liner, eyes scanning the familiar scar at the end of my stump. Sometimes when I looked at it, I was removed from the memory, only seeing it for what it was and what it wasn't. Other times, like that morning in New Orleans, I blinked and flashed back to the accident, to the blood, to the screaming, to the numb awareness that my entire life was about to change.

After my physical therapy had ended, I'd taken up yoga, deciding I would do it without my prosthetic leg. I wanted to build strength, both externally and internally, and I also wanted to find inner peace and understanding.

Closing my eyes, I started my practice with long inhales and exhales, slipping away from reality for a while.

Yoga brought me comfort, and I slipped into my practice easily, slowly moving to standing position and through various poses with my eyes adjusting to the rising sun over the city. Before I knew it, I was on my back in Savasana, eyes closed as I braced myself for the new day.

Thoughts of my parents creeped into my mind, as they always did, and I would imagine myself stripping those thoughts from my mind and dropping them onto a cloud floating by, just like my yoga instructor had taught me when I was thirteen. Anything that didn't serve me, mind, body, and soul, I let go of in my morning practice. When my eyes fluttered open and I pulled my leg into place again, I felt at peace, walking back to the room with an easy smile and open heart.

The room was still dark when I opened the door, and it appeared Emery hadn't moved even an inch. I checked the time on the small alarm clock next to his fluff of hair, frowning when I saw it was already eight. Our plan had been to be on the road no later than eight-thirty.

*I'm not his mother,* I reminded myself, ducking into the bathroom to quickly rinse off. I didn't break much of a sweat that morning, so a full shower wasn't necessary, but I did want to freshen up before sitting in the car next to Emery all day.

I packed up my belongings as quietly as I could, taking Kalo for a walk and getting her fed and watered for the day ahead. When the clock read a quarter till nine, I flicked on the first light, just a small lamp in the corner, and cleared my throat.

Emery didn't stir.

I zipped up my bag, plopping it on the bed without care for being quiet anymore.

Still nothing.

Kalo watched me as I blew out a breath and I shrugged down at her, extending an open hand toward the ruffled mess of covers Emery still laid under. Kalo followed my hand, and then before I could stop her, she jumped up onto his bed, digging into the covers until she uncovered his face.

"Ack!" Emery groaned, rolling over with furrowed brows as Kalo assaulted his face with her classic puppy kisses. I scolded her, though I was laughing, and called her name until she jumped over to my bed instead, sitting with her tongue still flopped out.

"Sorry," I chuckled as Emery covered his face with his hands. "It is almost nine, though... want me to make you a cup of coffee or anything?"

He shook his head, palms still dug into his eyes as he rubbed them.

"I was thinking," I started, pacing. "Maybe we should make a plan. For the trip. Like, cities we want to hit, amount of miles we want to cover each day. Not that we have to stick with it to a T or anything," I said quickly. "I just mean it might be nice to know what to expect."

"Come here."

I stopped, watching as his hands fell exasperatedly to his sides on top of the comforter. It puffed with the weight of them, and his tired eyes found mine.

"Come here," he said again, patting the small patch of empty bed beside him. He was still practically in the middle of it, and he didn't make to move to either side.

I swallowed, fingers finding the cool metal of the ring on my middle finger. It matched the one on Lily's finger thousands of miles away, our promise to remain best friends no matter the distance between us. I spun it around and around as I sat on the edge of his bed, unsure where to look.

He didn't say another word, just reached out for me, hand wrapping around my elbow gently and guiding me down until I was lying on my back next to him, careful not to touch my body to his, heart thumping hard under my ribs.

"I had a strange dream last night," he said, voice gruff. It sounded different than last night, the baritone of it, and I caught the hint of sadness that underlined it like a shadow. "I'm not sure if I even slept at all, but I know I dreamed."

I wasn't sure if I was supposed to answer him, or ask about the dream, or just lie there. The third option seemed to be the only one I could manage, so I kept spinning my ring, eyes on the ceiling.

"I was an eagle, I think, or maybe a crow. A crow seems more likely. I know I had wings, and feathers, and a beak. And I was aware I couldn't *actually* be a bird, I still felt human inside, but I was building a nest. I had all these..." He threw his hands up in front of us, waving them around. "Sticks and shit. Leaves and sticks and mud and just all of it was a mess. And I kept trying to build this fucking nest." He was growing more and more agitated, his voice picking up volume as he spoke. "But nothing would work. The mud was too wet, it wouldn't hold, and the sticks were too fragile. Everything kept breaking. And there was this storm coming, I could hear it in the distance, and see the clouds and the lightning. And I needed to build the goddamn nest."

He paused, shaking his head. He shook it over and over, not speaking for the longest time. When he finally did continue, his voice was softer, almost broken.

"The storm was closing in, and I was still frantically trying to get the nest to stick, feathers flying everywhere from the exertion. And I was moving so slow, like I was under water. But then all of a sudden, I looked at the storm, at the clouds, at the lightning, and I realized I didn't know why I was working so hard to build the nest. I had no one to build it for, no one who needed it, no one I was protecting. And I wasn't scared of the storm."

I pulled my eyes from the ceiling, tilting my head just a little, enough to watch the slow rise and fall of his bare chest beside me. I was on top of the covers and he still rested under them, the comforter gathered at his hips. I just watched him breathe for a moment, wondering why he was telling me this, wondering what it all meant.

"What happened next?"

Emery let out a long breath. "The storm came, and it washed me away. I couldn't control anything, and the rain was so hard, it flooded me out of my tree and down into a low valley, the rapids dark and treacherous. But I wasn't scared anymore, I was only upset I spent so long trying to build that fucking nest."

The fingers playing with my ring stilled, and I folded my hands over my stomach. "That is a strange dream."

Emery nodded, rolling over until he faced me completely. He waited until I tilted my head a bit farther, until our eyes connected, and then I saw the sadness I'd heard in his voice before. His eyes, so gold the day before, were dull and tired, and they watched me with a plea for something, though I didn't know what.

"I don't want to drive today," he whispered. "I don't want to move from this bed. Can we just... can we stay here. I'm so tired." His eyes closed, the same two lines forming right above the bent ridge of his nose as he did. "I'm *tired*."

I swallowed. In that moment, the tall, confident man I'd met the day before reminded me more of my mother, helpless and sad. I wondered what had happened to him, what demons he battled in the dark of the night when no one else was around.

"How about I drive today?" I whispered back.

He opened his eyes slowly, watching me, pupils fluctuating in size as they flicked back and forth between my own. A hardness seemed to wash over them as we laid there, the vulnerability slipping away just as quickly as it had come. I'd offered to drive thinking it would help, that it would make him happy, but it was like I'd disappointed him, instead. Or, maybe it wasn't me at all. Maybe it was the dream, or himself, or life, in general. But suddenly I felt like I was the nest, a waste of his time, of his energy.

He didn't speak, but I heard his voice anyway, asking me that same question he did the day before.

*What makes you happy?*

I wanted to know his answer, too.

I wasn't sure how long we laid there before he finally nodded, his eyes still tired as he did. I opened my mouth to speak again but he was already up, covers thrown back, and I was alone in his bed. The ridges of the lean muscles that lined his back were all I saw as he dipped inside the bathroom, a stranger yet again, the door shutting behind him with a soft click.

# Chapter 6

## Lake Charles, Louisiana

We'd been on the road for three hours, and Emery hadn't said a single word.

The sun warmed our skin as we drove with the top down again, and this time I'd been smart enough to slather my shoulders and face with sunscreen. I was a little burnt from the day before, just a tinge of red on my otherwise tan skin, but enough to know it wouldn't be pretty if I didn't protect myself.

Kalo laid behind my seat most of the drive, finding shade there, and the music blasted over the sound of the wind as it whipped through the car.

I'd watched Emery from my peripheral most of the drive, glancing over every now and then to see if he'd look back at me. He never did. His eyes were either on the scenery as we passed through each town or on the pages of his journal as he wrote. Even when he wasn't writing, the book sat in his lap, pages wide open. He held the pen in his hand the entire time, too, the cap hooked on the top of it, always at the ready.

Emery wore a permanent scowl that day. Not just the easy lines between his brows, but a full-on, eyebrows pulled low and mouth in a thin line scowl. The edges of his clean jaw seemed even sharper, the sun and shadows battling for dominance when we passed under lazy Louisiana trees. I wanted to know what he was thinking, how he was feeling, but every attempt I'd made at a conversation had gone off about as well as a lighter in the rain.

We stopped in Lake Charles long enough to grab new snacks and use the bathroom. Emery still didn't speak, but he did take Kalo for a walk while I filled up our gas tank. I massaged my thigh gently and surveyed them together in the small patch of grass at the edge of the parking lot, Kalo hopping around in the grass with a goofy grin and tongue hanging out. Emery just stood and watched her, hands in his pockets, shoulders rounded.

When we were back on the road, I propped the bag of beef jerky I'd just purchased in-between my legs, ripping the top of it open and digging inside for the first chunk just as I noticed the bridge coming up in the distance. It was a steep incline, pointing us toward Westlake, and I chewed on the teriyaki snack with a glance toward Emery.

"Are there a lot of bridges where you live in Florida?" I asked, trying again to get some sort of conversation flowing. The awkward silence left between us from the morning was still hanging around, and I was ready to get rid of it.

Emery didn't answer, his eyes on the water as we started to ascend over the bridge.

"I used to be terrified of them," I continued, shredding another bite off a large piece of beef jerky. "My dad said when I was younger, I would literally scream at the top of my lungs anytime we crossed over one. I don't really remember that, but, ironically enough, I got into a car accident on a bridge. And ever since then, I haven't been afraid of them anymore."

Still nothing.

"Have you ever been in a car accident?"

He looked at me over his sunglasses then, brows gathered in a pinch of concern.

"Oh," I said, cheeks flushing. "I guess that's probably not the best topic of conversation on a road trip, is it?"

Emery looked at the road again, and I washed down the beef jerky with a drink from the large fountain soda I'd purchased at the gas station. Tapping my thumbs on the steering wheel, I racked my brain for what else to talk about.

"I bet this bridge would be so fun on a bike. I mean, not the way up, of course. That would suck. Calves would be on *fire*. But look at this hill down," I said as we dipped over the apex. "Could you imagine? You'd go so fast, just flying down with the wind in your face, wheels turning faster than you've ever seen them go before."

I paused, smiling.

"Do you have a bike?"

Emery sighed then, folding his hands over his journal with the pen still threaded through his fingers. He just looked at me, as if he was asking, "*Are you done yet?*"

"I'm talking too much, huh?"

He forced a smile, but not the encouraging kind. The kind that said, "*Yes, you are.*"

I laughed. "Just another reason why I'll be single forever. Add it to the list."

Emery had started turning his gaze back to the road, but he stopped then, facing me again.

"You say that like it's a bad thing."

*He speaks, ladies and gentlemen.*

"What? Being single?"

He nodded.

"Well, it's not exactly the *best* thing."

"Are you kidding?" He snapped his journal shut in his lap, sitting up a little straighter. "Being single is *literally* the best thing ever."

It wasn't exactly the conversation I'd had in mind, but he was talking, so I took it. Dipping my hand into the beef jerky bag again, I pulled out another nugget, popping it in my mouth.

"Oh, sure. It's super fun not having someone to kiss, or hold, or share good and bad times with. It would suck so bad to have someone who loved you during the holiday season, or someone who wanted to make you smile every day. Sounds *awful.*"

Emery snorted. "See, you have it all wrong. Those things you just said, those *fantasies,* they're just that. Your vision of what a relationship should or would be is warped from what it actually is."

"Mm," I mused. "Sounds like the pessimistic view of a guy who'd rather have sex with no strings attached, to me."

"Well, yeah," he agreed and I laughed, Kalo popping up from where she was hiding behind my seat at the sound. She seemed happy we were talking, too, and she hung her head between us. "That's part of it. You're telling me having mind-blowing sex with someone new, someone exciting, whenever you want doesn't appeal to you?"

My cheeks flushed a deeper shade and I cranked the dial on the air conditioning, giving the wind an extra boost. "I think I'd rather have someone consistent, someone who loved me when he touched me."

Emery stared at me long enough for me to glance his way and then regret that I did, because he was looking at me like he was a scientist and I was the gunk under the microscope.

"You're a virgin."

I scoffed, grabbing my drink and pulling the soda through the straw without breathing for a solid thirty seconds, shaking my head all the while.

"It's nothing to be embarrassed about," he added when I finally put the drink down, both hands finding the steering wheel. My knuckles turned white, and suddenly it was *me* who didn't want to talk.

"Just because I've never had sex before doesn't mean I'm naive or stupid. I know how relationships work, and I know casual sex must have its perks but... I don't know. I don't want to be single forever."

"Well, you should be," he said. "Maybe not forever, if you want kids or whatever, I get that. But you should spend time alone. Travel alone. Live alone. You should try new things, figure out if you like them not just because your friend or *boy*friend likes them, but because *you* genuinely do. And you should have casual sex," he added. "With as many people as you can before you settle down."

"That sounds unsafe."

"Condoms and birth control, my Little Penny."

I scrunched my nose at the reference to my nickname earned at the casino the night before. "You really don't ever want to fall in love? You don't want to know what it's like to have someone care about you so much it literally drives them crazy, and they would do anything to make you happy, and you'd do the same for them?"

"Do you know a single couple in your life who's actually like that?" he probed, and Kalo tilted her head, as if she was ticking through people she knew just like I was. "Not in movies or books, but actual people. Your parents? Their relationship beautiful and wonderful?"

I swallowed. "Hardly."

"Okay. What about your grandparents? Aunts, uncles? Teachers? Anyone in your town, any of your friends?"

I thought through the short list, especially since I'd never had a relationship with my dad's parents and my mom's parents had both passed away when I was young. Lily's parents had been happily married once, or so I thought, until they got divorced. They were still cordial with each other, but as her mom had put it, *the love had died.* Tammy left her ex because he hit her, and Ray was still in love with a woman who never loved him back.

Emery seemed to watch my wheels turning, and though he didn't smile, I felt the smugness rolling off of him from across the console.

"Okay, well, maybe relationships aren't supposed to be perfect. But you don't believe in love at all? Like, not even a little bit?"

He shrugged. "Love is real, of course. I know it exists. I've loved a lot of people."

I looked over at him then, a tinge of something touching the pit of my stomach. Jealousy, maybe? But I wasn't sure if it was of him, that he'd been in love, or of those who'd been on the receiving end of his.

"But most of it is chemical, Cooper. Lust and endorphins and all that crashing every logical thought for the first six months or so. Then reality sets in, and you

70

realize you actually hate living with that person. Or they want you to change all of a sudden. The *I love you just the way you are* turns into *I'd love you more if you got a stable job and a five-year plan.*" Emery paused. "It's almost impossible to find someone who really loves you — the real you — flaws and all. So no, I'm not sure I believe in a one true love or a soul mate. I do believe in loving as many people as you can, and experiencing them in all the ways you can before the chemistry runs out."

"Is that code for *have a ton of sex*?"

"Among other things."

I chuckled, shaking my head. "So, is that your plan, then? Stay single forever?"

Emery was quiet a long moment before he turned toward the road again, flipping his journal open. "Maybe. But forever isn't always as long as you think it will be."

He started writing again, reaching forward for the volume dial and cranking it up until an old Tom Petty song filled the space between us. I guessed the conversation was over then, and Kalo licked my arm before settling back into her place behind my seat, leaving just my thoughts to entertain me as we drove toward the Texas border.

We hit a bad storm right after we crossed the state line. I'd pulled over, getting the top up just before it started raining buckets. Traffic was awful, visibility was poor, and Emery and I were both so tense by the time we made it out that we were ready to stop for the day.

So, even though it was less than six hours from where we'd started that morning, we called Houston home for the night, checking into a modest hotel in Midtown. I took Kalo for a long walk, fighting back yawns that started hitting me hard after the storm. When I made it back to our room, Emery was already buried under the covers.

"I'm taking a nap. Want to grab dinner in a bit?"

I finally let myself yawn, unhooking Kalo's leash and digging through my bag for her food and water bowl. "A nap sounds perfect. Should I set an alarm?"

"I've got one set for an hour and a half. The concierge said there's a concert in the park nearby tonight and there are supposed to be a bunch of food trucks."

"That sounds fun."

Emery didn't respond, rolling over toward the wall and pulling his comforter over his head.

His soft snores were the only sound in the room until the air conditioning kicked on with a hum, and I flopped down onto the other bed, eyelids heavy. Kalo was clearly ready for a nap, too. She finished her food quickly, jumping up onto the foot of my bed and curling up into a ball of fluff before I'd even taken my shoes off. I reached for the lamp on the table between our beds but my hand froze in place when I noticed Emery's journal laying in front of the phone.

*Don't do it.*

But already my hand was reaching for it, my eyes flicking to where Emery was bundled under the sheets, the same leg sticking out like it had that morning.

Slowly, and as quietly as I could, I slipped my hand under the worn leather, wrapping my fingers over the bind and pulling the journal to my lap. My breaths were slow motion, heart in my ears as I glanced at Emery again before opening to a page near the beginning.

*Dad thinks depression is a mental excuse, not a mental disorder.*

*I listened to him and Mom fight about it the entire drive to therapy today. She was playing John Cougar Mellencamp's* Uh-huh *album way too fucking loud, and they yelled over it instead of turning it down. I told them I didn't want them driving me anyway, I'm twenty-three, for fuck's sake, but Mom insisted on dropping me off on their way to lunch and picking me up after. Bonding time, or whatever.*

*Dad and Mom never fight, not unless it's about me.*

*Mom is worried about me, and I hate that I upset her, but I'm not sure how not to.*

*Honestly, I think my dad is right. I don't have a reason to be depressed.*

*We have money, we always have. I went to a good school, a good college, all paid for. I have a job with my dad until the day I die — a good job, one I enjoy, one I excel at, one that will mean I'll have a life of fortune just like he did. I've had plenty of friends throughout the years, even if I did drive them all away. Sex isn't hard to find, neither is a girl to spend time with, if I want that sort of thing. I'm healthy. I'm not the most unfortunate looking dude, either.*

*All signs point to normalcy.*

*Most people would kill to have what I do. I think that's why Dad grumbles under his breath when my therapy comes up, when Mom tries to make him recognize I have issues. I hate the word, too. Depression. It sounds so fucking stupid, and I feel stupid. I don't want to go to therapy, or talk about my feelings, or question every fucking thread of my past looking for answers.*

*What if there is no answer? What if I am just not a happy person. Period. The end.*

*I think I could have gotten away with it, with just being a miserable prick, if I hadn't pulled the stunt that I did. That woke everyone up, most of all Mom, and now I have to pay for it.*

*I didn't even want to do it. Maybe the day I tried, I did. It was a bad day. Today, right now, I know it was stupid.*

*But today is a good day.*

*Even if I did have to listen to Dad tell me how ungrateful I am for a solid twenty minutes.*

*I think it's because he grew up with Grams for a mom. She's the only one who seems to get me, and it's because she's the same kind of crazy. People say I got my nose from her, and I guess I got this, too.*

*I still hate writing in this thing. And think all of this is pointless. And for the record, I fucking hate John Cougar Mellencamp.*

My hand found my mouth, fingertips ice cold on the skin of my lips as I glanced up at Emery. He was still sleeping, his breaths even and steady, his mind at peace — at least I hoped. I didn't know what he was dreaming, or if he even was at all.

I should have put it down, should have closed the journal and vowed never to pry into his private thoughts again. I should have had more respect for him, for the words meant only for him, but I was selfish. I wanted to know more. I wanted to know everything.

My fingers fell from my lips and flipped through the pages, all the way to the entry from last night.

*Grams told me when I took this trip, I needed to keep my eyes open. She said part of the journey would be doing things I'd never done before, taking chances, exploring. She wanted me to invite adventure into my heart.*

*So, I picked up a hitchhiker.*

I scoffed.

*Okay, not really a hitchhiker, but a girl who needed a lift.*

*I don't even think she realized it, not until the moment I asked her to come with me, maybe not even until we were two hours away from Mobile where I picked her up. But I knew the second I saw her.*

*She was a caged bird, and when I opened the door to let her out, she didn't know whether to fly or molt.*

*Her name is Cooper and she has a dog. The dog came with us, which I thought would be annoying since I hate anything that is adorable, but surprisingly this dog doesn't bother me. Her eyes are crossed a little bit and her fur is out of control, like she's never been to a groomer. I like that about her. She's the ugly kind of cute.*

*I don't know if I like Cooper yet.*

I chewed my lip, heat crawling its way up my neck.

*She talks a lot. She's naive. She's young. Her glasses are too big for her face. She's religious, but I don't know that I can blame her since she grew up in the Bible Belt. Mostly, I'm just perturbed because under all that, she's beautiful, and I find myself insanely curious about her.*

*I wonder how she'll be on my bad days.*

*She was my waitress at the diner in Mobile and I asked her my question. She couldn't answer. But unlike everyone else, she didn't tell me a bunch of stupid shit. She could have said her dog made her happy or her boyfriend or something else surface-level.*

*Does she have a boyfriend? I didn't even ask.*

*Actually, I really don't care, so I won't be asking.*

*But the point is she didn't look at me like the question was absurd, or like there were plenty of things in the world that made her happy, or like I was weird for asking. She looked at me like she couldn't answer because in order to list what made her happy, she had to know she was happy in the first place.*

*She also looked at me like I was serial killer when I asked her to come with me, not that I can blame her.*

*Still, she came. And now I'm on this trip with a girl and a dog.*

*Maybe this was what Grams was talking about, or maybe I'm just fucking stupid. Either way, I've got someone to talk to.*

*Poor girl.*

I smiled a little at that, yawning as I closed the journal and gently placed it where I'd found it. I tucked my legs under the sheets, gently removing my prosthesis once I was covered and moving it off to the side. Stretching my arms over my head and pointing my toe, I let exhaustion wash over me, closing my eyes just as Kalo moved to curl up by my side. I rolled over, one hand petting her long, soft fur as the other propped the pillow up under my head.

"You really are the ugly kind of cute," I whispered to her, and she licked my hand in agreement before laying it down on her paws.

I closed my eyes, thoughts still racing as his handwriting filled my mind. I shouldn't have read his journal, and I swore to myself then and there that I wouldn't read anymore. We were on a road trip together. If I wanted to know something about him, I should just ask.

*That is, if it's a day where he's talking.*

I wondered if he'd wake up after our nap in a better mood, with the smile I'd seen a few times the day before. I wondered if tomorrow would be another silent drive, if I would annoy him even more than I already do.

He'd called me a caged bird.

No one had ever pinpointed exactly how I'd felt my entire life until that moment, that sentence, that truth scribbled out in messy, honest, almost impossible to read letters.

I imagined Mobile as my cage, Emery's hand on the door of his car, holding it open for me to escape. And just before I drifted off to sleep, my breaths even and steady in my chest, I found myself wondering if the nest from his dream really was me, after all.

A few hours later, Emery and I were both rested and cheerily stuffing our faces with the most delicious barbecue pulled pork sliders in the world.

Well, I was cheerily stuffing my face. Emery still wasn't speaking, his brows furrowed over his bored eyes, but at least he was eating.

We wandered through the park together, stopping now and then to read a plaque or watch the street performers. Emery held Kalo's leash, and every time we walked by another dog she had to stop to sniff them out. Emery didn't seem bothered by it, though. He just watched her patiently, eating his slider, and he even shared his water with her once we'd found a place to settle in for the concert.

It was a lively Sunday night, and though it wasn't *much* better than Alabama, the night air did seem to be a little cooler in Texas. I even had on one of the light sweaters I'd packed, which made me smile even bigger. Maybe I was forcing it to be sweater weather, but as long as I wasn't sweating, I was happy.

Emery had purchased a large blanket from one of the vendors and spread it out on the lawn near the front of the stage. We both sat on the itchy fabric of it, Kalo plopped down between us, belly up. Emery lazily rubbed her fur with his eyes on the stage, though he didn't look like he was really waiting for the show to begin, just like he was there. Existing.

"Are you okay?" I asked, but it was just as the first long note played from an electric guitar, and the crowd cheered, welcoming the local band to the stage.

Emery turned to me, the lights from the stage casting him in a purple glow. He gave me a thumbs up, then his hand rested on Kalo's head again, and he faced the stage.

The band's energy was infectious, the crowd swaying and clapping along as they played a mixture of popular covers and their own music. They sounded a little like they were from the 80s, reminding me of Bruce Springsteen with the melodic flow of their voices and instruments. When they took a break and the DJ came on, I took Kalo for a walk around the park and grabbed a four-pack of doughnuts from one of the food trucks Emery and I had been eyeing earlier. But when I made my way back to our blanket, he wasn't alone.

There was a girl sitting next to him, right where I had been before, though calling her a girl felt stupid because she was more a woman than anything else. Her long, dark hair fell all the way down to her short jean cut-offs, and she tossed it back behind her shoulder with a laugh at something Emery had said. The closer I got to them, the more her beauty struck me — dark, exotic eyes, gold headband wrapped around her forehead, lips full and painted a deep, dark red. She looked like a modern day Pocahontas, and I was the girl with glasses too big for her face.

Emery looked up at me when I made it to the blanket, causing Pocahontas to follow his gaze. She didn't glare at me or eye me up and down. She just smiled, a beautiful smile, her eyes falling to the box in my hands.

"Oh, my gosh! Those doughnuts are the best, have you had them yet?" she asked with a light, airy voice. Kalo hopped into her lap and she laughed, petting her behind the ears. "Well, hello there!"

"Kalo, down," I scolded, tugging on her leash until she was on the other side of me.

The only empty part of the blanket was beside our new friend, so I sat down with as much grace as the awkward third wheel can. My leg made a clinking noise when it hit the heel of her boot and she eyed me curiously, but I just cleared my throat, tucking my legs to the side opposite her and opening the box of doughnuts.

"You can have one, if you want," I said, offering her the first pick. I glanced at Emery, who was watching me with eyes a little less dull now.

"You're so sweet! Thank you." She picked up the small vanilla one with lemon icing, taking a bite and wiping the frosting from her stained lips. "I'm Emily."

"Cooper."

"Cute name!" She smiled, turning back to Emery, and then she offered him the doughnut she'd just taken a bite of.

They seemed to have some inside joke I didn't know about, because his eyes flashed, a hint of something there as he leaned forward and took a bite. It felt more like I'd walked in on him pounding her against the wall in our hotel than just seeing him eat a pastry she held in her hand.

The band kicked up again, and Emily leaned into Emery, speaking into his ear over the sound of the music. I couldn't hear them now, but Emery was laughing, and that same unfamiliar zing flitted low in my stomach as I reached into the box and pulled one of the cereal-covered doughnuts out.

I was acutely aware of the two of them as the band played through their second set. She was so gorgeous, and even with her back turned to me now as she cuddled into Emery's side, I couldn't help but trace the lean lines of her frame, her long, tan legs, her shiny black hair. She had one hand propped back behind her and it slid closer to Emery's, her fingers just barely brushing the top of his.

*Why are you staring at them, creep?*

I shook my head, trying my best to ignore them. What did it matter? Why did I care she was here, sitting close to him, making him laugh? I didn't even know him.

His journal entries flashed in my mind and I shoved those thoughts down.

He was single. He loved being single — that much he'd told me. This was probably going to be a part of the road trip, so I needed to get used to it.

But I couldn't stop staring.

Emery leaned into her, whispering something in her ear as his fingers laced with hers on the blanket behind them. His eyes found mine and I blinked, turning back to the stage quickly and shoving another bite of doughnut in my mouth.

Suddenly, Emily stood, waving at me with flushed cheeks before walking slowly and purposefully toward the park exit, her doe eyes looking back at Emery as she tucked her hands in her back pockets.

"Emily wants to show me her album collection," Emery said, handing me the keys to his car.

"Oh." I took the keys from his hand, swallowing down the acid building in my throat. It was like he was speaking to me in code. I had a pretty good idea what *album collection* really meant.

He eyed me for a moment, like he was waiting for me to protest. When I didn't, he pushed himself up off the blanket and followed Emily's trail, hands in his front pockets, just as calm and confident in his walk as she was.

Except, unlike her, he didn't look back.

"Ugh!"

I tugged my over-the-shoulder bag off, slinging it into the desk chair across the room before sliding the half-empty box of doughnuts on top of the desk. Kalo didn't seem fazed by my temper tantrum as I hastily unclasped her leash, letting that drop to the floor with another huff.

Flopping down on the edge of my bed, I pulled off my sneakers, a juvenile curl on my lip as I replayed how sweet Emily had been to me. "I'm Emily. I'm a drop-dead gorgeous exotic free spirit with long beautiful hair who eats doughnuts and still manages to have a six-pack," I mocked, rolling my eyes and turning to Kalo for reinforcement.

She just tilted her head.

"God, they even *sound* cute together," I said with a sigh, flopping back onto the bed. "Emery and Emily. Em and Em. Ugh."

Kalo whimpered, her paw patting my hand like she understood. I ruffled her fur, still sour-faced as I reminded myself again how stupid I was being. *I just need a hot shower,* I told myself, sitting up on the edge of the bed again. *And a good movie.*

I texted Lily and Tammy both to let them know I was alive and well before stripping out of my clothes and letting the hot water from the shower wash away my frustrations from the day. It had been a weird one, especially since every other day of my life up until that point had been practically the same.

I still didn't know why Emery leaving with Emily bothered me as much as it did, even after I'd dressed and climbed into bed for the night. I turned on the TV despite the uncomfortable pain in my stomach, trying my best to ignore it as I flipped through the channels.

Finally settling on an old Lifetime movie, I pulled the fluffy white comforter up under my chin with a sigh, feeling marginally better now that I was clean and warm. Emery's journal was right where I'd left it earlier, and I peeked over at it, eyeing it like it was a giant bowl of pasta and I was on a no-carb diet.

"No, Cooper. Don't even think about it."

I spoke the words out loud, as if that would stop me, like Kalo would hear them and prevent me from grabbing the damn book even if I wanted to.

The air conditioning kicked on and I adjusted the comforter over my shoulders again, watching as the main actress in the Lifetime movie grabbed a knife off her kitchen counter, dropping to the floor with wide, terrified eyes. The man she'd once dated was crazy now, and he'd just broken into the house.

My eyes flicked to the journal and back again.

The actress screamed. He'd found her.

Kalo's leg twitched with her dream and I reached for her, soothing the fur on her belly, eyes skirting off the screen again and back to the bedside table.

"Whatever," I huffed, flipping the covers back and grabbing the journal off the desk. I looked around me, like there were cameras ready to catch me in the act. But it was just me. He was with *Emily*, I reminded myself.

And then I cracked open the leather binding, flipping to the third entry.

*Marni is disappointed in me.*

*That's my therapist's name — Marni. I told her Grams gave me this journal three weeks ago, and she was excited I was finally going to give writing a chance.*

*Since then, I've only written two entries.*

*And so, Marni is disappointed in me.*

*I told her to join the club.*

*Today was a bad day. She knew it when I walked into her office and didn't crack a joke or ask about her cat. I just sat down in the same chair as always and waited for her to ask how I was, to ask how I'd been. And when she did, I just said I was fine. Everything was fine.*

*Marni knew it was bullshit.*

*She wants me to write about that day. She thinks not acknowledging it is holding me back and preventing me from moving forward. She said writing about it will be easier than talking about it, because writing is free of judgement, writing is just for me to see and to think about.*

*I still think all of this is fucking stupid, but I'm tired of adding people to the list of those I disappoint, so here's my attempt to write about it.*

There was a break in the page, a little star between the two paragraphs, and my throat was tight as I continued reading. It was there in my stomach before I even read the next word, the knowledge that what I was about to see would change everything.

*I just took a nap. Even thinking about writing about that day exhausts me. Even now, after sleeping half the afternoon away, I'm still just so... tired.*

*That day feels like a dream.*

*It's been almost two months now, and it feels like forever ago and like it was just this morning. It feels like it was someone else and like it was me, too. It feels like I dreamed it and like it happened and I'm no longer here, even though I am.*

*There was nothing particularly shitty about that day. It was just another bad day, another day where everything felt pointless. I was a month away from graduating college, with a degree I could take or leave, a degree I got because it's what was expected of me. I had a lot of people who called me a friend, but not a single one of them knew a thing about me aside from my name and what kind of beer I drank. There was a girl in my* bed that morning, and I barely remembered the night with her. Her name was stitched onto the little backpack she had with her and her tits were fake. That's all I knew about her when she left that morning, telling me to call her, knowing that I wouldn't.

I remember lying there, not blinking, just staring up at the ceiling. I didn't want to get out of bed. I didn't want to go into the kitchen and have to make small talk with my roommate or go to my capstone class at one-thirty or meet the guys from my fraternity out at the bar that night. I didn't want to move. I didn't want to live.

That's how easily the thought hit me.

I was just sifting through everything that sounded awful in my mind and the sheer pointlessness of it all steered me right to that simple truth: I didn't want to live.

I didn't think twice about it. I didn't tick through any of the reasons why I needed to live, why I should want to. I just thought it, and then I walked into the bathroom I shared with my roommate, opened the medicine cabinet, and grabbed the bottle of hydrocodone he was prescribed after his oral surgery earlier that month. He'd only used a few of them, and there were six left in the bottle.

I took them all.

Marni wants me to write about how I felt after I swallowed the pills. She wants me to write about what was running through my mind as my breaths got shallower, as the light slowly faded away, as I closed my eyes for what I thought would be the last time.

But Marni doesn't get it.

I didn't feel a single damn thing. I didn't feel sad, or angry, or scared. I didn't feel relief, either. I didn't wonder *what people would say or do when they found me. I didn't think about how it would break my mom's heart. I should have thought all of those things, but I didn't.*

*The last thing I remember thinking was that living was exhausting.*

*And then I closed my eyes.*

My lips quivered as my fingers traced the ink on the page, the cursive lines that made up that last sentence, and then a tear fell from where it had trickled down my cheek and splatted on the page.

I turned to the next one.

*When I woke up, for a split second, I thought maybe I was wrong about religion. Everything was white and blinding, but it was because I was in the hospital. I hadn't taken enough. They pumped my stomach and I woke up. I lived.*

*So, there it is. I wrote about it. Assignment completed.*

*Marni said after I finish I should let it digest and write about how I feel tomorrow, after I've let it sit for a day.*

*It'll probably be another three weeks before I write in this thing again.*

The date on the next page was the day after the one I'd just read, but I couldn't read anymore. My eyes were blurred by tears I held onto as I closed the journal and held it to my chest. I felt so dirty for reading that entry, for being selfish enough to want to keep reading even when I knew it was private, when I knew it was something never meant to be read — least of all by me.

He'd tried to kill himself.

My heart squeezed and I closed my eyes, letting the tears fall halfway down before I swiped at them, and then I tossed the journal back on the bedside table like it was on fire. Flicking off the lamp and the television, I rolled over to face the window, hugging a pillow to my chest.

I couldn't hold onto a single thought before another one raced into my mind next, quickly replacing the first. Who had found him? Who told his parents? What happened next? Why did he do it? Was he seeing Marni before that day, or was she part of his treatment plan? Was he on medication now? Was he *okay* now?

Was he still alive?

Suddenly, the fact that he was with Emily didn't bother me anymore. Annoyance turned to worry in a flash, and I checked the time on my phone, seeing it was nearly midnight. I didn't know if he would come back to our room that night. I didn't have his phone number. I didn't have any way to reach him, or find him, or make sure he still had a pulse.

I could only wait to see if he showed back up.

I swore I didn't sleep at all that night, but I must have at some point, because I woke to Kalo licking my face and the smell of sausage McMuffins. With a groan, I rolled until I was facing away from her, pulling the covers over my head.

"Morning, sunshine."

At the sound of his voice, I sat upright.

Emery was sitting at the edge of his bed, which was still exactly how it had been left after his nap yesterday. He was halfway through his breakfast sandwich and he tossed one at me before I could register it. My hands flew up, catching the greasy paper before it smacked me in the face.

"You're here," I said, setting the sandwich on the bedside table with my eyes on him.

His hair was messy, his sexy smirk just barely playing at the edge of his lips. It was infuriating to me in that moment, that he could look that good that early in the morning. Especially because I had a pretty good feeling as to *why* he looked so happy.

"Of course, I'm here. Where else would I be?"

*With Emily*, I almost said, but I just stared at him and shrugged instead.

"I fed Kalo and took her for a walk. I'm all showered and ready to go whenever you are."

He was perky and cheerful, and I was annoyed. Where was this guy yesterday? Was *Emily* the reason he felt so great today? What happened to wanting to stay in bed?

My eyes glanced at the bedside table where I'd thrown the journal the night before, but it was gone, packed away.

*Well, he made me wait yesterday, so he can do the same*, I thought, waiting until he was typing a text in his phone to slide my leg into place. I rolled my pant leg down while still under the covers before swinging my legs over the edge of the bed.

I coughed to cover the sound of it clicking into place, the little black pin popping into the hole as I bent for my yoga mat.

"I'll be back."

"You don't want your sandwich?" Emery asked as I passed him, heading for the door. "It's sausage, egg, and cheese. It's a delicious heart attack in a bag. And I got you OJ to wash it down with."

"I'm not hungry," I answered, and then I let the door shut behind me, heading to the gym with thoughts of last night replaying in my head.

I focused on meditation more than poses that morning, spending almost double the time in Savasana before finally making my way back to the room. My shower was hot but short, then I changed quickly and packed my bag, slinging it over my shoulder and heading to the car with Kalo in tow. I didn't tell Emery I was ready to go, or ask him if he wanted me to drive again, I just gave him the same silent treatment he'd given me the day before and decided I didn't care if it bothered him.

Part of my silence was driven by my stupid girly emotions over him hanging out with Emily all night. I was annoyed not only at him, but at myself, because there was absolutely zero reason for me to be upset. I had no right, and yet, still I was.

But the other part stemmed from what I'd read in his journal.

My eyes were still puffy from the tears I'd spilled, and I pressed my cold fingers underneath them as Emery pulled onto the highway, studying my reflection in the small mirror on my sun visor. I looked like shit, and felt like it, too.

Popping it back into place, I chanced a glance at Emery, suddenly seeing him in a completely new light. I wanted to ask him about a million questions that morning, but instead I just stared at him until he returned my gaze, and then I turned to look out the window.

Eight hours passed without a single word between us.

Unlike me the day before, Emery seemed completely content with letting me be silent. He was too busy jamming out to his music, which ranged from classic rock to modern day country, to ask why I was sulking. I'd never heard such an eclectic taste in music, and had it been a normal day, I would have been laughing and singing along with him.

But it wasn't a normal day.

The more I sulked, the more frustrated I became. I *never* sulked. I was always the happy girl, the positive girl, the silver lining girl. Tammy would always get annoyed at how positive I was. She would roll her eyes and scoff at me when she wanted to rant and I just gave her solutions, and positive quotes, and meditation mantras. The way I saw it, life was too short, too delicate to spend time and energy being miserable.

It was the first time in a long time, maybe ever, that I was alone with my negative thoughts.

I went from being ecstatic about leaving Mobile and chasing my dream to cursing myself for being so stupid. I ticked through all the reasons getting in the car with Emery was a terrible idea as we drove through Texas.

*I don't have a place to stay in Washington.*

*I don't have a job lined up.*

*I don't even have an acceptance letter to Bastyr.*

Ever since I could remember, I'd saved and prepared for what would be the life-changing move for me. And then I threw all that out the door and jumped in a car with a stranger, a stranger who I now knew was suicidal — *is* suicidal? — and took a chance like it was exhilarating and fun and the stuff life is made of.

*Stupid.*

We passed a sign that said forty miles to Amarillo, and my eyes roamed the colors of all the fallen leaves surrounding the highway. Some trees were already completely bare, ready for winter, while others were still bright with yellows, oranges, reds, and browns. I personally liked the ones with just a few leaves left, those persistent ones that were holding on for dear life, not ready to leave summer yet.

The music died in the car, and I turned to Emery, who just pulled his hand back from the dial and placed it on the steering wheel again. He glanced at me, and we watched each other for a moment before I propped my chin on my hand again, eyes flashing over the sea of color.

"It's kind of ironic, isn't it?" he asked, speaking over the sound of the wind whipping through the car. "How beautiful everything is when it's dying."

I didn't answer, but I glanced at him over my shoulder, eyes surveying the sad smile on his lips before I turned back toward the road.

"So, did we trade places?" he tried again. "Is this payback for me being a prick yesterday?"

"At least you admit it," I murmured.

Emery chuckled, cutting around a Honda. "So, it is payback. An eye for an eye, huh?"

"I'm allowed to have a bad day," I said, facing him as I crossed my arms over my chest.

"I never said you weren't," he mused. He was watching me through the dark tint of his sunglasses with an amused smirk on his stupid face. "It's just that you're usually so... sunshiney."

"Don't act like you know me. You don't."

"Fair point," Emery agreed, shifting his hands on the wheel. "Let's change that. Tell me more about you."

At that, I laughed. Full-on, head tilted back, deep from the belly laughed.

"You are so.... ugh!"

"Frustrating? Annoying? Unfairly charming?"

"Yes," I grunted, and then I realized the last thing he said. "No!"

Emery laughed. "Just get it all out, Little Penny. You've been stewing for eight hours now, that pot has got to be ready to blow."

Huffing, I turned in my seat, tucking my prosthetic leg up under my other knee so I could face him more. "Fine. You want to know what I've been thinking?"

He nodded.

"I've been thinking about how stupid I am. Not just for jumping in a car with a guy I don't know and leaving literally everything behind other than my yoga mat and a few changes of clothes, but for doing so without making any kind of plan at all. I don't have anywhere to stay in Washington, no job, no idea if I'll even get into my dream school that I based this whole..." I paused, hands flitting around my face. "Hair-brained plan around. And, quite frankly, *you* make me feel stupid, too."

His brows pulled inward at that.

"Because for some unknown reason, I like you, and I want to know more about you, but yesterday you made me feel more like a nuisance than anything else. Not only did you not talk to me all day, but when you finally did, you put me down for wanting to find love in my life, like it was a naive fantasy for little girls. Then you left with *Emily*," I added, throwing my hands up to stop him from saying anything when he opened his mouth to interrupt me. "And that's fine, because you don't owe me anything, and she was gorgeous and sweet and fun and I get it. You're a guy, you... wanted to have a fun night. Fine. But I'm not like you, okay? I've never done this before."

He watched me have a mental breakdown in his car, and I swear it was like he was seeing me for the first time.

"I'm not accustomed to sleeping in a room with the opposite sex, or driving across the country without a plan, or sharing this much space with someone whom I can't tell if I annoy or intrigue. And it may sound stupid to you but I was worried last night. I didn't know where you were, or if you were coming back to the room, or if I would have to somehow try to hunt down your body and find your phone and call your mom to tell her you were dead."

My heart slipped into my stomach at that admission, because I knew it stemmed from reading his journal, from prying into his private life that he hadn't invited me into.

I sighed. "And I don't know, I just... I just feel stupid. I feel like a stupid little girl with stupid little dreams and a stupid little belief that life will turn out to be everything I've ever wanted it to be, because it sure as hell hasn't been even anything remotely close up until this point."

My chest deflated along with the hope I'd held onto for so long, and I sank into the seat, staring through the front windshield at the cars ahead of us.

Emery was still looking at me, his attention bouncing from the road to me and back again. He was quiet for a moment, then he cleared his throat, shifting in his seat.

"I'm sorry," he said softly. "You're not stupid. Sometimes I have bad days, and yesterday was one of them." He swallowed, and my throat was tight again, his handwriting still fresh in my mind. "I can't promise it won't happen again, but I just want you to know it had nothing to do with you. You don't annoy me." He made sure to look at me again when he said that part. "And I'm an open book. So, what do you want to know? Ask me anything."

"An open book," I challenged, face flat. "Like the kind from *Harry Potter* with the teeth the size of my head inside?"

He laughed, the sound warming me from the inside out. "Careful, your nerd is showing."

"I like my nerd."

"So do I," he answered quickly, and a blush creeped its way up my neck when he pushed his sunglasses up, his eyes connecting with mine.

I didn't mind when he looked into my eyes. I didn't mind it at all.

"Well, first thing's first, what's your phone number?"

Emery chuckled, listing it off as I typed it into my phone.

"When's your birthday?"

"Hey, it's my turn. Don't be greedy."

I threw my hands up in mock surrender.

"You keep talking about your dream school," he said as we pulled back into the passing lane. "Which school?"

Kalo popped up from her seat in the back, excited we were talking again. She licked his ear and we both laughed as she climbed into the front seat and onto my lap.

"Bastyr," I answered, rubbing behind Kalo's ears. "I want to go into Naturopathic Medicine."

"I don't even know what that is."

"Voodoo," I joked. "Basically medicine without stuffing people full of pills. Trying to use what the earth gives us naturally to live a long and healthy life."

"This from the girl who devoured an entire bag of beef jerky in front of me yesterday."

I sighed. "Yeah, well, I'm sure my diet will change once I'm there. In my defense, it's kind of hard to eat anything even remotely healthy in Alabama."

"Fair," he said with a smile. "So, you want to help people. I'm shocked. Never would have guessed."

I swatted at his arm. "Funny. When's your birthday?"

"June first."

I squinted one eye, thinking through the calendar as Kalo hopped out of my lap again and into the back. She propped herself between our seats, her tongue blowing in the wind.

"Gemini," I finally said, and it all clicked together. "Oh, yeah, I can totally see that."

"See what?"

"It just tells me a lot about who you are," I explained. "The need for adventure, the charming personality, the habit to go from light and fun to pensive and deep in a split second."

Emery threw his head back in a laugh. "Oh God, please tell me you don't actually believe that my *sign* tells you who I am? Let me guess, you're an Aquarius and have it tattooed on your foot."

My mouth popped open and I sat up straighter. "I am an Aquarius, actually."

"Of course, you are," he laughed the words. "I promise you, there's nothing my sign can tell you about me, nothing that's actually substantial, anyway. Horoscopes and all that? It's bullshit. Say something vague enough and you can apply it to anyone's life."

"That's not true!" I argued. "I am a textbook Aquarius. Like, it's scary how much my sign is accurate for who I am."

"That so?" he asked, and he pulled his phone from his pocket.

"Don't text and drive."

He frowned. "I've got it, Mom. Okay," he said, eyes on the road again, but they kept flicking down to his phone.

"So, you'd say you're loyal and kind, and hardworking, but that your weakness is that you tend to worry and you're overcritical of yourself? And you'd also say that you love books and nature, but you dislike being the center of attention."

I nodded. "Yep, that's me to a T."

"Congratulations. You're a Virgo."

He tossed his phone to me as I scoffed, rolling my eyes. But when I looked down at the screen, it was the same astrology site I referenced all the time, and the traits he'd been reading were for a Virgo, not an Aquarius.

My mouth popped open again.

Emery eyed me from the driver seat, a shit-eating grin on his face as my eyes scanned the screen. Even Kalo seemed in on the joke, licking my shoulder, and I just tossed the phone back to him and crossed my arms. "You're an asshole."

"Is that a Gemini thing, too?"

I tried to fight it, biting my lip so hard I left an indent, but in the end I gave into a loud laugh, one that rolled through me in a mixture of embarrassment and amusement. "Jerk."

Emery laughed, too, before tapping my chin gently with his knuckle. "Hey, you say you're an Aquarius, I believe you. No judgement. To each their own."

"Mmm-hmm."

"I'm serious," he said, and his eyes were more sincere then. "And for the record, you're not stupid for having dreams and taking crazy risks just to see if you can make them happen." He swallowed. "You're brave. And you're living. That's more than most people can say."

There was an honesty so real it hurt under that last sentence, his amber eyes searching mine, his hands tightening on the steering wheel. I wanted to ask him if he was living, if he had dreams, too.

But I didn't get the chance.

Suddenly, Emery's eyes narrowed, like something felt off, and as soon as he looked back to the road, there was a loud pop. I screamed like I'd just been set on fire. Kalo jumped from her spot, ducking behind Emery's seat, and my heart raced in my ears as the car thumped along with the smell of burnt rubber assaulting my nose.

"Shit," Emery mumbled, pulling off onto the shoulder. I was still trying to calm down when we finally stopped and he jumped out, jogging over to my side of the car and cursing again. "We blew a tire."

Cars and trucks were still whizzing by us, each one rocking the car with force. I grabbed Kalo's leash and we both got out, too, surveying the damage. The rubber on the back passenger tire was completely shredded, the car resting most of its weight on the bum leg. I sighed, peering up at Emery, who was already typing out a number on his phone from a card he held in his hand.

"Who are you calling?" I asked.

"Roadside assistance."

I nodded, Kalo plopping down in the long, overgrown grass next to me. "What are we going to do now?"

Emery went to answer me but then paused, his call being connected to a human being. Once he was finished telling the person where we were located, he tucked his phone back in his pocket.

"They'll be here in about thirty minutes or so, closest shop is right off that next exit, so we shouldn't be too far behind."

"And then what?"

Emery looked at me like the answer was obvious, shrugging his shoulders. "We grab dinner at a weird diner while they fix the tire."

"But we have to pay them," I pointed out.

"That's usually how that works."

"Okay, so…" I waited for him to connect the dots, but he didn't. "We have to earn some money. We've got to do something crazy and weird to get back on the road, like how the girls in *Crossroads* did the karaoke contest."

Emery watched me with a blank stare, blinking twice before he threw his head back in a laugh.

"I'm serious!" I defended, smacking his arm.

"I have my parents' credit card, Little Penny. We're fine."

I scoffed. "But we can't just *charge* it. That's no fun, it goes against all the road trip rules."

"Rules?"

"Yes, rules!" I started counting on the fingers on my right hand, tapping each one with my left. "Survive on potato chips and beef jerky, never pick up hitchhikers, and if you break down, figure out some crazy way to make the cash and get back on the road."

"None of those are real."

"They're unwritten."

Emery laughed, crossing one arm over his chest and balancing his elbow on it, hand finding his smooth chin. "It's just a tire. It'll take maybe two hours to fix, and that's only if they have to go somewhere to pick up a part. And it'll be like three-hundred dollars max."

"Your point?"

He couldn't stop smiling at me. "You're not going to let this go, are you? You really just want to make this difficult."

"The *rules,* Emery."

I didn't say his name often, and the sound of it, the way it felt rolling off my tongue made me pause, my eyes flashing to his, cheeks warming when I saw the same pause in him.

He tucked his hands in his pockets, looking down at Kalo before his eyes surveyed the car and the highway again. After a moment, he turned back to me, shaking his head with his signature smirk creeping out. "Fine. What's our next move, game maker?"

I squeaked, clapping my hands together in excitement as Kalo popped her head up to look at me. My heart deflated a little when I realized I didn't *actually* have any idea of what our next move was, but then the universe sent a sign, as it so often does.

My eyes locked on the billboard behind Emery's head and I grinned. "Let's get the car to the shop, and then I have a plan."

# Chapter 9

## Just Outside of Amarillo, Texas

"This is insane," Emery said again as he opened the door for us, guiding us under the large neon sign that read Big Earl's Wing House.

"Scared?" I teased.

He rolled his eyes, letting me lead as we made our way to the hostess. She was a middle-aged woman who reminded me of Tammy, except this girl was a little more round, and a lot more smiley.

"Hey, y'all! Booth or table?"

"Actually, I have a question about your wing eating challenge," I said, and Emery shook his head beside me. I narrowed my eyes at him before continuing. "Can you tell us a little more about it?"

"Sure!" She balanced the menus in her arms, opening one up to the wing challenge page and showing us what it entailed. "There are twenty-five wings total, each one dipped in one of our twenty-five famous sauces. You have to eat all of them — including the one rolled in our hottest sauce, Big Earl's Inferno. And if you can do it, your meal is free. Plus, you get this t-shirt to brag to all your friends." She pointed at a framed t-shirt behind her that said *I survived Big Earl's Wing Challenge* and flashed us a wide smile. "So, booth or table?"

"Wait," I said, trying to piece it all together. "So you eat all the wings and they're free, if not you pay for the meal... is there any..." I looked to Emery, who was just grinning, and I knew he would be of absolutely zero help. "Is there a cash prize or anything?"

The hostess looked a little appalled by my question, her brows pulling inward. "No, sweetie. Just the t-shirt."

I chewed my lip. "Just give us a minute." When I turned back to Emery, he looked smug, and I glared at him before pulling him to the side.

"See? They don't even pay if you can do it," he said. "Let's just grab dinner and put the charge on my card."

"There's got to be a way..." I tapped my chin with my finger, looking around us like I would find the answer from one of the other patrons in the restaurant, or from the hostess who was watching us closely now, one eyebrow hooked up high on her forehead.

"There is a way. We eat, go back to the shop, pay for the fix with my card, and go back to the hotel room — where we left your dog, might I add."

"She's fine. Watered, fed, walked, and probably sprawled out on my bed by now."

"Still, they don't have a cash prize. Might have to break the rules just this once," he teased.

I sighed, pushing the breath through flat lips. It was all too easy, and not at all fun, but if they didn't pay the winner of the contest, my idea was pretty much shot.

I was just about to give in when it hit me.

Maybe *they* won't pay us if we win, but what if...

"Can I borrow this?" I asked the hostess, pointing to a white bucket filled with paper menus and crayons for kids.

She definitely thought I was insane.

"Uh, sure?" she said, her accent thick as she peered over her shoulder at the other hostess who had joined her, both of them shrugging.

"Thanks." I grabbed the bucket and pulled the menus and crayons out, making sure they were neat and tidy on the side of the hostess stand before making my way toward an empty table right in the middle of the restaurant. Emery called out my name but I didn't stop, so he followed, and my heart beat thick and fast in my throat as I climbed on top of an empty chair. I made sure I was balanced and sturdy on both legs and then I stood, booth after booth turning their attention to me.

"What are you doing?" Emery whisper-yelled at me through the corner of his mouth, but I ignored him, shaking slightly as I forced a smile.

"Ladies and gentlemen of Big Earl's Wing House, may I have your attention for just a moment?"

Those who weren't already staring at me paused, some of them mid-bite, some of them drinking beer from glasses shaped like cowboy boots, and all of them looking at me with curious eyes, including the hostess we'd left behind us.

I cleared my throat, wringing my already damp hands together. "My name is Cooper and this is my friend, Emery. Say hi, Emery."

He waved, his smile tight as he watched me.

"Emery and I are on our way up to Washington, but our car broke down, and now we're in a predicament trying to get back on the road."

"No, we're not," Emery argued under his breath.

Again, I ignored him.

"Now I know you all have places to be, and I know the last thing you expected was some..." I laughed, gesturing to myself. "Some little girl from Alabama standing on a chair, asking for your help, but here I am." A few people chuckled, and I used those laughs as fuel for hope. "Some of you may have heard of Big Earl's Wing Challenge."

Whistles and hollers rang out from various booths, others looking around confused. I could tell just from that who the locals were and who was passing through.

"Well, my friend Emery here is ready to take the challenge. But," I added, holding up one finger. "That all depends on y'all. You see, right now you're just getting dinner — which is great, I can tell just from the way it smells — but for a small donation to get us back on the road, you could have dinner *and* a show." I glanced down at Emery before holding up my hand to hide my mouth from him, pretending to whisper, but loud enough that everyone could hear. "And between you and me, Emery here's a wuss, so it would *definitely* be a good show."

More laughs surrounded us as Emery crossed his arms over his chest, shaking his head at me, though I saw the smile he hid.

"So, what do you say, folks?" I hollered, standing straighter and holding the empty bucket into the air. "Are we going to have to hitchhike our way across the great US of A, or are y'all ready for a show?"

I expected a roaring round of applause and cheers, but instead I was met with silence, someone coughing near the front door as everyone else looked around, most of them avoiding my eyes. My cheeks flushed red with heat and I glanced at Emery, who was still shaking his head.

He was right. This was insane.

Emery reached a hand up, ready to help me down from the chair as I offered an embarrassed smile to the ones still looking at me. But just as I stepped down, a loud whistle came from the back of the restaurant.

Emery and I both turned, along with the rest of the joint, to find an older man seated in the far back booth holding up a twenty-dollar bill in his hands. He wore a Navy Veteran hat and a grin.

"Let's get him a bib, boys."

His buddies cheered, all of them digging into their wallets for cash, too.

And that's all it took.

Every booth joined in on the cheers as the hostesses cleared off a table in the center, seating Emery down and prepping the table with wet naps. I took the bucket through the crowd, gathering the cash as Emery watched me. I gave him a thumbs up sign with smile too big for my face as I held up the bucket for him to see. He just laughed, tucking the bib they handed him into his shirt with a promise for paybacks on his lips.

Twenty wings in, Emery hated me.

The entire restaurant was gathered around him, chanting his name and promising him beers to celebrate the win. His beautiful lips were slathered in different colored sauces, his hands covered in the same, and his eyes were murderous on me, though he was still smiling.

"Come on, guys. Keep up the energy!" I encouraged, and more people chanted his name as he picked up the twenty-first wing, getting hotter with each bite as he neared the Inferno.

"This is impossible," he said when he finished that one, staring at the four left in the basket in front of him. "My mouth is on fire."

His eyes were red and watery, his shoulders slumped until the guy with the Navy hat clapped him on the back and rubbed some life back into those shoulders.

"Come on, kid! You can do it!"

The crowd cheered with him, and I just laughed as Emery shot more daggers straight at my forehead.

He cursed.

He screamed.

He nearly cried.

But by God, he did it.

When he opened his mouth and showed the last of the twenty-fifth wing was gone, the restaurant erupted into a battle cry of sorts as two waitresses rushed in, one with a tall glass of milk to ease the burn and the other with his victory t-shirt. They snapped a picture of him with us all standing around, and even though I knew he was hurting, he smiled through it all.

When the pictures were taken and the chaos died down, I stood on the chair again, thanking the crowd. They all wished us well, and when Emery helped me down from the chair, he didn't say a word, but he watched me with a mixture of awe and hatred.

"You did great," I tried, nudging him with my elbow. "Wear that t-shirt with pride."

A short, almost silent laugh came from his lips, but his eyes were still on mine, something there that wasn't before. "You're something else, you know that?"

I blushed, hands reaching back to pull my hair over one shoulder. Before I could answer, the man in the Navy hat who'd started it all came up beside us.

"Thanks for a fun evening," he said, his voice low and gravelly. "I'm John, by the way. I frequent this place, so if you ever come back through town again, make sure you stop in to say hi."

Emery nodded, reaching out to shake John's hand. "Will do, sir. Thanks again for supporting our crazy idea."

He laughed. "You kids remind me of my younger days. This is the stuff life is made of. Don't blink, or you'll miss it, and wake up seventy-two and grumpy."

Emery and I exchanged glances, sharing a smile between us before turning back to John. His eyes were old and kind, eyes that had seen more than we could even imagine.

"Thank you for your service, too, by the way," I added, nodding to his hat.

"It was my honor. I actually wondered... did you serve, too?" His eyes fell to my prosthetic leg, the one hidden under my jeans, one obviously not hidden to him.

"Uh, no sir," I stammered, face red again as I braided my hair with shaky fingers.

John's brows furrowed. "Well, losing a limb isn't something you should be ashamed of, my dear. You're beautiful and you've got a good spirit about you. I don't know what happened, but you should show that scar off with pride. Most people wouldn't be such a ray of light after something like that."

Emery was watching me now, and I felt his understanding click into place as John patted my shoulder with a strong hand.

"Take care, you two. Be safe."

"We will," Emery murmured, his eyes still on me. "Thank you again, John. Have a great night."

I waved to John with my embarrassment still on full display as Emery guided us back out into the parking lot. The hotel we booked was connected, and we walked in silence most of the way. I was waiting for it, for the question, the pity, the new way he would look at me now that he knew. But when we were almost to the hotel, the teal doors connecting the rooms to the outside coming into view, he nudged me.

"I can't believe you actually pulled that off."

A small sigh left my lips, relief washing over me. Maybe he hadn't picked up on it. "Me? You're the one covered in wing sauce."

He glanced down at his shirt, various stains still showing regardless of the bib he'd worn. He grinned. "Worth it. But I've decided that you owe me."

"That's fair," I conceded with a laugh. "How much did the shop say it would cost to fix the tire?"

"After labor, we're looking at just under four hundred dollars."

It was my turn to smile. "Well, we raised a little over five, so it looks like we got the tire covered *and* breakfast."

"You going to eat a hundred dollars of pancakes?" Emery challenged, one brow rising as we dipped around the back of the hotel toward our room.

"You doubt me?"

At that he laughed, looking at his shoes as his hands slid into his pockets again. "Not even a little bit."

We were silent again as we walked toward the rooms at the back end of the hotel. Ours was down at the very end, the small pool directly in front of our door. I was pulling our key from my pocket when Emery stopped me, the feather-light touch of his hand finding my elbow.

"Would it make you feel better to make a plan for the trip?" he asked, golden eyes taking on a green hue from the blue reflection of the pool light.

I smiled. "Honestly? A little. Even if it's just a rough plan of which cities we'll hit along the way and when we'll get there... especially since I need to find a place to live and a job."

Emery nodded, and he was looking at me that same strange way, like I was something between a shooting star and a freak show. "Okay. We'll make a plan tonight, then."

"Okay," I replied, and then I stifled a laugh, reaching up to thumb a smear of sauce off the side of his neck and showing it to him. "You're a mess right now."

"Always have been. But you know... I think I know a way to get us both cleaned up quickly..."

A mischievous grin was painted on that gorgeous face of his as his hands wrapped around my wrists. He slowly started walking backward, tugging me with him, and I just looked at him, confused.

Until I realized he was steering us toward the pool.

"Ohhhh, no," I argued, trying to pull away from his grasp. "Don't even think about it. I'm not the one covered in sauce."

Emery launched at me, wrapping his arms all the way around me and crushing me to his chest as he picked my feet up and walked even faster. "You are now!"

The sauce that had previously been only on him smeared on my clothes and skin, too, no matter how I tried to wiggle away. I shrieked, laughing and protesting with my tiny fists hammering on his chest, but it was no use. With just enough warning to hold my breath, we tipped over the sidewalk and into the cold water, his arms still wrapped around me until we both went under.

The cold of it was a shock to my system, and it took a second to actually get my body to inhale once I emerged again, eyes and mouth wide. My glasses had come off in the tumble and I slapped at the water frantically until they were in my hands and back on my face, the heat from my face making them steam up a little.

Emery just laughed.

"H-h-hate you," I chattered, but I couldn't fight off the smile. "You're d-d-dead."

"Yeah? You're going to do the killing?"

I nodded, which only made him laugh harder, so I splashed him.

It was so cold I couldn't think. I needed to get out, not only to find warmth but to dry my leg, which wasn't exactly built for water sports. But my feet wouldn't carry me toward the ladder to get out, because at the exact moment I went to move, I noticed Emery's tight, wet t-shirt.

It was just a heather gray t-shirt with a simple logo in the top right corner, but now, it was clinging to his chest, hugging his arms, outlining the defined ridges of his abdomen beneath it. His normally messy hair was wet and dripping, one strand of it falling in a slant over his left eye as he moved toward me. Those eyes were locked on mine, the smile he'd worn before fading more and more with every inch he closed between us.

"Cold?" he asked.

I swallowed, which was enough of an answer I supposed, because he didn't stop until our chests were touching. His arms wrapped around me again, pulling me into the heat of him, and I just stared at the wet fabric stuck to the middle of his chest, breath as shallow as a rain puddle.

"Cooper."

He rasped my name, the sound of it vibrating his chest still pressed against mine. My arms were crossed tight over my stomach, which meant they were brushing his abs, and I felt his breaths coming strong and steady, like the fact that we were wet and touching didn't bother him in the slightest.

My eyes followed the crease lines marking his soaked shirt up to his neck, his set jaw, until I met his gaze.

Emery looked so dangerous in that moment, like a warning sign on a barbed wire fence. *Keep out*, his eyes warned, but my hands grazed the hard muscles of his abdomen under the water, anyway. I was drawn to that wire, my skin not yet shredded from the barbs, from thinking I could climb over, the lesson not yet learned.

"You were jealous last night, weren't you?" he asked, voice low and rough. "Of Emily."

My fingertips twitched to reach up for my hair, but they were still pinned between us. I couldn't hide from him in that moment. I wasn't sure I ever really could before.

"A little," I breathed.

Emery swallowed, and then the eyes he'd had fixed on mine fell slowly to my lips, and my stomach fell quickly to the bottom of the pool.

"Don't be."

The inches between us turned to centimeters, his gaze still on my lips, and all I could do was inhale a breath and close my eyes. The water, so icy cold before, was hot and still around us, the mere proximity of him serving as a heater. Time seemed to stick, the second hand caught in a glitch, unable to move forward until the next move was made. And I waited — though I wasn't sure what for. A kiss? A new breath? A promise?

But none of them came, just a pained sigh as Emery's forehead leaned against mine, and I felt the air leave his lips and touch my own, though nothing else did.

"Come on," he said after a moment, pulling back until it was only his hand that grasped mine. My eyes fluttered open, lids heavy, heart like an anvil in my chest. "Hot showers, cold beers, and new plans. In that order."

Emery smiled, though it seemed strained to me, and then he turned, guiding me out of the pool in what felt like slow motion.

We were both shivering when we stepped inside, Kalo bounding up to the both of us immediately and licking at the water dripping from our clothes. Emery told me to take the first shower and all I could do was nod, still in a daze. When the bathroom door was a barrier between us, I pressed my back to it, letting my head drop to the wood, and took one long, deep breath.

As if oxygen could save me.

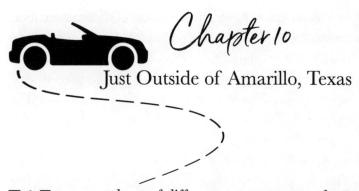

*Chapter 10*

## Just Outside of Amarillo, Texas

**W**ater poured out of different compartments of my prosthetic leg when I took it off, and I dumped it into the bath tub, laying the various parts out flat on the counter. I stared at the scattered pieces as I filled the tub with hot water, all the while cursing under my breath. Now that the adrenaline had faded, I realized getting thrown into the pool with my leg still on wasn't exactly the best thing to happen to me. Insurance helped me pay for my leg back when the accident happened, but as I grew, I had to pay for my own upgrades — and getting one that was waterproof wasn't at the top of my list.

It would be fine, I knew that because I'd been caught in the rain more than a time or two on my bike. It just needed to air out and I would have to change my liner and socks. Still, I had to take the foot shell completely apart, which meant I'd have to walk out of the bathroom on one leg.

In front of Emery.

Nerves assaulted me the entire time I bathed, mind racing with how he would react when he saw it. Would he cringe or pretend he didn't see it? Which would be worse?

I sighed, towel still wrapped around me as I studied the leg on the bathroom counter after my bath. I had a feeling he already knew about it, if not before John's comments at Earl's, then definitely after. But was I ready to *show* him?

I guessed it didn't matter now.

Creaking the door open just a crack, I peered out at Emery, who was sitting on a towel on the floor at the foot of his bed, writing in his journal.

"Hey, can you hand me my bag?"

He looked up at me, eyes catching on my towel before he snapped into action, grabbing my bag off my bed and handing it through to me, making sure to turn so I could open the door wider and slip the bag through.

"Thanks," I said when I had it, closing the door again. "I'll be right out."

"Take your time."

My hands were shaking again as I dressed, pulling on the one and only pair of gym shorts I'd packed. They were short, the edges of them hugging my thighs. The fabric was tight around my right thigh and loose around the left, and I eyed my imbalance in the full-length mirror, stomach rolling at the thought of Emery seeing me like this. No one had really seen me without my leg on, other than my parents, who didn't notice, and Lily, who didn't care.

But I didn't have a choice, so I threw my bag over one shoulder and tucked the parts of my leg under my other arm, ready to lay it out to dry on the desk in our room. Then, with an unsteady breath and my head held as high as I could manage, I opened the bathroom door again, standing in the frame of it as Emery's eyes landed on me.

It was impossible to ever get used to the way he looked at me, especially when those two lines formed between his brows. Every time his eyes pinned me, I swore I never wanted to move again.

Pushing my glasses up the bridge of my nose, I watched as his gaze flowed down my body, catching for just a moment on the bare leg that still existed before flicking to the one that was absent. I opened my mouth to say something but he was already on his feet, taking my bag from my shoulder and the parts of my leg from my other hand. He dropped my bag near the foot of my bed and laid out all the pieces of my prosthesis on the desk, and I just stood frozen in the door frame, watching him.

"Here," he said when he finished, moving to my side. He grabbed my left arm and hooked it around his shoulder, bending to my height and helping me to my bed.

"I can do it on my own," I whispered, but we were already across the room.

"I don't doubt that."

Emery made sure I was settled on the bed, my good foot on the floor while my stump hung down, the cut just below the knee. His eyes roamed over both of my legs as he pulled up the desk chair, laying the towel he'd had on it since he was still wet before sitting down and rolling closer to me.

He wasn't grimacing, or studying it like it was a science project, or looking at me with pity. He just seemed to be taking in the lower half of me for the first time, his eyes tracing my thigh, my shin, my ankle, before finally landing on my scar, on the most vulnerable part of my entire body.

"You already knew, didn't you?" I asked after a moment.

He found my gaze, nodding slowly. "I suspected, but I figured you would tell me when you were ready."

"I'm never ready to tell anyone about it," I said quickly. "But... I didn't really have a choice tonight." I eyed my leg drying out on the desk.

"Fuck, I'm so sorry, I didn't even think about it when I threw us in the pool."

"It's fine. It'll dry."

Emery swallowed, eyes searching mine. "John was right, you know. You are beautiful. With or without your prosthetic."

Everything about the situation made me want to crawl right out of my skin. I didn't want him to see me like this, or tell me I was beautiful when all I felt was broken. I tucked my wet hair behind my ear, eyes on the carpet between us. "You should go shower."

"I will," he said, voice low. "Can you tell me what happened? Is that... would that upset you?"

A shudder rushed through me and I shivered with the force of it. Emery reached out, his hands finding the outer edges of each of my knees, and he rubbed the skin there. I watched his thumb rub the normal, toned muscle of my right leg and the thin, damaged muscle of my left. The warmth from his skin made me shiver again, and when my eyes found his, my stomach flipped at the heat I found there, too.

"It's hard," I whispered, and my eyes watered, though I tried to fight against the tears.

Emery just squeezed my thighs a little tighter, the pad of his thumb tracing the skin in smooth circles, eyes resting on mine as he waited.

I took a deep breath, folding my hands on my lap and staring down at them as I spun my ring. "It was my twelfth birthday. My parents forgot. Again," I added, and my heart stung with the familiar ache of being forgotten, a feeling I knew too well. "It was the first year I didn't care to remind them."

I was still watching my hands, but I felt Emery staring at me, felt his gaze on me. I pushed out another breath and kept going.

"My dad didn't come home from work that evening, and my mom thought he was cheating again. So, she threw me in the car to go look for him. I begged her to stay home, but she insisted, and she had been drinking. I knew better than to argue with them when they were drinking.

"I was reading my book in the back seat, *A Wrinkle in Time*, so I don't really know what happened. All I remember is my mom cursing, and then the car jerked, over and over again. It felt like we were hitting the biggest speed bumps to ever exist. Then we flipped, I don't know how many times, and I blacked out. When I came to, there was smoke everywhere, and I looked down and there was just... blood. So much blood."

Tears flooded my eyes again, and I tried not to blink, not to let them fall, inhaling another shaky breath.

"My left leg was pinned by the door, it had been crushed in, and the car had landed on that side. So, I was just... stuck. I didn't notice the pain until my mom started screaming. Then it all hit me — the blood, the smoke, the pain — and I blacked out again."

I shrugged, a mixture of emotion and complete numbness washing over me, each of them fighting for dominance.

"I woke up in the hospital, and by that time, they'd already amputated my leg. My mom walked away completely fine. She was too drunk to even tense up, so other than some bruises and cuts from the seat belt and airbag, she was fine." Two tears slipped from my eyes at the same time, rolling down over my cheeks and hitting my thumb in unison. "She was fine, except she was angry at me, because she knew the hospital bill would be outrageous."

"Jesus Christ," Emery breathed, and his hands moved to grab mine. He held them tightly as I closed my eyes, more tears seeping through.

I shook my head. "It's weird how much of it I don't remember. Tammy, my friend from back home, says I repressed it all. But I don't really recall much of the physical therapy, or getting used to my leg. I know it was hard, I know I hated it, but one day it was just... easier. And every day that passed, it became more and more normal. When I started doing yoga, that's when I really found peace with it. With everything, really."

"You do yoga without your leg on?"

I nodded. "I wanted to build strength and balance. Sometimes I do it with my leg on, just to test it, but I like doing it without it more. It's nice to remind myself that I can still be strong, even if I am missing a limb."

Emery was silent for a moment, then he dipped his head down a little lower until my gaze met his. He was completely surrounding me now — his knees on either side of mine, elbows resting easily on my thighs, hands covering mine, eyes piercing through my ghosts. "You are strong, Cooper," he whispered. I looked away, but he moved until he was blocking my view again. "You are. And the fact that something like this happened to you and you're still here, *living*, smiling and spreading light... it's incredible." He paused, swallowing. "I couldn't do that."

"You'd be surprised."

"No," he cut me off. "I'm serious. I know myself, and I would have given up years ago." He watched me for a moment. "I hope you never do."

I closed my eyes, his words settling around me. "I'm a little tired, could we maybe make plans in the morning?"

"Of course," Emery said softly, backing out of my space. He released my hands and I immediately wrapped them around myself. "I'm going to jump in the shower. Want me to shut off the lights?"

I shook my head. "I'll wait until you're out."

"Okay, I'll be fast."

With that, Emery jumped up, digging through his bag for his toiletries before dipping inside the bathroom. I let out a long, loud breath once he was gone, the memories of the crash still fresh in my mind as I fell back against the cool, rough, Native American print comforter. Kalo moved closer to me, whimpering a bit as she nudged me with her nose. She could always tell when I was sad, and I just rubbed the fur on her paw, reassuring her I was fine.

I was tempted to read another passage from Emery's journal, knowing it was still sprawled out on the floor from where he'd been writing, but after talking about the accident, I was too tired to even lean up again. Instead, I wiggled until my head was on the pillows, tucking my legs under the sheets.

Kalo curled up beside me, and though I said I would wait, exhaustion pulled me under while the shower was still running. I faintly remember hearing the water cut off, and then the door opening. A few seconds later, the lights were off, and then I must have started dreaming, because I swore I felt a hand brush my hair back from my face.

I cracked one eyelid open, but Emery was already in his own bed, scribbling in his journal by the light from his phone. And I fell back asleep to the sound of the page turning.

"Okay. So, we have Colorado Springs and the Grand Canyon," I said around a mouthful of banana muffin, washing it down with iced coffee as I continued planning our route the next morning. "What else?"

The sun had barely risen, but Emery and I had been up for an hour, eating breakfast from the hotel lobby and figuring out our next moves. Emery seemed to have woken up in a good mood again, which I was thankful for, since I needed his patience and cooperation to figure everything out.

"I want to drive up the Pacific Coast Highway," Emery said. He was playing fetch with Kalo, though she rarely brought the toy back, usually flopping down in the same spot and chewing on it, instead.

"Okay, let me see..." My tongue stuck out of the corner of my mouth as I studied the map on my phone, making notes in the notebook Emery had bought from the lobby when we grabbed breakfast. "Done."

"Don't you need to make plans for where to stay and stuff, too? For Seattle?"

I nodded. "I do. Next hotel we stop at, we should make sure it's one with a business center. I can just spend a day putting in apartment applications and job searching."

"Sounds like a boring way to spend a day."

I rolled my eyes. "It's called *being responsible*. You should try it."

"Nah." He winked at me, tugging on Kalo's toy until it was freed from her jaw before throwing it again.

"Should we hit Vegas?"

Emery paused then, Kalo nipping at his hand still holding her toy. She'd actually returned it to him this time. "Fuck yeah, we should go to Vegas. And we're staying right on the strip, too."

I chuckled, marking it down on the list. Once we had everything we *wanted* to do listed out, I made us a driving route, calculating eight hours of driving max per day, though most days would be less.

"If we go this way, it'll take us..." I did the math in my head, pulling up the calendar on my phone. "Eleven days to make it to Seattle, but that's if we're driving every day. So if we end up wanting to stay more than one night somewhere—"

Emery coughed. "Vegas."

"Like Vegas," I repeated, laughing. "Then it might be a little longer."

"So, about two weeks?"

"About two weeks."

Emery tossed Kalo's toy before smiling at me from where he sat on the edge of his bed, his hair still messy from sleep, muffin crumbs gathered in his lap. "Let's do it, Little Penny."

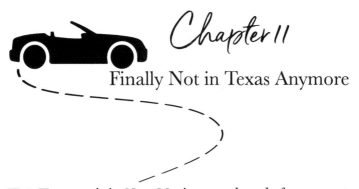

# Chapter 11

## Finally Not in Texas Anymore

We weren't in New Mexico very long before we cut right across the Colorado border, and finally, it felt like fall.

Actually, it almost felt like winter.

We didn't have the top down anymore, and I was bundled up in one of the two sweaters I brought, my arms tucked tightly across my stomach to keep the warmth in. I'd never seen anything like that before — the mountains stretching up in the distance to our left, the prairies flat and dry to our right as we crawled our way to Colorado Springs. I didn't know how Emery was keeping his eyes on the road with everything so beautiful around us. There was snow on the tips of the mountains, and I traced the outline of it in wonder as we drove.

"I've never seen snow before," I said absentmindedly, petting Kalo's head. She had crawled into my lap somewhere in New Mexico.

"Ever?"

I shook my head. "I've never been outside of Alabama."

Emery glanced at me then, watching me for a moment before his eyes found the road again. "It's pretty, if you don't have to shovel it. I stayed with a college buddy once over winter break. His family lives in Pittsburgh." He shook his head. "It was awful. We had to shovel so much snow, and you have to put on so many fucking layers when you go outside, and then peel them all off when you're back inside. And everything is *wet*." He grimaced before a soft smile found his lips. "But it was something, to see it fall from the sky. And it's so soft at first. It's pretty. And *quiet*, everything is so quiet when it's snowing."

"That sounds magical," I said in awe, closing my eyes and trying to picture it. "I don't think I would mind shoveling, if it meant I got to see that first fall."

Emery scoffed. "You say that now. But if your feet were frozen numb and your hands raw and red from the shovel, you'd change your mind."

My thigh started to tingle under where Kalo was resting, and I moved my hand under her fur, rubbing my thigh in small circles, my eyes still on the scenery as we passed.

"Do you have something for that?" Emery asked, nodding toward my leg. "For the pain?"

I shrugged, still working the muscle under my fingertips. "I used to. They gave me pain meds, but they just... they took all the light out of me. I started looking up more natural remedies when I was fourteen. That's kind of what lead me to Bastyr, actually."

"That makes sense. I don't think I would want to be doped up all the time, either."

He said it like he knew, his eyes softening under the weight of his brows, and my mind flashed to his journal entry, to the hydrocodone he took to try to end his life.

I swallowed.

"I was basically a zombie when I was on them. Pain relief is a hard thing to study when it comes to naturopathic medicine, though. I tried acupuncture, and that didn't really work for me. I brew willow bark in my tea and that helps sometimes, but other times the pain is so severe that it almost feels like nothing will help."

"And you just ride it out?"

I nodded. "Usually. I figure it's my body's way of reminding me what was once there, and sometimes I don't mind having that reminder. Even if it is painful."

Emery was silent a moment, his hands fisting the steering wheel.

"Sounds almost like that love you were talking about."

I tilted my head. "How so?"

Kalo readjusted herself on my lap, huffing as if our talking was keeping her awake. I chuckled, petting behind her ear.

"Well, it's like with my grams. Sometimes I smell something or hear something that reminds me of a time with her, and it hurts, but... in a good way. In a way that reminds me she was here, and alive."

My chest ached with his admission, and I was tempted to reach for him, to wrap my hand around his own, but I kept petting Kalo, instead.

"Yeah. I think it's exactly like that." I paused. "Or like when you love someone and they break your heart. It hurts to remember them, but it would hurt worse not to."

"You've experienced that heartbreak?"

I flushed then, eyes back on the road. "Well, no. But I think I can imagine what it would be like."

"Have you ever been in love?"

I swallowed. "Not yet."

"Ever had a boyfriend?"

"Not unless you count Trevor Baker in the fourth grade. He kissed me by the swings."

Emery laughed. "I'm sorry, it's just... I find that so hard to believe."

"That Trevor Baker kissed me? Hey, I was a looker in the fourth grade. That was before I needed glasses."

"No." He laughed again. "I mean that you've never had a boyfriend, a real one."

My heart squeezed, and I looked back out the window. "Yeah, well, no one in my town really wanted much to do with me once I lost my leg. Add in the fact that my family didn't exactly have the best reputation and, well..." I shrugged. "But it's fine. I had my books, and this fluff ball here." I scrubbed Kalo's head.

"What's your favorite book?"

It was my turn to laugh. "You can't just have *one* favorite book. That's like me asking you to choose a favorite arm."

"My right one, of course."

I rolled my eyes. "I'm serious. I've read thousands of books, there's no way I could ever pick a favorite."

"Okay, well which one got you hooked on reading."

Smiling, I reached into my purse by my feet, pulling out the worn copy of *Catcher in the Rye* I'd brought with me.

"No shit," Emery said, eyeing the book. "You're a Holden Caufield fan?"

"He was my first crush."

Emery laughed again just as we rounded a corner to reveal another breathtaking view of the mountains. "Most girls were crushing on Leonardo DiCaprio, and you were lusting after Holden Caufield."

"He's a stud. He's smart and witty, and foolish."

"And you like foolish men?"

I shrugged. "I *liked* foolish *boys*. Past tense."

"And now?"

I didn't know why heat crept its way up my neck, or why I had to fight back a smile at him asking me what kind of guy I preferred. It felt like he was asking me another question altogether, one he'd asked with his eyes, already.

"I don't know. I want someone I can laugh with, and go on adventures with. Someone who will challenge me to be better but also support me when I'm weak. I want someone who shares their deepest fears with me, shows me their scars willingly — someone who trusts me to heal them, just as I trust them." I bit my lip. "And I want to feel a rush every time our skin touches. I want to lose entire afternoons with them under the covers. I want someone who I can't wait to share good news with, and someone who I know will hold me when the bad news comes."

I knew I was rambling, but I couldn't stop. The want for a love I'd never experienced consumed me. My eyes were still tracing the mountains as my voice lowered, my hands finding my hair, braiding it over my shoulder.

"I want that kind of love that leaves you breathless when it hits you, and makes you want to throw up at the thought of losing it. The kind that makes you *so happy* that it hurts at the same time, like it's painful to think that out of all the people in the world, you somehow found the one meant for you." I sighed, tossing my braid back behind me. "But really, I don't know what I want. Not completely. I've never come face to face with it." I shrugged, lost in my thoughts, in the unknown of it all. "I guess I'll just know when I find it."

Emery watched me for a long moment, so long our tires brushed the bumpy edges of the shoulder before he turned his attention back to the road. And then he was quiet.

"Go ahead," I said, poking his arm. "Say what you want to say. Tell me I'm stupid and that fantasy doesn't exist."

He didn't smile, didn't spout off a cynical list of reasons why I was wrong. He just drove, one hand on the steering wheel, the other brushing over the soft bit of stubble that had grown on his chin overnight.

"You're not stupid," he finally said. "And I hope you find all of those things with someone, Cooper. I really do."

I smiled. "I hope you do, too."

Emery didn't respond, pointing instead to a sign up ahead. "I need a restroom break. You hungry or anything?"

"I think I can wait until we get there."

He nodded, pulling us off onto the exit. A few minutes later we were parked at a quiet old gas station, and he hopped out, taking Kalo's leash. I couldn't help but watch him as he walked with her, and once she was finished, she was back in the car and Emery was headed inside.

His journal was tucked in between the driver seat and the console, and my eyes flicked down to the leather before I tore them away again.

My right knee bounced.

I unbraided my hair.

I texted Lily.

And then I gave in and picked it up, anyway.

My stomach was in knots as I glanced up at the gas station, watching for him while my fingers flipped to the page from last night. It was bookmarked with a small, dark red ribbon, and my name jumped off the page as soon as I opened it.

*I saw Cooper for the first time tonight.*

*We've only been together a few days, but still, I thought I had her figured out. I thought I had her nailed down as this stupid, naive little girl who had never been hurt before. But she has been hurt. She's been through more than most people I know.*

*More than me.*

*I knew something was off with the way she walked, with some of the noises I heard her make, but it was still a shocking sight to see her standing in the frame of our hotel bathroom on one leg. Half of the other one is gone. She lost it in a car accident with her mom.*

*Her mom was drunk. Her mom didn't lose a damn thing, but Cooper lost her leg.*

*Now I'm sitting here on the bed opposite her, and she's asleep, tears still staining her cheeks because I asked her what happened. And she told me, she opened herself up to me even though I was a complete fucking asshole to her yesterday. And why, because I was having a "bad day" as Marni would say?*

*Stupid.*

*I don't know what bad days are, not really. I don't know what it's like to wake up in a hospital without a leg, or to learn how to walk again, or to look at my drunk mom who doesn't have a single scratch on her and know she's responsible for my new life.*

*Grams would have liked Cooper.*

*I wish she could have met her.*

Emery pushed through the gas station door, flicking his sunglasses back down over his eyes as I carefully slipped his journal back into place. When he dipped back down into the driver seat, I was smiling, and I just looked at him.

"What?" he asked, the corner of his mouth quirking up, too.

"Nothing."

I couldn't stop smiling, though I didn't know why. Maybe it felt good that he had seen me, *really* seen me, or that he'd written about me with such respect. Or maybe it was that he'd said his grandma would like me, and I knew that was a big deal for him. Either way, I couldn't erase my goofy grin, and Emery just cocked a brow, shaking his head as he started up the engine.

"Okay, weirdo, you're DJ. Less than two hours until Colorado Springs."

And then we were back on the road, and I was back in my thoughts, wondering more and more with every mile just who Emery Reed was.

We stopped at the first diner we saw in Colorado Springs for a late lunch, asking our waitress what her top recommendations were for our visit. The first place she mentioned was a hike called Seven Falls, so when our bellies were full, we drove to the Broadmoor Hotel to buy our tickets and prep for the hike.

"Think you're ready for these stairs, Little Penny?" Emery teased as I tightened my sneakers. We were waiting for the tram to pick us up from parking and take us to the falls, and I was already inhaling the fresh mountain air, taking in the scenery around us.

"Hey, I can do everything you can with this leg of mine," I said, thumping it with my knuckles. "I am slightly worried about the cardio aspect, though. Not exactly getting the heart rate up much in yoga."

He laughed. "Don't worry, I'll carry you up if I have to."

"Oh, yeah, because I'm sure the drinker is *super* healthy."

"Whiskey doesn't stop me from having abs, now does it?"

I blushed at that, eyes skating down to his abdomen even though it was currently covered by his beige knitted sweater. The tram pulled up, saving me from a response as we climbed aboard, Kalo in tow.

It didn't take long before we were at the foot of the falls, being guided through what to expect during our climb. Emery bought a simple black backpack from the store at the bottom and packed a couple of waters for each of us, along with trail mix, and then we were on our way.

Kalo was hopping up the stairs as fast as she could at first, nearly choking herself with the leash as she tried to run faster, but by the time we'd climbed the first long set of stairs, she slowed to match our pace.

"It's like a never-ending stair master," I said, exasperated. I paused at the little lookout over the first waterfall, catching my breath and taking in the view. My leg was okay, my extra socks helping take some of the brunt of the hike, but I knew it would be sore the next day.

I was thankful it was chilly but not *too* cold as we stood by the spraying water, little drops peppering my cheeks.

We'd only climbed up part of the way and already I found myself breathless in wonder.

"It's amazing, the way nature carved this place. These mountains, these waterfalls," Emery said, pointing to the different grooves in the rock around us. His nose was pink from the cold, his eyes wide and bright. "We think we know the world, but we're only seeing a tiny second of its journey."

We stood there, Kalo with her head through the railing looking down while Emery and I looked up and around. And I'm not sure why it hit me in that moment, but I realized then that I wasn't in Alabama anymore. I realized then that I was finally on *my* journey, and it may only have been a second for the Earth, but it was time frozen still for me.

"Strange," I said, voice low, mixing with the rushing water. "It makes me feel small and free all at once."

Emery nodded in agreement, pulling a water bottle from his bag and offering me a drink before we started for the stairs again.

We were silent as we climbed the rest of the two-hundred and twenty-four steps, stopping several times along the way to drink water and let Kalo rest. I attempted to take a photo on my phone a few times, though it never did the actual scenery justice, so I opted for keeping it tucked in my back pocket, instead. When we reached the top, both of us out of breath, Emery nodded toward the sign for Midnight Falls, and we took the less than half-mile hike down to see that part of the falls up close.

We were the only ones on the trail when we reached the end, save for an older couple studying their map. Kalo was antsy from being on her leash so I let her off for a second, laughing when she ran straight for the water and hopped around on the rocks, her tongue hanging out and flopping around with her.

"How long have you had her, anyway?" Emery asked as we watched her play.

I smiled, thinking back to the day she came into my life. "I adopted her as a puppy right around my sixteenth birthday. Hard to believe I've had her for almost five years now."

Emery inched a little closer to me, his hands tucked in the front pockets of his jeans, elbow just barely brushing mine. His hair was a little damp from the falls, his skin still pink from the cold. "And her name? How did you come up with that?"

"*Kalos* is a Greek term for astounding beauty, inside and out. I read once that there isn't an English word that can be used as a synonym, because of the level of beauty the word is said to describe. I liked that, a word that didn't have an equivalent. I liked that only one culture took the time to give that kind of beauty a name."

Emery frowned. "But her eyes are crossed."

I laughed, smacking his arm.

"What? I mean, she's kind of goofy looking, you have to admit."

"She is," I laughed the words. "But she's also beautiful. And different. And mine."

Just as I said the words, the older couple who had been looking at their map was posing for a selfie near the foot of the falls, and I watched in slow motion as Kalo darted toward them, tongue hanging out, paws skipping across the wet rocks.

"Kalo, no!" I jetted after her, but it was too late. She startled the woman and, though he tried, the man couldn't stop her from slipping and falling on the rocks.

"Shit."

Emery sprang into action, sprinting past me to help the woman up as I wrangled Kalo back on her leash. Emery and the older gentleman were on either side of the woman, escorting her to a dry rock nearby to sit.

"I'm so, so sorry," I said, Kalo still pulling against her leash to try to lick the poor woman. "I know I should have kept her on the leash, she's been cooped up in the car all day, I thought she'd be fine. I'm so sorry."

"Oh, it's alright," the woman said, a wide, toothy smile on her pleasant face. She had long gray hair that hung down to the middle of her back and eyes that crinkled at the edges. Her frame was slight, and she wore a Native American print dress over black leggings and boots. If I had to guess, I'd have said they were both in their sixties or so. "I may look fragile, but these old bones are a lot more sturdy than they appear."

"You just wanted an excuse to get in the waterfall, Nora. You don't fool me," the man teased, his gray-blue eyes twinkling as he handed her a bottle of water. He was taller and rounder than her, but his hair was the same silver, and he watched her with love and adoration. "You okay, dear?"

"I'm fine." She swatted at the bottle, signaling him to put it away. Then her eyes trailed up Emery's arms, locking on his face. "And you've got it all wrong. I didn't want to get in the water, but I did want to be saved by a strong young man."

It took everything in me not to laugh as a red tinge shaded Emery's already pink skin. I didn't think it was possible for him to blush.

"Well, I can't blame you there," I said.

"What's her name?" Nora asked, holding out her hand for a very impatient Kalo. She licked it immediately, tail wagging against my legs.

"Kalo."

"Australian shepherd?"

I nodded. "Yes ma'am. She's a mix."

"She's beautiful," the man said. "You two from around here?"

"Just passing through, on our way up to Washington," Emery answered, petting Kalo's head along with Nora.

"Ah, we love that state. So many beautiful things to see. Newlyweds?"

Emery and I both laughed at that, his a little more genuine than my high-pitched panicked one. I opened my mouth to tell him that we had really just met, but Emery cut me off.

"Yes, actually. But you wouldn't know that, since she wears her ring on the wrong hand," he said, eyes on my best friend ring as I just gaped at him. "We're from a small town and our parents don't exactly approve of us being together, so we eloped."

Nora smiled up at her husband, their hands intertwining where his rested on her shoulder. She turned her attention back to us after a moment. "That will be some coming home party."

"You're telling us," Emery agreed with a laugh.

I was still gaping.

"I'm Glen, by the way," the man said, extending his hand to shake Emery's first before mine. "This is Nora. We're passing through, too. On our way down to Florida."

"That's where we came from," Emery mused. "What part are you heading to?"

"Whatever part isn't freezing," Nora answered quickly, and I chuckled. They were running *to* the heat while I was running to escape it.

"Are you guys staying in Colorado Springs for the night, then?" Glen asked.

Kalo finally plopped down on the ground next to me, and I rubbed behind her ear as Emery answered.

"Yeah, I think we're going to get a room up at the resort where we parked the car."

Nora looked up at Glen, the two sharing a knowing glance before she waved her hands at us. "You two should join us for dinner. We're camping not too far from here, and we've got plenty. It'll help save a little more money for a real honeymoon."

I flushed again, and Emery grinned at me, clearly finding joy in my discomfort. "What do you think, *honey*? You down for a little camping?"

I murdered him twelve times with my eyes in that moment, but smiled nonetheless. "As long as you keep me warm by the fire, *sweetie*."

"It's settled then!" Glen said, clapping his hands together with a wide smile. "Let's get down those stairs and we'll take you guys to our site. I think we could all use some dry clothes and a good dinner."

"And a stiff drink," Nora added.

We all laughed at that.

# Chapter 12

## Colorado Springs, Colorado

Glen and Nora turned out to be the best hosts ever. They not only invited us into their campsite for dinner, but they had an extra tent for us, one Glen and Emery popped up in no time once Nora had convinced us to just stay with them instead of driving back into town to find lodging. It turned out Nora had sort of a thing for strays, which we learned after being introduced to the three cats traveling the country in their camper with them.

"Makes no damn sense," Glen said, petting the white one behind the ear as it curled against his leg where he was seated by the fire. That one was named Valentine, after the town in Arizona where they'd found him. "Traveling with a bunch of cats. Thank God, we finally trained them to do business outside. You don't want to know what it was like having a litter box inside that thing," he said, nodding toward their camper.

Emery and I shared a smile, one that warmed my cheeks more than the fire.

"They needed a home, and we had one to give. It's just that simple," Nora argued, her eyes on the other two cats who were curled up on the mat below the camper steps. They were both tabbies, striped with different shades of gray and black, and one of them had a bite mark shaped piece missing from its left ear. That one was named Toledo, and the other was Faith. I loved that they each got their names from where they came from, like those places were still a piece of who they were, no matter where they traveled. As much as I never wanted to set foot in Mobile ever again, I knew the same was true for me.

"I just can't say no to her," Glen explained, eyes catching Nora's affectionately. "Never could."

"That's why I married you," she said, reaching out to squeeze his hand with her own. "That and your dashing good looks, of course."

We were all gathered around their fire pit, each of us indulging in a large bowl of the amazing chili Nora had whipped up that made me feel like I was really experiencing fall for the first time in my life — a *real* fall. In a strange way, they felt like home, those two strangers. They were kind and gracious and entertaining.

They were also hilarious.

Emery and I learned quickly that Nora was a little eccentric, and Glen kept her grounded. The way the two of them played into each other was adorable, and I couldn't help but ask them about every aspect of their lives. I wanted to know how they met, when they got married, how many kids they had, when they retired, why they decided to travel — everything. And they loved to tell the stories.

"So, that was it," Nora said after dinner, finishing the last of her chili and handing her little bowl to Glen. "There we were, about six months retired and watching Netflix all day every day because our darling daughter had showed us how to work it on our television, and I just saw our lives slipping away. I hated it. So, we bought this old camper, made it our project to fix her up, and as soon as she was good to go, we made our first trip."

"That was three years ago," Glen said, taking both mine and Emery's bowls, too. He even picked up Kalo's, who was spoiled with the scraps that evening. "We've seen a lot of the country and even some of Canada since then."

"See what happens when you listen to me?" Nora teased.

"Forty-two years together and I'm still learning, dear."

"You're lucky I'm patient."

They shared a loving glance, Glen winking at her before disappearing inside the camper with our dishes. It was a small, pull-behind one with a full bed they shared and a low-key kitchen. Nora told us they still carried the tent they were letting us sleep in just in case they camped somewhere where they'd want to be outside, like the time they slept right on the edge of a cliff in Canada and overlooked a crystal blue lagoon.

"What about you two?" Nora asked when it was just the three of us around the fire. Kalo was by her feet, already sleeping, her belly full. Nora rubbed her fur with a content smile as she waited for our answer. "Have you made a list of your hopes and dreams for your life yet?"

Emery and I glanced at each other, my eyes wide and his amused as ever as he reached forward and folded his hand over mine. His was warm, mine like ice, and chills sprang from his touch all the way down to my toes.

"We're still figuring a lot out, but our first stop is Seattle. Cooper here is going to Bastyr in the spring."

*If I get in*, I thought, but I just smiled.

"She was telling me a little about that on our hike back up," Nora said just as Glen rejoined us. He handed Nora another Michelob Ultra before taking the seat next to her. "And what are your plans, Emery? Your dreams?"

I looked at him just as intently as Nora, wondering the same thing myself, but when I saw the discomfort on his face, I squeezed his fingertips draped over mine, letting him know I was there.

And he squeezed back.

"My dad wants me to take over his business. Well, he wants me to be his partner first, but eventually take over."

"What business is that?" Glen asked.

"We create start-up companies and then sell them, so kind of like flipping houses, except flipping businesses. He's been successful at it his entire life, and I've found out in the past few years that I'm pretty good at it, too."

"Well, that's wonderful," Nora said, but I was still watching Emery, because something in his eyes told me it didn't matter if he was good at it. Something told me it wasn't all he wanted. "So, you've got the job parts figured out, but that's such a small part of it. What else? What's on your list?"

"What do you mean?" I asked.

"Oh, Nora loves lists," Glen said with a smirk. "To-do lists, goal lists, pros and cons lists."

"They're practical and help keep your brain centered," Nora defended. "I made Glen sit down with me and make one when we were first married, all of our hopes and dreams. Kids, house, travels, etc. We still have it in a scrapbook at home."

"That's so sweet," I said, leaning a chin on my palm as I sat forward. "Did they all come true?"

Nora grinned, cheersing her beer with her husband's. "They did, in their own way, but we'll never check the whole list off. That's not the point. In fact, we add new items to the list every year."

"It's about growing together. Changing. And figuring life out along the way," Glen agreed, and I smiled.

I liked them.

"You guys should make a list," Nora said. "We can start it right now."

"Great idea! And I have just the thing to get the creative juices flowing." Glen pulled a long, cigar-looking thing from his pocket, waggling his eyebrows as Nora chuckled.

"What is that?"

"It's a joint," Emery answered, and now he was watching me with that same amused smile, as if he was curious as hell over what I'd say next.

"Oh."

Nora and Glen's faces dropped.

"I'm sorry, dear, are you okay with it? We don't want to offend you. It's legal here, of course, but we know some people still have opinions about it."

"No, no," I assured Nora. "It's fine, honestly. I've just never... I don't really drink. By choice. And I've never really been around... *this* before." I gestured to the joint in Glen's hand.

"Weed," Emery said. "It's just weed, Cooper."

Glen lit the joint after making sure several times that I was okay with it, and I watched in fascination as he smoked it before handing it to Nora, who took two hits herself. Then she leaned up in her seat, passing it around the fire to Emery, and his eyes caught mine before he put the end of the joint to his lips and sucked in a breath.

I'd never been into guys who smoked cigarettes, but seeing Emery's lips around the paper, the smooth way the smoke left them when he exhaled, the cool, confident manner he had as he took another hit like an expert — it sent a warm rush over me, and I swallowed, adjusting my position in the folding chair.

He went to pass it back to Glen but I stopped him, my hand finding his forearm. "Wait."

Emery paused, smoke still seeping through his lips as his eyes connected with mine.

Listening to Nora and Glen share their stories had me looking at my own life up until that point, the twenty years I'd had on Earth and all I'd experienced — or rather, the lack thereof. Something about that night, that fire, or maybe those people had me wishing for more. I wanted stories of my own to tell, and I knew that wouldn't happen if I didn't step out of the box I'd lived in so comfortably my whole life.

My hand was a little shaky where it rested on Emery's arm, and when the next words left my lips, my voice followed suit. But I was more sure in that moment than I had been at any point up until then.

"Can I... can I try it?"

I couldn't stop giggling.

It didn't matter what happened, or what anyone said, because I was stuck in my own thoughts, and everything was funny. And when I tried to explain *why* it was funny, I just laughed harder, and barely got a word out.

"You are so high," Emery whispered into my ear, his elbow leaning on my chair's armrest.

"I am," I agreed, and then another fit of giggling started. "I'm so *hot,* too. Is it hot to you?"

I knew I sounded ridiculous, since it was in the forties that night, but the fire was warm and so was my sweater. I picked at the neck of it, searching Emery's low, red eyes. He was watching me with a soft smirk, his hair mussed as always, his eyes curious.

"Want to take a walk to cool off?"

I nodded, and before I knew it, he was standing and pulling me up with him. He told Glen and Nora we'd be back, making sure it was okay to leave Kalo with them, and then we were walking by the light of the flashlight on his phone. I tripped on a rock, nearly falling as I laughed loudly, catching my balance with a firm grip on Emery's arm.

"Hold onto me so you don't fall," he said, chuckling, too. "Are you okay? Do you feel okay?"

"I feel amazing."

He laughed again, and I threaded my arm through his, leaning into him. He smelled like fire and citrus.

The farther we got from the fire, the more settled I felt. I was cooler, my skin tingling with the transition from the warmth of the fire to the icy night air, and the urge to laugh seemed to be left behind at the campsite, especially once we reached the edge of a small cliff at the end of the park. The moon and stars were bright, illuminating the edges of the mountains in the distance, and Emery clicked the light off on his phone, letting the night surround us.

The sky almost seemed sea blue instead of black, and I watched our breath float up in front of us in little puffs of white. It didn't feel real, standing there with Emery, knowing I wasn't in Alabama anymore, that I never would be again. I'd already seen more in the past four days than in my entire life before, and I knew it was just the beginning.

"That was fun," I finally said, nodding back toward the campsite. "Making that list with them. They're funny."

"Everything's funny to you right now."

I nudged him. "Don't make fun of me! Are you high, too?"

Emery looked down the bridge of his nose at me, one side of his face shrouded in the darkness, the other illuminated by the moon. "I am."

"It's a weird feeling."

"It is. I remember my first time, too. It doesn't affect me the same way anymore, though."

I frowned. "What do you mean?"

A loud, long breath left his chest as he turned his eyes back toward the mountains. "I used to laugh like you, and now I just get..." He faded off, mouth flattening like he didn't know if he should say anything more, like he wasn't sure he could trust me.

I squeezed his arm, letting him know he could.

"I get in my head," he finished after a moment. "And that's a dangerous place to be."

Suddenly, I felt sober, though I knew I wasn't yet. His words struck that chord inside me, the one that warned me, that buzzed to life when something was a threat. I didn't want him inside his head, not if it was the same dark mind that almost took his life.

"Maybe it's only dangerous because you're the only one there. You could..." My voice faded along with my confidence. "I'm here, if you want to talk."

Emery smiled, though it fell quickly, and he tucked his hands into his pockets. My own hand was still wrapped around his bicep.

"It's nothing specific, honestly. I just get to thinking... like tonight, making that 'list of hopes and dreams' with them. You were so happy making it, laughing and listing things off. And it made me... sad."

"Why?" I whispered.

He shrugged. "That's the kicker. I'm not sure."

My thoughts were fuzzy in my head, and I suddenly wished I could come down from my high, that I could be sober and present. I fought through the cloud, trying to find the right words to say.

"Do you think it's because making a list like that takes something as grand as life and simplifies it? Makes it so... small?"

Emery turned to me then, his brows pulled together, my favorite lines forming between them. "Kind of," he admitted, as if it surprised him that I understood. "It was also hard for me, to even come up with those few that we did to start the list."

"You think you don't have any real hopes and dreams."

"I don't."

I shook my head. "Yes, you do. You're just figuring it out. It's not easy for everyone."

"It was for you."

I laughed then, but not because I was high — because the thought of anything in my life being easy was hilarious.

"Nothing in my life has been easy, Emery. Sure, I know that I want to go into natural medicine, but that's only one part of life. A *tiny* part of it. Maybe it was easy to make my list because life hasn't disappointed me yet. I'm still lusting after things you've already experienced and been let down by."

"Like love," he said, and it wasn't a question. It was a statement, one he punctuated with a turn in my direction, with a stare down into my eyes that felt like a piercing needle.

"Yes," I whispered. "Like love."

Emery wouldn't take his eyes off me, not even when I blushed and looked away, or when I found his unwavering gaze once more, my breath suddenly hard to catch.

"It's such a shame," he finally said, voice as smooth and calm as the sky above us. "That you've never been really kissed."

"It is?" I breathed.

His Adam's apple bobbed once in his throat as he nodded, stepping closer to me, and the hands that were in his pockets had somehow found their way to my neck. They crawled up, framing my face, his thumbs by my ears as his fingers curled into my hair. My mind rushed like the waterfalls we'd seen earlier, my heart racing along with it, our breaths meeting between us in a mixture of white puffs.

I expected him to ask, or to maybe change his mind halfway through, but Emery was steady and sure as he leaned down, his eyes not leaving mine until our mouths connected.

And in that moment, with that kiss, everything changed.

We both inhaled the moment our lips touched, and I stepped into him, my arms wrapping around his middle. I pushed up onto my toes, desperate to get closer, to get *more* — of his lips, of his breath, of his warmth, of him. When I opened my mouth, his tongue swept inside, and

I didn't even try to fight the moan that came next. That moan made Emery grip my hair, tugging it lightly, just enough to tilt my head back and allow him better access.

He wanted more, too.

My first kiss wasn't anything like I thought it'd be. I didn't see fireworks or feel butterflies in my stomach. No, I saw the stars, and the mountains, and the rushing water. I saw messy script writing and a wet t-shirt stuck to muscular arms. And I felt fire, hot and burning in my core, my breath more like steam than just an exhale into a cold night. I felt warm hands and cool lips, thick sweaters and thin inhibitions, and when he finally pulled back, his forehead pressed to mine, I felt empty and elated all at once.

"Wow," I breathed, my hands still fisted in his sweater. "Was that... is kissing always like that?"

Emery swallowed, the muscle over his jaw flexing as he shook his head slightly. "Never."

We were both quiet a moment, my thoughts still going faster than I could keep up with. I wasn't sure if it was the high or the kiss anymore. When Emery pulled all the way back, his hands brushing down the sides of my arms before he hooked his hands with mine, I asked the only question that was clear above the rest of the noise.

"Can we do it again?"

So, we did, all night long. Emery wrapped us up together in the same sleeping bag, our bodies hot and slick as he kissed me like it was his job, like it was number one on his hopes and dreams list. He didn't lift my shirt, or sneak a hand down my sweat pants, or thrust his hard on against me, though I knew it was there. I could feel it even when he tried to hide it from me.

He kissed me like it was a privilege, like he didn't want to rush, like we had forever.

I think I knew even then that we didn't.

I woke up alone in the sleeping bag the next morning, rubbing my eyes with a slight ache behind them. I felt around on the floor of the tent until I found my glasses, and when I pushed them into place, every moment from last night rushed back all at once.

A smile found my lips as I closed my eyes, remembering the feel of his hands, the taste of his lips, the sounds he made when we were both driving each other so crazy it was unbearable. When I opened my eyes again, Emery was in the opening of the tent, watching me with a lazy smile.

"Good morning."

"It really is," I said, and his smile grew.

"Glen and I are going to go for a morning hike around the park, probably get some firewood. I figured I'd take Kalo to get some of her energy out. You want to come?"

My leg protested with a strong, tingling ache before I could even open my mouth to answer.

"I'm a little sore from yesterday, so I think I'll stay back."

He eyed my leg, a flash of concern on his face, but I smiled to assure him I was fine.

"Okay. Nora is making breakfast burritos. And there's coffee."

I hummed at that. "I'll be out in a sec. Have fun on your hike."

Emery's eyes trailed over me, the strap of my layering tank top slid off one shoulder, my legs still covered by the sleeping bag. When his gaze found mine again, I knew my blush was like a neon sign, and he just smirked before letting the tent flap close.

I bit my lip, falling back into the sleeping bag with a puff, my stomach giddy, heart fluttering.

*What does this mean?*

It was a question I didn't let myself ask last night, at least not out loud, but it was sounding in my head on repeat now that the morning light was shining. I'd never been kissed before. Emery knew that, and he kissed me. He was my first kiss. That had to *mean* something, right?

Or was it just for fun? Was it just Emery being him, kissing girls like it was no big deal, like everything would be normal the next day?

Were we just friends?

Were we even *that*?

My smile faded when I realized we'd known each other for less than a week, and here I was getting butterflies over a make-out session. He probably did this all the time — he probably usually did *more*.

Desperate for reassurance, I eyed the tent opening before pulling Emery's journal out of his bag and into my lap. I heard his voice fade along with Glen's, and even though my heart thumped with a mixture of adrenaline and guilt, I opened to the last page.

But there was nothing new.

*Of course, he hadn't written about it yet. When would he have had time?*

But I needed something, needed his words, needed to be inside that beautiful brain of his. So, I flipped back toward the beginning, reading an entry not too long after the one about *that day*.

*I stopped taking my medicine.*

*Marni knows, but my parents don't. They think it's the only way to save me from myself, to dope me up to the point of basically not living at all. Marni gets it, she knows why I don't want to take them. She still thinks I should, but doesn't press me to. She says it's my choice. My parents make me feel like I don't have any of those, anymore.*

*Grams has been on medicine all her life, the exact kind they prescribed me. She said she doesn't know how she would have survived as a mother, as a wife, without them. But after Gramps died, she stopped taking them.*

*I liked her better then.*

*Maybe she's a little crazy, maybe she talks about darker things than most preferred — but she's here. She's alive, and alert, and real. Uncensored. I appreciate that.*

*So, when I told her about not taking my pills anymore, she didn't judge me, either.*

*She told me how to get rid of them and make it look like I was taking them when I wasn't.*

*Anyway, I stopped taking my medicine, and I feel a little better and a little worse. Dad wants me to step up in the business, and I'm trying, but my heart isn't in it. My heart isn't in anything.*

*When I was little, I used to love the swings. It was the only place I wanted to be on the playground. I spent my entire recess on the swings. I loved that feeling, of flying, of falling. Marni said I should focus on things that make me happy, so I went to the park today. I went to the swings.*

*They don't make me happy anymore.*

*Maybe today is just a bad day.*

"Whatcha reading?"

I jumped at the sound of Nora's voice, tossing Emery's journal across the tent like it'd bitten me. One eyebrow raised on her face as I pressed a hand flat to my chest.

"Sorry, you startled me," I said on a laugh, crawling out of the sleeping bag to retrieve his journal. I tucked it back into his bag, but when I faced Nora again, I saw suspicion all over her face. "Just the map we have for the trip, figuring out the next stop. We're thinking Rio Grande National Park."

"Mm-hmm," she said, eyeing me. "Great park, definitely worth the stop." She paused, her lips rolling like she was tasting her next words before she said them. "I've got coffee and breakfast out here. Care to join an old woman?"

"I'd love to. Let me put something warmer on and I'll be right out."

She nodded once, eyes flicking to Emery's journal before she ducked out of the tent. I cursed under my breath, dressing quickly and pulling my hair up into a messy knot on top of my head before joining her by the fire.

Nora poured me a fresh cup of coffee, adding a little pumpkin spice flavored creamer to it before handing me the steaming mug. I inhaled the scent, a wide smile finding my lips.

*Fall.*

"There was one summer when I thought Glen was being unfaithful," Nora said, and I nearly choked on my coffee.

I managed to swallow it down, giving her my full attention, not sure where that confession came from. "Really?"

She nodded, sipping from her own mug. "It was dreadful. We were young, married only a few years, and those years were rough. In fact, the first five years of our marriage were the hardest. But I didn't know there would be brighter days then, and I thought he had found comfort in another woman." Nora shook her head. "I went crazy, badgering him about where he was when he wasn't home, listening from the other room when he was on the phone, even following him once."

I didn't know what to say, or why she was telling me the story, so I stayed quiet, drinking my coffee.

"He wasn't. Cheating, that is." She smiled then. "No, he was planning a surprise party for our fourth wedding anniversary, and it was one of my best friends he was talking to on the phone so late at night. He was helpless when it came to planning anything, still is," she added with a chuckle. "So my friend Barbara helped him. When I found out, when they surprised me, I burst into tears. Not for the party though, but for the fact that he was still mine."

I smiled a little then, hands wrapped around my mug.

"Sometimes, we have to trust the ones we love, the ones who love us, even when it's hard to do." Her eyes skirted to my tent, to the journal, before they found mine.

"Because even though marriage brings us together as a unit, there are still two individuals who make that whole. And they need to be able to have their own things, their own time, their own privacy."

She said the last word with a raise of her eyebrows, and I flushed, lowering my coffee until it rested on my knee.

"It's not that I don't trust him," I admitted, glancing around us to make sure he wasn't around. I couldn't tell her that I barely knew him, that I wanted to, that I knew more than I should because I'd snooped already and now I couldn't stop. "He's just... his mind is complicated. Sometimes I read just to know him more."

"I know it seems impossible, but you have to have patience, Cooper."

I felt like I was getting a scolding from a mother I'd never had, and I dropped my head.

"There may be things he hasn't told you yet. Hell, there may be things he will *never* tell you. But you don't get to decide which thoughts are which, or when you get to learn more about him, or when that trust goes deeper than where it is already. You only get to be there for the ride, holding on, showing him you're not going anywhere. And every now and then, you'll get to see inside him — *really* see inside him — and you'll cherish it. And your love will grow. And you'll realize why you waited."

I nodded, thumb tracing the black porcelain of my mug. "You're right." It was all I could manage without telling her the entire situation, because even though she was speaking to me as if I were his wife, I heard it as his friend — as his *new* friend.

I hadn't earned those script confessions yet.

"Thanks, Nora."

She smiled then, lifting her mug and tilting it toward me from across the fire. "Unsolicited advice is my forte, sweetie. Now, drink your coffee before it gets cold."

The conversation was easy and light after that, and we were laughing when the guys returned. Glen swooped down to kiss Nora's forehead as soon as they reached us and Kalo licked my cheek with the same enthusiasm, but Emery disappeared straight into the tent. When I followed, he wouldn't look at me. He just started packing, saying we should get on the road.

When I asked if everything was okay, he assured me it was, but that assurance wasn't sealed with a kiss or a hug or even a smile.

We couldn't thank Glen and Nora enough for their hospitality as we loaded up the car and hugged them goodbye, exchanging numbers to keep in touch. Emery seemed back to normal in front of them, but as soon as we headed toward the car, he handed me the keys, climbing into the passenger seat and pulling his hoodie up over his head as Kalo climbed over him into the backseat.

It was a bad day.

I didn't need to ask this time, or pry, or beg him to talk. I knew from the look on his face, from the way he desperately tore his bag apart for his journal, letting it rest in his lap, pen at the ready.

So, I fired up the engine, ready to drive in silence. But before we pulled away, I reached out with a shaky hand, my cold fingers finding his wrist.

He stiffened.

When he didn't pull away, I slid down farther, and he turned his hand up, letting me lace my fingers with his for just a moment, just long enough to squeeze and let him know I was there.

Then, I pulled my hand back, put the car in drive, and we were on the road again.

## Chapter 13

### Rio Grande National Park, Colorado

It wasn't just a bad day.
It was a really, *really* bad day.

The warmth and playfulness I'd felt from Emery the past two days was completely gone, replaced by a shell, by skin stretched over bones and hollow eyes and lips that didn't open.

I knew the drive would be long and quiet, so I just listened to the radio for the four hours until we made it to Rio Grande. But even when we were there, surrounded by another natural wonder in Colorado, Emery didn't seem to care.

We did a short hike through the park, but he didn't talk, didn't hold my hand, didn't even offer to hold Kalo's leash. So, once we made it back to the car, I didn't even ask if he wanted to stay for the night, just loaded us all back in and settled in for a long night drive to the Grand Canyon.

Emery held onto his journal the entire time, but didn't write down a single word.

# Chapter 14

## Grand Canyon Village, Arizona

It was almost midnight by the time I pulled us into one of the historic hotels near the Grand Canyon, and Emery just stood beside me with our bags as I checked us in. The only sound he'd made all day came when I tried to put the room on my card and he simply said, "No," before shoving his own card forward.

The room was small, and Emery dropped his bag on the bed, stripping his shirt off and immediately making his way to the bathroom. It locked with a click behind him and I exhaled long and loud, flopping down onto my bed with Kalo already at my feet, ready to be fed. I rubbed her ears, stretching out my muscles that were tight from driving all day. I hadn't even had the time to do yoga that morning, since Emery had been so eager to get on the road, and I felt the difference — not just physically, but mentally, too.

When Kalo was fed and watered, I rummaged through my bag, pulling out the last set of clean sleep clothes I had and laying them on the bed. Emery emerged not too long after, steam billowing out around him as he dried his hair with one towel, the other tied around his waist. I swallowed as I watched the water droplets drip down his chest and over his tight abdomen, but he didn't notice.

He wouldn't look at me.

I was quiet as he sat on the edge of his bed, clicking through his phone. But after a few minutes had passed, I was ready to break the silence, so I cleared my throat, gathering my clothes off the bed.

"After we check out the canyon tomorrow, I think I'm going to do a load of laundry. The concierge said they have a little laundromat on site." Emery didn't respond, nor did he seem like he was even listening, his fingers still working over the keys on his phone. "Want me to add any of your clothes in with mine?"

"Sure."

I nodded, heart stinging from his icy response. "You okay?"

He huffed at that, tossing his phone on the bedside dresser with a loud thud before his eyes finally met mine. They were hard as stone. "Fine."

I think part of him saw the hurt in my eyes in that moment, because he forced a long breath, running a hand roughly through his hair and tearing his gaze away. I waited for him to say something else, but he didn't — he just stared at the floor where his bare feet rubbed against the carpet.

Swallowing, I held my head as high as I could, adjusting my clothes in my arm. "Okay. I'm going to take a shower."

I took my time, washing my stump and soaking my sore muscles in the bathtub for a while before draining the water and running the shower. The hot water stung a little as it hit my back, but still I stood beneath the stream on one leg, holding onto the bar at the back of the shower for balance.

*Maybe he's regretting last night. Maybe I'm a terrible kisser and now he's thinking about how stuck he is with me. Maybe I said something when I was high, something I don't remember. Maybe he just doesn't like me.*

My mind raced until the water ran cold, and I stepped out of the tub with a heavy sigh, knowing it was no use. I wasn't exactly an expert in depression, but I knew enough to understand that whatever he was going through today, it wasn't because of me. There was a war raging inside that head of his tonight, and only he could see it. Only he could fight.

But only if he wanted to.

Emery was already asleep by the time I let myself out of the bathroom, so I hopped on one leg over to the bed, finding balance on the desk along the wall as I did. I laid my prosthesis beside the bed, set an alarm for seven so I could get up to do yoga before we went for our hike, and then I curled in beside Kalo and turned down the light, praying tomorrow would bring Emery back to me.

"I can't believe it," Lily said over the speaker phone the next morning.

My eyes were closed, back pressed to my mat, and a stupid grin was plastered on my face. I was still lying down from Savasana, my body aching yet satisfied after a great yoga session, and I had a feeling today would be a better day.

"Honestly, neither can I."

She sighed longingly. "I hope you know not all of your first kisses will be like that. Like, he ruined you. He set the bar too high. You're going to be so disappointed next time. My first kiss was Robby MacIntyre, remember? He tongue punched my mouth and slobbered all over me behind the bleachers our sophomore year. At least *I* could only go up from there."

"You should write him a thank you card."

"I really should. He set the bar low. But seriously, what are you even feeling right now?"

I shook my head, trying to figure out how to put it into words. "I don't even know. I feel... high. God, Lily. His lips... they're just... magical."

"Like I said," she reiterated. "Ruined."

I chuckled, sitting up on my mat. "Anyway, I just wanted to tell you. We're hiking the Grand Canyon today so I need to get back to the room and get him up and going."

"Think he'll be in a better mood today?"

My smile slipped, fingers picking at the loose strings at the hem of my tank top. "I hope so. I think yesterday was just a bad day."

"You don't think he's overanalyzing the kiss? Do you think... is he maybe freaked out by how good it was, too? You said he was more of a *single forever* type of guy."

"Well, I don't think we're necessarily getting married just because we kissed," I combatted with a laugh. "Maybe it was just a fun night and it'll never happen again."

Lily scoffed. "Yeah, right. You guys will just continue to drive across the country, spending every waking moment together and sleeping in the same room and you'll never kiss again. Totally. Makes sense."

"Shut up."

"Just be careful, okay?" Lily paused, and I imagined her fidgeting with the straps of her backpack like she always did when we were in high school. She was walking to class, and for a moment I had a longing desire to be there with her, to be at the same college as my best friend. "Your first kiss might have been incredible, but your first heartbreak is going to suck — especially if he's the one to hand it to you."

"It was just a kiss," I lied. "I'm fine. If he wants to just be friends, I'm cool with it."

"And if he wants to make out and take your shirt off?"

I blushed, biting my lower lip. "I mean, I wouldn't be mad at that, either."

"I'm sure," Lily laughed the words. "Okay, go hike the Grand Canyon. I'll just be here, in Illinois, drowning in homework, studying in the library with the other nerds and wishing I was on a cross-country trip with a boy who kisses like a god."

"I'll send a postcard."

"You better."

There was another pause, and my heart squeezed. I wondered what it would be like to be there with her, what my life would have been like if I'd had a normal childhood and parents who cared about me. I wondered how the diner was doing, how Tammy was holding up while they filled my position. I even wondered about my parents. Were they going to be able to pay rent? Were they thinking of me at all?

But I knew that answer already.

As if she could read my mind, Lily spoke my thoughts out loud. "Miss you, bestie. You wearing your ring?"

I sighed. "Miss you more. And like you even have to ask."

"I've got mine on, too. I'm with you in spirit. Call me anytime, okay? Even if it's the middle of the night."

"I'll check in again soon," I promised, and then I ended the call, rolling up my yoga mat and heading back to the room.

It was still dark when I let myself in, but Kalo was wide awake, hopping around my feet as I used the light from my phone to find my way through. I took her for a long walk, my excitement growing as I saw the ridges of the canyon in the distance, but when I tried to wake Emery after we were back, my mood soured instantly.

He was still in bed, covers pulled up over his messy hair, and when I turned on the lights, he groaned.

"Ready to hike, sunshine?" I tried to tease, but he just huffed from under the comforter.

"I don't want to go."

I was tempted to roll my eyes, but then I remembered his journal, how he wrote about the days when everything just felt pointless. I'd never experienced it myself, but I imagined it would be an awful feeling. He'd asked me to understand, and I wanted to, I wanted to give him what he needed.

Steeling all the sympathy I could, I sat on the edge of his bed. "It's really nice outside, and I promise you'll feel better once you get out of bed. You're just tired, but—"

He sat upright in a jolt, cutting my words short, especially when his hard eyes connected with mine. They were bloodshot, like he hadn't slept a wink.

"You're right, I am tired. Too tired to listen to your sunshiney bullshit. So, if you want to go hiking, go. I'm not leaving this bed."

My nose flared, eyes tingling, but I sniffed back the thought of crying just as regret slipped over Emery's face. Clearing my throat, I stood, gathering the backpack he'd bought in Colorado and packing a couple of bottles of water in it along with a few protein bars.

He sighed behind me, flopping back into the bed. "I'm sorry. I just... I can't today, okay?"

I peered at him over my shoulder, but his eyes were on the ceiling, and even though I was hurt, my heart ached for him. All I wanted was to help, to make everything better, but I knew I couldn't. The battle was inside his head, and I couldn't help fight from the outside.

"It's okay," I said softly. "Would it be okay if I left Kalo with you, then? It would probably be hard to do a tour with her, and she's a pretty good cuddle buddy, if you want one."

Emery didn't look at me, but he nodded, his eyes still glued to the ceiling as I strapped the bag onto my shoulders.

"I'll see you later." And with that, I kissed Kalo's head and slipped out the door, leaving him alone in the dark room.

I wanted so badly to spend the day with him, to laugh with him, to talk with him... especially about what happened in Colorado. But I couldn't force him to talk, and I couldn't force him to be okay. Like Nora said, sometimes I just needed to be patient with him — and this was one of those times.

So, I shook him from my thoughts as I checked with the concierge on which hikes he recommended. Deciding I wanted to do the Skywalk more than anything, I signed up for the Grand Canyon West Tour, and a shuttle scooped me up from the hotel a short half hour later.

I used the time on the shuttle to text Tammy, letting her know I was still alive. I told her I had stories for her and she freaked out, making me promise to call her as soon as I could. Then, I checked my social media, which reminded me again how lame my life back home was when I had a whole ten notifications — most of them from Lily tagging me in memes. When I tucked my phone back in the front pocket of the backpack and looked up as the shuttle pulled to a stop, I gasped.

For a second I just sat there, even as the other passengers around me started shuffling off the bus, cameras at the ready. When I finally stood, it was like I was in a trance, my feet moving me out the door on autopilot while my eyes adjusted.

There was a reason they called it the Grand Canyon.

It was grand. There was no better word for it.

The depth of it, the magnitude — it was breathtaking. I couldn't see it all, couldn't take it all in at once, so I just stood there, eyes grazing each and every inch of the canyons while the cool Arizona breeze whipped through my hair.

"Amazing, right?" a soft voice said from my right, and I turned to find a girl about my age, maybe a little older, smiling back at me. She had fire-red hair and freckles lining her cheeks, with blue aviator glasses hiding her eyes and a friendly smile aimed right at me.

"It's... I don't have words."

"I know. This is my second time here. I did the south bend last time, but I had to come do the Skywalk." She pulled a bottle of water from the side pouch of her bag, taking a sip. "I'm Zoey."

"Cooper."

She smiled. "Want to be hiking buddies today? I heard there are some picnic tables down this way if we want to venture along the edge for a while. Do the skywalk last? I've been driving alone for a few days and would love some company."

Zoey seemed so genuine, the way she smiled and waited for my answer, and truthfully, I didn't want to be alone that day, either. So, I nodded, offering her a smile of my own as I pulled the straps of my backpack tighter.

"Actually, that would be great. The friend I'm with is..." My voice faded. "He's not feeling well, so I came out by myself today."

"It's kismet then," she conceded, then she looped her arm in mine and tugged me toward the canyon.

And so I set off with my new friend, and the great day I'd been feeling that morning in yoga started to bloom, even if it was without Emery.

Zoey loved to talk — even more than me. We were quite the pair, jabbering the entire time as we walked the edge of the canyon, pausing here and there to take photos. I found out Zoey was from a small town, too — in Rhode Island, of all places — and she left as soon as she turned eighteen. She'd been traveling the country ever since, writing a travel blog to sustain herself. It was fascinating, hearing about her loyal readers and supporters. I pulled up the site when we stopped at a picnic table, bookmarking it to explore later.

"So, you just started writing about the local places in your home state," I said, scrolling through one of her posts on her blog. "And people started following? And then requesting places they wanted you to go?"

She nodded, biting off a big hunk of an oat bar. "Mm-hmm. It started with them wanting me to come to their towns, to little places they loved, and then they started picking places on the map. Before I knew it, they were donating on my website to help sustain me, and then when I put together my first book, they were rabid. Since then, I've started doing pod casts and motivational speaking. It's crazy," she said, shaking her head. "I haven't lived in the same place for longer than three months since I turned twenty-one."

"Wow," I breathed, trying to imagine what that would be like. I was in awe just from what I'd seen since leaving Mobile and crossing six states. What would it be like to travel the *world*?

Zoey told me about her first trip to Europe, about how she fell in love for the first time with a German university student. She told me about their first kiss in front of the remains of the Berlin Wall, and I teared up a little as her eyes glossed over, the memory leaving her lips and finding my ears. It was magical, just like my first kiss with Emery, but she had only known him for two weeks before she was off to the next place.

"I fell in love with him, even though I knew I'd be leaving," she confessed. "I've never been scared of love, of feelings, of falling hopelessly for another human being. Yes, it hurts to leave, or to lose it, but it's also amazing to live it. It's worth it, to me, to have the experience."

When we started our hike back to the Skywalk, I also learned that Zoey had had several boyfriends all around

166

the world, and she told me about each of them, showing me pictures on her phone. I loved listening to her stories of how she met them, of their time together, of how they kept in touch when she left. Some of them she sees when she passes through their cities, some of them are married now, and some of them fell apart when she left.

One thing was for sure — Zoey was no stranger to boys or the messes that came with them.

Maybe that was why I tossed through every question I had for her as we neared the Skywalk, and when we were waiting for our turn to go out, I kicked at the dirt, a little nervous.

"Hey, can I ask you something?"

"Haven't I proven that nothing is off limits by now?" She laughed, taking a swig of her water before offering it to me. I declined, holding up my own, and she screwed the cap back on. "What's up?"

I shifted. "I've never had a boyfriend before, but, there's this guy..."

"Always is," she mused, offering me a knowing smile.

"We haven't known each other long, but we kissed the other night."

"And let me guess, now he's being weird?"

I balked. "Yeah. Exactly. How did you know?"

Zoey chuckled, tightening the straps of her bag. "Trust me, they *all* do that — especially if you knock them on their ass, which I'm sure is the case with you and this guy. You're beautiful, smart, funny — boys don't know what to do with that when they actually have it."

"I don't think that's it," I said, pushing my glasses up the bridge of my nose. "He's... complicated. It was amazing, the night we had together, but now he will barely look at me. I'm not sure what to do."

"Hmm," Zoey hummed, tapping her pointer finger on her chin. "Look, I don't know the guy, but I'll give you the advice that saved me. Every guy plays by *their* rules — so pay attention. What does he respond to, and how does he communicate? Even if it's out of character for you, you might have to play his game now and then to knock some sense into him. Now," she said, holding her finger up. "This does *not* mean change who you are — because you should never change, not for anyone, least of all a guy. But, if you like him, and you think he likes you, then let him know you're not going anywhere. And don't be afraid to step out of your comfort zone to show him you can play his game just as well as he can."

My wheels were turning, trying to think of what *game* Emery would play, but I came up blank. Maybe he was different from the guys Zoey had been with. It wouldn't surprise me.

Emery was different from everyone.

"Thanks," I said, though I wasn't sure exactly what to do with what she'd told me — at least, not yet.

She smiled. "Sure thing. You ready?" She nodded toward the skywalk, and we looped arms again, boys forgotten for the moment.

We made our way toward the horseshoe-shaped glass bridge that hung over the edge of the canyon, and when we stepped out onto it, our dusty sneakers hitting the glass, a new kind of magic found me.

Up until that point in my life, there had only been three moments when something shifted in me — the day I lost my leg, the day I realized what I wanted to do for my career, and the night Emery Reed kissed my lips. All of those moments had changed me, had propelled me into a new chapter, a new version of myself.

None of them compared to what I felt when I walked out onto that bridge.

It was completely made of glass — the walls, the railing, the floor — and my breath caught in my throat as I eased my way out, hands shaking as I pulled my arm from Zoey's. My fingers trembled still as they slid along the smooth glass stabilizing me, eyes trying to find a focus that felt impossible to grasp. I looked all around, yet I couldn't see everything — I would have had to stand there for years. The canyon was so beautiful, the sun beginning to set in the distance, casting the red rocks in an orange, heavenly glow. It seemed to span on forever, the dips and valleys and peaks, every inch of it rich in age and history.

I stopped at the apex of the horseshoe, leaning my elbows on the railing and peering over the edge. There were other tourists around me, most of them snapping selfies with the canyon in the background, but I left my phone tucked away, trying my best to take it all in with my eyes, instead.

I felt everything in that moment — the beat of my heart in my chest, the breath as it left my lungs before I inhaled again, the breeze through my hair, the sun on my cheeks. I felt everything I had been up until that moment, and somehow, I felt everything I would become after. It seemed like that was a turning point for me — before and after the Grand Canyon. And before I even realized it was happening, a tear fell from my wet cheek onto the railing where my hands gripped tight.

No one seemed to notice me as life rocked through me for possibly the first time on the edge of that canyon. No one asked me if I was okay, or offered me a tissue, and I was thankful. It was my moment, one meant for no one else, and for the first time, I felt alive — truly, one-hundred percent alive.

It was my rebirth.

I'm not sure how long I stood there, but it was long enough for the sun to fade away, settling the canyon in a purple dusk as the tour guides ushered us back to the busses. I hugged Zoey in a sort of trance when we had to part ways, and she just smiled, because she got it — she knew.

"Keep in touch, okay?" she said, squeezing me tight. We had to board opposite busses, hers heading to a different hotel, and I hugged her with a thanks I couldn't voice.

"Will do. Take care, Zoey."

We shared a smile when we pulled back, and then just as quickly as she had come in, Zoey walked out of my life.

But I'd never forget her.

# Chapter 15

## Las Vegas, Nevada

Emery didn't get out of bed the entire time we were in Grand Canyon Village.

The next morning, when it was time to make the short drive to Las Vegas, he seemed to be slowly coming back to life. He woke up early and showered, bought us breakfast, and walked Kalo. After I finished our laundry, we packed up and checked out, driving along the canyon for as long as we could so Emery could at least get a look.

Still, even though he was alert and driving, he wasn't talking much. Other than asking me if I was ready or if I had any music preference, we were still on the silent treatment, and I hated it.

I felt refreshed from seeing the canyon, and I had to physically bite my tongue to keep from telling Emery all about it. I wanted to share the experience with him, but I knew better than to try to talk to him when he was in this mood.

Been there, tried that, binge ate the doughnuts alone in the hotel room while he hooked up with another girl.

No, thanks.

But more than anything, I wanted to know where his head was at. What did our kiss mean to him? Did it mean anything at all? Nausea haunted me at the thought that I may never get the answers.

It was only about a five-hour drive into Sin City, and I kept my eyes on the desert the entire time. When the lights glowing in the low valley came into view, the sun was just beginning to set, and for the first time in two days, Emery smiled.

"Welcome to Vegas, Little Penny."

My heart fluttered at the nickname, at the warm tone, and I glanced at him, his smile infectious as we closed in on the oasis city. It was literally in the middle of the desert, but it was bright and loud, the energy buzzing from the strip all the way down the road to our car still just out of town. I couldn't tear my eyes away the closer we got, and once we were actually on the strip, I just hung one arm out the window, staring in wonder.

It might as well have been daytime for how bright it was, and there were thousands of people littering the strip. I watched as bachelorette parties stumbled over the bridges crossing the strip in ridiculously tall high heels, all of their dresses matching, the bride standing out in white. There were street performers of all varieties, club promoters passing out cards for clubs, and when we paused at a stop light, a man grinned at me, handing me a playing card with a scantily clad woman on the front.

Scratch that — she was naked.

I held it up with wide eyes, and Emery laughed from the seat beside me as I freaked out and flicked the card away from me, letting it float down to the floor board. Narrowing my eyes at him, I punched his arm playfully, and the smile fell from his face just as the light turned green. Now that I was looking at him, I couldn't stop — not with the lights shining over him, casting him in a different colored glow every second that we drove, his hair blowing back behind him with the top down.

He was coming back.

Or, so I thought.

We checked into the Cosmopolitan, which was right in the center of the strip, and I nearly ran into Emery six times as I looked around at the casino, the high-hanging chandeliers, the shops, the *glamour*. Kalo seemed lost with me, the two of us stumbling around like we were hypnotized as Emery led us in confidence. It was absolutely unreal, and though Emery fit right in with his fashionable sweater and designer jeans, I was still in yoga pants and an oversized long-sleeve shirt, and I felt completely out of place.

Emery ripped his bag open as soon as we were in the room, and I got Kalo set up with her bed, food, and water, turning to Emery just as he reached back for the neck of his sweater, pulling it up and over his head. Heat tinged my cheeks, and I pulled my hair over my shoulder, twirling it in my fingers as I looked around the room — at literally *anything* but his bare, toned back.

It was stunning and modern, with a glass shower right between our room and the bathroom, a long chaise with a view of the large windows overlooking the strip, and a wide balcony. I ran my fingers along the plush purple runners at the edge of the bed before opening the sliding glass door and stepping out into the night, the breeze sweeping up from the strip and taking my hair with it.

Kalo came out to enjoy the view with me, and I tucked my arms tight around my middle, teeth chattering just a bit. It had been warm driving in the desert, but now that the sun had set, it was in the fifties, a dry kind of cold.

"I'm going out," Emery said, and when I turned to find him standing in the doorway, I froze.

His hair that was so messy from the wind in the car was tamed, combed over in a stylish wave, the sandy blond strands framing his golden eyes. His jaw was set, hands resting comfortably in the front pockets of his beige dress pants, a wintergreen button up hugging the muscles of his arms and drawing my attention to where the top few buttons were left undone. The sleeves were rolled up to his elbows, and the whole outfit made him look casual yet completely put together. He was a walking *GQ* model.

And I had a ketchup stain on my shirt.

"You wanna come?"

The way he asked, I wasn't sure if he actually wanted me to join him or not, but the thought of spending the night alone in Vegas was enough to make my stomach do a somersault.

"I do, but..." I pulled at my clothes, eyes on the stretched-out fabric. "I don't have anything... like... that," I said, gesturing to him.

Emery watched me, waiting, and I stared at him, waiting, too.

But no answer came from his lips, and no reassurance, either. He didn't have to say anything for me to realize that it was my problem, not his.

"I'll check out some of the shops downstairs and I can just text you when I'm ready, and meet up with you then?"

He nodded, and the words had barely even left my lips before he turned and jetted out the door.

Kalo tilted her head at me, as if to ask me what the hell I was going to wear to go out on the town in Las Vegas. Her ears flopped over, tongue following suit, the wind blowing at the shaggy strands of her fur.

"I don't know, Kalo pup," I said, bending to press my forehead to hers. With a sigh, I ruffled her fur and stood again, eyes on the fountain springing to life below. "It might be time to dip into the savings."

After perusing the elegant shops in the Cosmopolitan and finding out very quickly that they were entirely out of my price range, I was ready to give up and stay in my pajamas for the night. I figured renting a few movies and cuddling with Kalo wouldn't be so bad.

But then I remembered I was in Vegas, and I mentally slapped myself.

Thankfully, a sweet middle-aged woman heard me asking the cashier at one of the boutiques if there were any other shops nearby, and she pointed me across the strip to the Miracle Mile Shops.

It was a different kind of wonder, being on the Las Vegas strip. It wasn't the Rocky Mountains or the Grand Canyon, a natural, earthy beauty that stole my breath away. The lights were the stars here, the hotels were the mountains, the sidewalks the valleys, and the people who flowed through them were the wildlife. Sin City seemed to whisper to me as the wind swept my hair back and I watched those who passed me, their eyes set on winning money or dancing the night away. Their electricity buzzed through me, and I bounced a little as I walked through the doors to the Planet Hollywood entrance to the mall.

Las Vegas was welcoming — warm and bright and loud — and I had my heart set on making just as many memories on the strip as I did hiking Seven Falls.

I scanned a few of the stores before finally seeing one that seemed a little my style, and as soon as I pulled one long dress off the rack, a charming, impeccably dressed man rushed to my side.

"Can I start you a fitting room?" He was all smiles, his voice light and airy, dark hair styled to perfection.

"Yes, thank you," I said, handing him the one long dress I'd found. The other ones I'd spotted were all short, so I followed him back, but he paused.

"You're not done shopping, are you?"

I shrugged. "I was looking for a long dress, and this seems to be the only one you have."

The man waved a hand at me, and I caught the name on the tag fastened to the front of his vest. *Antonio*.

"With your figure? Short is the way to go. Or a tight pair of jeans to show off that tiny frame. Here, why don't you try this on and I'll grab you a few other options. Is it to go out, for dinner, casual?"

I shifted, realizing I hadn't even asked Emery where he was going. "Um... I'm not sure. I'm meeting a friend out tonight, but he didn't tell me where. I think it'll probably be a bar of some sort."

"Oh, honey," he said on a laugh. "There are very few *bars* on the strip. It's all clubs, and that means we need to get you all glammed up." He hung my dress on a hook in the back dressing room, holding back the fabric curtain for me to step inside. "I'll be right back. Trust me, you won't leave here until you're looking fabulous, doll."

He clapped his hands together with an excited giggle before leaving me alone in the room, and I just chuckled, tucking the curtain closed.

It turned out Antonio was *my* lucky penny, because the only dress I'd managed to pick out myself swallowed me like a burlap sack. But he had plenty of outfit choices for me to try on, and a few of the other female associates joined in, bringing me shoes and accessories, all of them joining in a mixture of *oooh's* and *aaah's* every time I emerged in something new.

Still, nothing seemed to be sticking. Not until I pulled on a short, black dress, one I'd been saving until last. I'd tried on the jeans, and the pant suits, and even the leather leggings — but wearing this meant one thing I wasn't sure I could handle.

My prosthetic leg would be visible.

The dress was long sleeved, with a draping neckline that accentuated what barely there breasts I had before tapering at my waist. There were swirl-patterned strips of fabric missing on the side and at the bottom, each of them covered in a mesh lace, and the hem cut off halfway down my thighs, leaving me way more exposed than I was used to.

Every part of me that I saw as a flaw was on full display — my nude socket, the silver pylon leg, the foot that matched my skin tone as much as it possibly could. It was all I could see as I pulled back the curtain with a shaky breath, ready for the stares, for the questions, for the looks of pity. But when I stepped in front of Antonio and the two other associates, they stared alright — but not at my leg.

At me.

"Oh. My. God," Antonio said, punctuating each word as one hand covered his mouth.

"That's the one," the girl to his left said, shaking her head like she was in disbelief. "Wow. You look *killer*." She snapped her fingers together. "I have just the shoes."

She disappeared before I could tell her I wouldn't be able to wear heels, but it didn't matter, because I turned to face the three angled mirrors, and when I stopped looking at my leg, I saw what they saw, too.

It was like the dress was made for me.

"Antonio, I can't wear this," I whispered, though my fingers ran over the smooth fabric with longing, brushing the mesh lace along the edges.

"The hell you can't," he said, stepping up beside me. He lifted his arms over my head, dropping them down to lay a gold necklace over my collarbone. It was a layered choker, several thin chains making an elaborate design that seemed to accent the dress perfectly.

"But..." I looked down, wiggling my leg.

"But nothing. What, you're worried about *that*?" he asked, nodding to my leg in the mirror as his female counterpart handed him a pair of bedazzled ballet flats over his shoulder. "Honey, no one is going to be able to focus on that with your tits pushed up to the heavens and your thighs singing hallelujah like that. Here, just try these."

I sat on the small cushioned bench and pulled the flats on, cringing a little at the way I had to stretch the delicate fabric over my prosthetic foot. But both shoes fit, and when I stood again, wiggling my toes and admiring the unique way the flats strapped over my arches, they all gasped.

When I turned back to the mirrors, all I could do was shake my head. "This is crazy."

"It's *perfect*," Antonio corrected. "Do you have contacts?"

I cringed, but nodded. "I do. I packed a pair in my purse just in case. You think I should wear them?"

"Definitely. And, what are you going to do about that hair? There's a blow-out place a few stores down. You should see if they can get you in. And stop by Mac for makeup."

I pressed my hands flat to my stomach, feeling a little overwhelmed. "How much is this going to cost me?"

Antonio added up the shoes, necklace, and dress, and when he told me the total, I nearly passed out. It was more than I made in three shifts at the diner. I sighed, bending to remove the flats, Antonio and everyone else protesting the entire time.

"I can't, guys. It's too much." I sighed again. "It's all too much." Suddenly, I felt defeated, and I had no idea why. "I don't even know what I'm doing."

Maybe it was battling with Emery for three bad days in a row, three days of him not talking to me, not acknowledging what had happened between us. Maybe it was that I was miles away from the place I'd called home my entire life, and I'd lost who I was, yet hadn't quite found the new person I'd become. I was in a strange purgatory, stuck between the before and after, unsure of every move I made.

Antonio exchanged a look with the two girls beside him, then he smiled down at me. "Oh, my *gosh,* I can't believe you work at our sister boutique in LA!"

I cocked a brow, eyeing him as he shared knowing looks with the other two.

"Of course we'll give you the employee discount. That brings your total down forty percent. Oh, and, *what do you know* — that dress just happens to be off our clearance rack!"

They all just watched me, their flawless smiles surrounding me in the dressing room, and it was all I could do not to fall apart. I didn't know whether to cry or hug them all, but I settled for the latter, whispering a thank you in Antonio's ear.

"My pleasure. Now, go fix that hair and get your face done, and show that *friend* of yours what you're working with."

# *Chapter 16*

## Las Vegas, Nevada

It was late by the time I got my hair and makeup done and changed into my new clothes. My palms were sweaty as I texted Emery, asking him where he was, and when it took him almost twenty minutes to answer, I started to panic at the thought of going all out only to end up partying by myself.

But my phone eventually lit up with his name. He'd gone down the strip, but was on his way back to the club inside our hotel. Marquee.

I sighed a breath of relief that I wouldn't have to find a cab — or worse, walk down the strip. I'd already walked Kalo when I got back from the mall, but I wanted to wait a while before making my way down. No way was I showing up before him. So, I sat on the edge of the bed, completely dressed and ready, petting my dog.

So cool.

When I'd managed to burn another twenty minutes, I checked my reflection one more time in the mirror.

The dress fit like a glove, just like it had in the store, and my fingers played with the gold chains of the choker as I took in the whole ensemble. I'd picked up a black clutch to match at the last second, and I held it in the hand not touching the chains. My hair was curled in soft waves that fell down my back and over my shoulders, and my glasses were tucked in my toiletry bag, leaving my eyes bare for the first time in years. I had fake lashes and more makeup than I even knew existed on my face, courtesy of Mac, and even though I looked completely different, I didn't feel weird.

I felt beautiful.

I wondered how many girls experienced this every day when they looked in the mirror as I slipped the hotel key into my clutch, letting the door click softly shut behind me. My eyes studied the rhinestones on my flats as they carried me to the elevator, my hands fiddling with my curls. I was anxious to see Emery, to see his reaction to me. Maybe he wouldn't care — after all, he'd been attracting drop-dead gorgeous women his entire life. But maybe he'd see what I did. Maybe he'd see the girl he kissed under the stars in Colorado, the girl waiting for him to tell her what the hell was going on in his head.

It was like playing a game of chess where none of the rules I'd learned applied anymore. There were new pieces, new movements, new strategies — and I had no idea how to play. All I could do was watch and learn from my opponent, which put me at a steep disadvantage.

The club was inside the hotel, the entrance located on the second floor, and the line was wrapped around the thumping dome that surrounded it as I rounded the hallway that housed the elevators. I stepped up to the back of the crowd, forcing a shaky breath and holding my clutch in both hands as I waited.

A group of girls in front of me was laughing when I approached, all of them visibly drunk, but after a moment,

I noticed them whispering to each other, their eyes flicking to me every now and then.

More specifically, to my leg.

I stood as tall as I could, trying to ignore them and keep my eyes trained on the bouncers checking IDs at the front. It was working until one of them turned to me, blinding me with a smile so bright against her bronze skin I almost squinted.

"Sorry for staring," she said, a thick Spanish accent curling the words, and I was surprised by the sweet tone of her voice. She was still giggling with her friends, but still, I waited for the insult, for the *bless your heart* kind of comment that would come next. She only shook her head with awe in her eyes as she gave me another once over. "We just can't stop talking about how amazing you look."

"Me?" I nearly choked.

She laughed, the other girls succumbing to another fit of giggles. "Yes, you. That dress is stunning, and your hair... I wish I could get mine to look like that."

"Seriously," one of her friends added. "It's so shiny. Like a shampoo commercial."

More giggles.

I blushed. "Thank you, but all credit goes to the hair place across the strip. This mess is usually in a braid," I said, running a few fingers through my curls.

"Mine is usually in a messy bun, so I get it," the first girl said. "Well, anyway, you look awesome. See you inside?"

"Sure," I said, and I couldn't fight the smile creeping its way onto my face once she turned around again.

Lily once told me there's nothing more genuine than a compliment from a drunk girl, and I held onto that as the line moved forward. My confidence was still roughly the size of a pea, but they'd made me feel as good as when I'd looked in the mirror upstairs. Maybe my leg wasn't the only thing people saw, after all.

The line moved quickly, and before I knew it, I'd had my ID checked and I was ushered inside. My nerves were on high alert when I handed the bouncer my fake, but he barely glanced at it, seeming much more interested in my attire than my age. I was inside before I could put my ID away again, but it wasn't a club I found on the other end of the door.

It was a concert.

Bright neon lights flashed, rays of green and purple stretching across the crowd on the dance floor and bouncing off the walls in the back. Dancers lined the railings on the left and right of the dance floor, each of them wearing platinum wigs and glowing makeup, dressed in nothing but what appeared to be black underwear and bras as they danced in time with the beat of the electronic music.

The bass thumped through me and my heart rate accelerated with it.

*How the hell am I going to find Emery in here?*

I hooked my fingers over the leather of my clutch, holding it in front of me as I slowly moved through the crowd, eyes on the bar. The music was so loud I couldn't think, couldn't process, the lights flashing bright over the sea of faces before they disappeared again. When I found a small clearing, I stood still, gathering my bearings.

And then I saw him.

Emery was at the bar, just like I'd suspected, seated at the far end of it on a barstool with people crowding on either side of him trying to get the bartenders' attention. His hand rested on the lower back of some platinum blonde girl, and that was all I could see of her from the back — that and her sky high, red-bottomed heels that matched the crimson sequin detailing on her dress.

His hands were on her.

But his eyes were on me.

The blonde leaned in to talk in his ear over the music as his gaze fell from my eyes down over my chest, my ribs, my legs. I thought I saw him swallow, though I couldn't be sure. All I knew was he was scowling, and when he met my gaze again, he didn't move. He didn't get up and come to me or call me over. His eyes didn't widen at my dress. His jaw didn't drop.

He just stared.

And my heart sank all the way down to the dance floor.

I thought he was coming back to me, I thought the bad day was over, but he was looking at me like he didn't want me there, like he was annoyed I showed up at all. It was clear to me in that moment that our kiss meant absolutely nothing to him, and that likely, I didn't either.

*Stupid girl.*

I wanted to cry. I wanted to scream and throw a fit and pack my bags and catch the next flight out of town. I didn't even know where I would go — back to Mobile? On to Seattle? To wherever the first flight would take me? It didn't matter, but I couldn't stay in that club another minute letting him make me feel like I didn't belong.

My bottom lip quivered as I ripped my gaze from his, but I held my chin high, biting back any emotion as I started making my way through the crowd again. He didn't deserve my tears, especially since he clearly wouldn't care if they fell.

I was nearly to the door when a hand wrapped around my wrist, gentle yet firm as it pulled me to a halt.

I turned, my eyesight blocked immediately by a wide chest, and when I craned my neck up to get a good look at the man hooked to the hand still holding me in place, my pulse ticked back to life.

He was ridiculously tall, especially next to me, with midnight skin and jet-black eyes. Those eyes were drinking me in, his full lips settling into a smirk as he pulled me just a little closer to him.

"I'm sorry, but there's just no way."

I stared at him, confused, my head tilting a little as I leaned in so I could hear him better. "I'm sorry?"

"There's no way," he repeated, taking my cue and stepping closer.

My eyes jetted to the left, then to the right, before finally finding his again. "I... I don't understand."

"It's just, I saw you from where I was sitting at the bar, just standing out there on that dance floor. You walked in, stood there, looked like someone broke your damn heart, and then you turned to leave. I almost thought I imagined you, because there's no way you got all dressed up, that you walked out of your hotel tonight looking like *this,*" he said, eyes trailing my body slowly again. "Just to leave the club before midnight."

I'd never blushed so furiously in my life, and I prayed he didn't see it as a bright flash of light found us in the dark before quickly shading us again.

"I was supposed to meet someone here, but..." I paused, unsure how to finish the sentence. "Well, it doesn't matter. I was just heading back up for the night."

He shook his head. "You're right, it doesn't matter. And there's not a chance in hell you're leaving yet, not before you let me buy you a drink."

I sighed, looking at the exit longingly. It was my way out of here, out of this dress, out of my head.

"Come on," the guy pleaded, squeezing my hand in his. "Just one drink, and if you still want to leave when it's gone, I'll walk you to the door."

I looked up at him again, finding nothing but a genuine smile, a genuine guy who thought I was pretty and wanted to buy me a drink. And maybe it was the thousands of miles between me and the parents who made me not want to ever touch alcohol, or maybe it was the embarrassment I felt from Emery's rejection, or maybe it was just not wanting to waste a dress I thought I'd never wear and makeup I knew I'd never know how to do again — but whatever the reason, I let out a long exhale, my worries riding it like a wave.

For once, a drink seemed like exactly what I needed.

"You've got a deal."

His grin doubled, eyes lighting up with my permission as he held my hand a little tighter, tugging me through the crowd again and back to the bar. When he found a space to squeeze in, we were pressed together, my chest hitting just under his as he placed a warm hand on my lower back.

"I'm Trey," he said, leaning in to yell over the music.

"Cooper."

"What's your drink of choice, Cooper?"

I balked, glancing at the rows of bottles lining the shelves behind where the bartenders rushed around filling orders. I'd never had a drink in my entire life — how the hell was I to know what my drink of choice was?

"Um..." I pulled a curl over my shoulder, twirling it in my fingers. "You know, I'll just have whatever you're having."

It was his turn to raise an eyebrow. "You sure?"

I nodded. "I trust you."

"Famous last words."

I laughed at that, and he watched me a moment with that same sexy grin before knocking on the bar, grabbing the attention of the next bartender who whizzed by.

"Two Manhattans, please. Bulleit. Oh," he paused, eying me mischievously and holding my gaze as he finished the order. "And two Vegas Bombs."

The bartender nodded and got to work, pulling bottles from the shelf, her hands flying faster than I could watch.

"You said one drink," I reminded him.

"Vegas Bomb is a shot, not a drink. And you also said you were having whatever I was."

His smile was infectious, and I mirrored it as I leaned in a little closer. "Sneaky."

Trey shrugged. "Or innovative, depending on how you look at it."

He slid me two shot glasses as soon as the bartender set them in front of him, the larger one filled with Red Bull and the other with two types of whiskey. When our Manhattans were made, Trey told the bartender what name the tab was under before turning to me with a devilish grin.

"Drop the shot glass in the Red Bull, then chug. Ready?"

Excitement swirled with fear low in my stomach as I laughed, shaking my head and lifting both of the glasses. "As I'll ever be."

"One... two..."

But before Trey could say three, a hand snatched the whiskey shot glass from mine, and Emery slid right between us.

"Hey!" I squeaked, frowning as I tried to grab the glass back. Emery held the shot right out of my reach, his eyes hard on mine, those two lines creased between his brows, jaw set.

"What the fuck, bro?" Trey stole the shot back, but Emery still didn't move.

"You don't drink."

His entire body was pressed against mine, his breath hot on my lips as he stared down the bridge of his nose at me.

"We're in Vegas," I reminded him.

"So now you drink?"

He was challenging me, his chest puffed out, fists clenched tight. Trey tried to move him out of the way again, but even though he was taller, Emery was solid. He didn't budge.

I narrowed my eyes. "What does it matter? Seemed like you had your hands full over there." I nodded toward the other end of the bar where he'd been sitting before. "Maybe you should worry about whether or not *she* drinks instead of me."

"I don't give a fuck about her."

"Oh," I mocked. "And you give a fuck about me?"

He blinked, as if my cursing surprised him, or the fact that I'd called him out. And since I'd finally shocked him silent, I reached around him, taking the shot glass from Trey's hand. Then I leaned over the bar enough that I could see him behind Emery, raising my glass to his.

"To Vegas."

Trey eyed Emery, a little pissed, a little confused as he tapped his glass to mine. Then as he took his, I stood straight again, my chest still touching Emery, and with my eyes hot on his, I dropped the shot in the Red Bull and chugged.

All my senses were attacked violently in that next second, my eyes and throat burning in sync from the whiskey, but I didn't cringe against the fire. I let it consume me, let it slide all the way down into my stomach as I wiped the corners of my mouth and stacked the empty glasses on the bar. Trey stepped around Emery, though we were still staring at each other, at least until Trey's hand slipped between us with my Manhattan.

"Wanna dance?"

"Love to." The words were like arrows lashing from my lips, and I aimed them straight at Emery as I snagged my clutch from the bar and tore my eyes from his, following Trey out to the dance floor.

I chugged half of my drink before Trey stopped, pulling my body flush against his. I was completely at a loss for why anyone actually *enjoyed* drinking as another burn sliced its way through me. I shook my head, eyes squeezed shut, my hands holding tight to Trey's arms for balance.

"I take it that was the person you were supposed to meet?"

"Doesn't matter," I said, still fighting the roll of my stomach as I added more alcohol to it.

Trey smirked, pulling me even closer, the hand not holding his drink sliding confidently down to my ass. "I think that's our theme for the night."

"We should get tattoos."

He laughed at that, but then his eyes fell to my lips, and neither of us were laughing anymore. "I think I want to leave my mark on you in a different way tonight, Cooper."

I swallowed, my heart thumping against my rib cage like it wanted to flee, like it didn't want to see what would happen next. Trey squeezed his hand, bunching my dress with it, and then our bodies were moving, his leg between mine as we rolled and dipped. I'd never danced before — not unless you counted the times I was alone in my bedroom with a fake microphone and Taylor Swift on the radio — and this was *definitely* not that kind of dancing.

Sweat rimmed the roots of my hair the longer we moved, and I drained the rest of my drink, abandoning the empty glass on a nearby table as Trey followed suit. Then we had both hands to touch, to roam, to pull, to feel. Trey's hands were enormous, his thumbs nearly touching above my navel as he gripped my waist, swaying me with him.

The alcohol buzzed through me like a lightning storm, hitting me in flashes along with the laser lights streaming from the DJ above the dance floor. I closed my eyes, reveling in the feel of the music, the base, the hands, the night. Trey leaned in, his voice barely audible as he spoke over the music and told me he'd be right back, he was grabbing us another drink. I nodded, eyes still closed, my hands lifting above me once Trey wasn't there to hold onto anymore.

It was surreal, dancing in the middle of a crowded club in Las Vegas, the music vibrating through every vein as I moved in time with the rhythm. A week ago, I was just a little girl in Mobile, Alabama, serving pancakes to the same people I had since I was sixteen. Now, I was a vixen, sexy and confident, wearing a dress that showed my most sensitive scar.

And it was the last thing on my mind.

Trey's hands slid around my waist from behind and he pulled me back into him, his hips matching my rhythm as he molded himself to me again. His abs were hard against my back, and I arched into him, running my hands through my hair and pulling it all to one side to cool my neck. But when he ran his nose along the skin I'd just exposed before sucking my earlobe between his teeth, my eyes shot open.

Because I knew then that it wasn't Trey at all.

"Emery."

I breathed his name like a curse, and his hands squeezed my hips in affirmation as he rocked against me from behind. My eyes fluttered shut again at the rush from his touch, my knees suddenly weak, and I leaned into him, letting him take my weight. His hands were everywhere — wrapping around to grab my own, fingers laced between mine before he dragged them up my ribs, under the wire frame of my bra, and then they were on a hot trail back down to my waist.

My lips parted as he picked up our pace and I let my head fall back onto his shoulder, eyes still closed as he kissed along my neck. Every part of our bodies was sewn together, and his heart beat hard and steady through the fabric of his shirt, the bass to the quick, light beat of my own.

Cracking my eyes open, I turned in his arms, staring at his chest. As soon as I lifted my eyes to his, I heard my name.

"What the fuck, man?" Trey shoved Emery away from me, his fresh drinks crashing to the floor with the movement. "I thought she made it pretty clear at the bar that you needed to back off."

"She's here with me, asshole," Emery said, bowing up to Trey.

"Oh, you're the guy she was supposed to meet here, huh? The one who left her standing heartbroken on the floor when she first got here?"

The color drained from Emery's face, and his eyes flicked to mine, but Trey stepped even more between us.

"Well, sorry bro, you fucked up, and now she's with me. So take a walk."

Emery's face screwed up, his hands shoving Trey back. "You fucking take a walk, *bro*."

Trey went to shove Emery again but I jumped between them, pressing my hands into his chest.

"Stop! It's fine, Emery was just leaving."

"Not without you, I'm not."

I spun, rushing toward him. "What is your deal? You've ignored me for the past three days, including an hour ago when you had another girl wrapped around you at the bar. Go find her and leave us alone."

"I. Don't. Want. Her." He stepped right back into me, into my space, his chest heaving. "And you don't want him."

"You don't know anything about what I want."

"I do," he argued. "Which is exactly why I haven't said a word since the night we kissed. Because I know what you want, Cooper, and I also know that I can't fucking give it to you."

He pulled back, the heat from him leaving me in a rush as I watched him push through the crowd toward the exit. My heart beat loud in my ears, louder than the music, louder than the voice in my head that told me I was in deeper than I could swim. Trey grabbed my hand from behind but I ripped it away, and before it registered in my cloudy mind what I was doing, my feet carried me through the sea Emery had already parted.

"Emery."

It was the seventeenth time I'd called his name, and he still hadn't stopped. His strides were twice that of mine, but I pushed to keep up as we crossed the second floor of the casino toward the elevators.

"Emery, just wait."

But he wouldn't, and when he made it to the elevators, he punched the up button over and over until the doors to one finally opened. He rushed in, but I had already caught up, and I slipped inside with him before the doors could close.

"Talk to me," I said when we were finally alone, both of us winded as the elevator shot us up to our floor. His hair that was so perfectly styled before he left earlier was a mess again, like he'd had his hands in it all night, and his eyes were red and weary.

"I'm sorry, you should just go back. Go have fun."

"You're sorry," I deadpanned. "Sorry for what, exactly? For giving me the best kiss of my life, for letting me open myself to you in that tent only to completely blow me off the next day?"

"It was your first kiss."

"And?"

Emery's eyes met mine. "And you can't say it's your best if you have nothing to compare it to."

"Oh, so I should just jet back downstairs and make out with Trey, huh? Is that what you want?"

He gritted his teeth, and I knew I'd struck a nerve, so I stepped into him.

"You want me to, what, have more *experience*? Will that make you feel better about kissing me, about touching me? Do you need me to break under someone else's hands so you don't have to be the one to do it first?"

The elevator doors opened again and Emery bolted off without an answer, but I was hot on his trail.

"That's it, isn't it? You don't want the responsibility of being my first kiss."

Emery tapped the key against the reader on our door, shoving inside, the door already closing behind him as my hands caught it. He went straight into the bathroom and shut the door, so I beat my tiny fists on it.

"Emery!" I screamed his name like it would somehow fix everything, like just saying it would force him to admit it. But when he didn't answer, my forehead hit the door in defeat and I closed my eyes on a sigh. "Please, Emery. Please talk to me. You at least owe me that."

It was quiet a moment, but I could hear him breathing on the other side, and then the door flew open and my head lifted, eyes meeting his.

"Yes."

We both cracked with the word, his nose flaring as he stepped toward me, but I was already moving back.

"You're right. I don't want to be the one to break you."

"So don't."

He shook his head as if I'd asked him not to breathe.

"You want love. You want romance and fairytales and happy ever afters. You want *I love yous* and whispered promises and growing old together. And you know what? You *deserve* that. You do." My back hit the wall, but he kept moving, advancing on me until we were just inches apart, his hands pressing into the wall around me. "I'm sorry I was selfish enough to kiss you the other night, because I can't give you any of that. I wish I could, but I can't."

"Why does it have to be all that? Why can't we be what you *can* give, what I can give. It can be casual. Why can't we just try?"

"Because I don't do this," he said, motioning between us. "I've wanted to kiss you from the second I saw you, Cooper, and I figured I'd have your legs on my shoulders and your head hitting the wall that first night in New Orleans."

I swallowed, heat rushing from somewhere in my core up to my cheeks.

"And I don't say that out of disrespect," he added quickly. "Because I realized almost immediately when you got in my car that you aren't that kind of girl... You aren't like any kind of girl I've ever met."

Some of his anger slipped away then, his eyes brighter, voice softer.

"I also realized that none of the rules I've set in relationships before you would work anymore. Not with you. I can't disconnect from you, and I can't treat this like it's casual because it's not. You're not. And I can't—" His voice broke, his eyes shutting tight as he shook his head before they popped back open again. "There are so many things I want to do to you, Cooper." He said it quietly, like it hurt, like it was ripping him apart from the inside. "Things you've never experienced, but I *can't*. Because you deserve more than that, more than what I can give you." He pushed back off the wall, his eyes falling to the floor. "More than me."

Emery's back was to me, one hand covering his mouth as he looked out the window across our room.

"But I want you," I whispered, pressing my hands into the wall behind me. I used it for leverage to stand taller before crossing the space between us. Hesitantly, I wrapped my arms around him from behind, my forehead burying into his back as he let out a pained sigh.

"You don't know me," he countered, voice rough. "And if you did, you'd be running right now."

His journal entries flashed in my mind, and I shook my head against the warmth of his back. *If only he knew.*

"How do you know that if you don't give me the chance?"

I moved around him, my hands sliding from his waist to hook behind his neck. I pulled him down into me, our eyes closing together, foreheads touching like they had the night of our first kiss.

"*Try*, Emery. That's all I'm asking. Let me in on the bad days, in here," I said, tapping his temple before my fingers trailed down over his chest. "And maybe, in time, here, too."

"And if I can't?"

I swallowed, but then pulled back until he opened his eyes, faking my next sentiment as best I could and punctuating it with a shrug. "Then you better at least give me the best damn casual sex of my life."

He smirked, but the curve on his lips died quickly, his eyes igniting with a mixture of passion and warning. My fingers tangled behind his neck, and I took the last step, closing every inch of space between us as I looked up at him.

"Kiss me," I whispered. "And this time, don't stop."

Emery blew out a breath, hands moving to frame my face. I closed my eyes as soon as his skin hit mine, mouth falling softly open, chin tilted up, waiting. His thumb brushed my jaw line before the pad of it skated across my bottom lip, and he groaned, making my eyes flutter open.

His honey eyes were locked on my lips, his brows bent together as he shook his head like he was about to commit a crime that would put him away for life. He swallowed, catching my eyes for just a second before he caved, a guilty man accepting his punishment as his mouth fused with mine.

And though I would have sworn it was impossible, he tasted even better the second time.

The room pulled away and snapped back in a rush, my hands flying into his hair as he lifted me. I wrapped my good leg around him, hiking the other thigh as high as I could before his hand slipped under it for support. He was still scolding me with hot, unapologetic kisses as I rolled my body into him, doing everything I could to get closer, to get more.

When my back hit the puffy comforter of his bed, my hair fluttered out around me, every inch of us sinking deeper into the bed as Emery kissed my neck. His hands were hard on my hips, gripping with a force that made me gasp his name. He told me he wanted me with that grip, confessed his sins with another kiss, and with a groan low in his throat and a roll of his hips against my middle, he threw every reason he should stop out our window and down to the Vegas strip.

Emery slid my dress up and over my hips, exposing the simple thong I wore underneath, and when his fingers ran along the lacy fabric, he paused. His forehead hit mine, a frustrated grunt leaving his lips. I thought he was going to stop, but he simply slowed, his fingers more gentle as they traced the edge of my panties, his kisses softer on my lips.

"Wait here."

In the next second, his warmth was gone, and I lay alone on the bed. I pulled my dress back down a little, my breaths as loud as a train while I watched Emery take his phone from his pocket. He pressed a few buttons, connecting to the speaker on the night stand, and then a soft acoustic song flowed out.

He seemed to be catching his breath as he removed his wallet from his other pocket next, and his eyes were on mine as he pulled out a condom, setting it next to his phone on the table. Then, he crawled back in between my legs, and with our eyes still watching, he kissed me.

With that kiss, everything slowed down — his lips, our hands, my breaths. Emery balanced above me on unsteady elbows, his eyes connecting with mine between each long, soft kiss.

It was my first time, but his shaky hands brushing my hair back told me he was just as nervous as I was.

My heart was the only thing still hammering, beating wildly, thoughts of what was to come rushing through me like a rip tide. He was going to touch me. He was going to touch me where no one had ever touched me before.

Emery pushed up from the bed, his arms stronger now as they held him up on either side of me. He watched me there for a moment, chest heaving, before he took a steady breath and leaned back until he was on his knees. His throat tightened as he swallowed, hands reaching down, palms flattening against the hot skin of my thighs before he pushed up. His wrists caught the hem of my dress, bringing it up with them, and I lifted my hips, my back, my neck, helping him until the dress was gone, discarded somewhere behind him, his eyes raking down my exposed body.

He wet his lips, fingers popping the buttons on his shirt loose one at a time before he tugged it off his shoulders. I'd seen that chest naked before, seen him in nothing but a towel after a shower, but it was different this time. This time, he was exposing that chest for me, for my hands, for my lips.

I sat up, my own hands trembling slightly as I unfastened his belt, the top button of his pants, sliding his zipper down with my eyes crawling up until they found his again. Emery towered over me, his pants undone now, and

I traced every ridge and valley of his abdomen with my eyes first before my hands followed suit.

I'd never felt a man, not like that — not hard and hot and bare, not that close. Emery placed his hands over mine, guiding them up over his chest before he pulled my fingers to his lips. With a kiss to each hand, he pulled them up until they were above my head, and then his fingertips skated down my ribs, igniting another wave of chills. He pulled my small bralette over my head, my hair falling out of it in a waterfall down my back before he laid me down again.

I couldn't grasp a single thought before it was knocked out by the next, my brain on overdrive as Emery kissed me. I felt him kick out of his shoes, and he balanced easily on one elbow and then the next as he maneuvered out of his pants, all the while pressing his wet lips against my skin. When it was just his boxer briefs against my thong, the hard length of him pressing into me, I inhaled a loud, sharp breath, shuddering beneath him.

"Are you okay?" he whispered.

I nodded, arching into him. "Don't stop."

Emery pushed up again, sliding a hand down my left thigh until my leg was hooked over his arm, and then he slid his other hand down to the ankle of my prosthetic leg. His thumb pushed the black pin with a pop, his brows furrowed in concentration, chest moving steadily with the rhythm of his breaths. His touch was soft as he gently removed the limb, the socks, the liner, placing each of them to the side with care before his thumbs hooked under the lace of my thong. And when every layer was gone, he sat back on his heels, shaking his head as his eyes roamed every inch.

"Goddamn, Little Penny."

I blushed, fighting a smile as I reached for him, pulling him back down.

Emery granted my wish with a single, quick kiss before his mouth was moving down. He sucked the skin of my neck between his teeth, eliciting a hiss from me before his mouth found my breast next. And down he went, until the backs of my thighs were on his shoulders, and his lips were brushing the sensitive skin that no one else had ever seen.

My breath picked up speed then, having him below me, the sight of his mouth just inches from the most private part of me. Suddenly, I wondered if it would hurt. I wondered if the stories I'd heard were true. Would I bleed? Would it even feel good at all? But the thoughts were fleeting, muted in the next second by the tender, velvet skin of Emery's lips on my skin.

His kisses were featherlight on my inner thighs and hips, each one moving closer and closer to where I ached the most. I rolled my hips, squirming under the touch, and when I thought I would spontaneously combust with anymore foreplay, Emery cast one last heated gaze up my body.

And then his mouth was on me, hot and wet and new, and all the pent-up energy left my lips in a loud, pleading moan.

I squeezed my eyes closed, fists tightening around where I gripped the sheets, hips rolling of their own accord. A flurry of foreign emotions blew through me as his tongue worked, my breaths coming so hard I felt lightheaded. There was some sort of heat building low in my stomach, a numbness lashing out from it like the tips of fire, reaching down to my toes before it would retract again. For some reason, I wanted to catch that fire, but it was just out of reach.

Emery slowed, his tongue flat and hot against my core as one of the hands gripping my thighs snaked under his mouth, instead. He gazed up at me, eyes wide and worried and on fire all at once, and then the tip of his finger brushed my entrance. It tickled the wetness there, and when he slipped it slowly inside me, centimeter by centimeter, a burning rush of pleasure seared from the point of contact through every nerve in my body.

I gasped, back arching off the bed, and Emery withdrew the finger slowly, pressing it back inside with careful measure.

"Are you okay?" he asked again, and I could barely creak an eyelid open long enough to nod before my head was back on the pillow, my knuckles white from twisting the sheets so hard.

He worked me gently, and I was stretching for him, opening in a way I'd never been opened before. I didn't understand it, how he knew how to touch me there, in a place never touched before — not even by me. It burned at first, a strange, almost numbing fire that faded more with every push inside until I was okay, and then I was more than okay, and then I was chasing that feeling again — one I couldn't quite understand, but that felt closer and closer with every second.

Emery withdrew his finger all the way before his middle finger joined the first, and I peered down at him, my eyes as wide as his this time as he gently slipped them both inside. The burning was back, but more fleeting this time, the sensation only there for a moment before it was gone again. And when he pressed them a bit deeper inside me, the tips of his fingers curling, his mouth lowering to the sensitive skin above his fingers again, I whimpered.

My breaths were loud and tight, my eyes squeezed shut, and I was reaching for that fire again. It was so close, the lashes coming closer together now until all of a sudden, the flames caught, and my entire body burned in a rush. I moaned so loud one hand flew to cover my mouth, but Emery ripped it away, his mouth relentless on the part of me that seemed to be the source of the fire, the spark that ignited it all.

And I realized then that this was it, the feeling I'd always wondered about, the forbidden and foreign rush that came with a man touching me the way Emery was. I rode out my first orgasm, legs shaking and heart racing. It was an out-of-body experience and yet I was present for every blazing second of it.

It seemed to give me every ounce of energy available in my body all at once before it washed away, quickly and fluidly, and my legs fell lax, hips opening, hands releasing the sheets. I panted, a sore awakening touching each muscle as Emery withdrew his fingers and kissed me once more, light and tender, before moving his way back up.

His shoulder shook as he leaned his weight on it, his lips fusing with mine as my breaths evened out.

"Oh my God," I breathed into his mouth. "I think I... did I just..."

"You came," he said, his teeth nibbling at my bottom lip. "How did it feel?"

"Incredible," I breathed the word on a laugh, and Emery smiled, kissing me softly.

He pushed back carefully until he was standing, and when I saw the red stains on his fingers, my eyes shot open for a completely different reason. Emery followed my gaze, holding up his clean hand to stop me from speaking. "It's okay, it's fine, it's normal," he assured me. "One second."

He slipped into the bathroom, my heart still thumping hard and loud in my chest until he returned with a damp wash cloth and clean hands. Emery crawled onto the bed again, one forearm sliding under my shoulder, hips resting between mine. With careful movements, he reached his free hand between us with the cloth, the warm wetness of it running the length of me gently as he watched me.

"You are so, so beautiful, Cooper," he whispered as he cleaned me, and then his lips were on mine, the cloth gone and dropped somewhere on the floor. He rested between my hips again, the hardness of him pressed against me, and though I'd felt it the night we'd kissed in Colorado, this was different. He wanted me. He wanted me so badly his body was reacting to me chemically, in a way he couldn't control, and it filled me with an unexplainable yearning to make him feel what I'd just felt.

"I want you," I whispered, a bit unsure of my own voice. "I want you inside me."

Emery swallowed, his arms shaking again, forehead pressed to mine. I'd felt so spent, but when I bucked my hips up to meet his and he pressed against the tender center of me, want took over. My hands ran the length of his shoulders, fingertips digging into the flesh as I pulled him closer.

It was like I was a precious vase, historic in nature, beautiful and regal, and he was the handler. He was so afraid of marking me, of leaving fingerprints or worse — breaking me. But I had faith in his steady hands, in the way he watched me, and I rocked into him again, my lips finding his.

He kissed me in return, then just as he'd worked his way out of his pants, he did the same with his briefs, eyes on mine the entire time. Our lips were still connected as he felt for the condom on the table, and I tasted myself there, a sweet and tangy mix of him and me that fueled the fire in my stomach again.

The song changed on the speaker just as Emery settled between my hips, his eyes searching mine, a new acoustic melody filling the room. One hand slipped between us, positioning him at my entrance, but he paused.

*God*, the two creases between his brows were enough to kill me in that moment. He was looking at me like his next move would kill me, and maybe it would. But I wanted to die in his arms that night.

So, with the heel of my right foot, I pressed into his backside, and he took the cue, eyes fluttering shut along with mine as he filled me. Slowly, inch by aching inch, until we were together in every way we physically could be, in every way I'd never been with a man before.

Emery groaned as he retracted before pressing into me again, this time hitting me a little deeper, the searing pain I'd felt before back again. I opened for him, nails digging into the muscles of his back as I adjusted to the new sensations. I was full, *so* full, every flex of his hips rocking me with a new rush of all-consuming pleasure.

It was born where we touched, spreading through my entire body in waves all the way to my toes, to my breasts, escaping as little pants from my open lips before a new wave followed right behind it.

"Still okay?" he whispered, kissing me softly as he rocked into me again.

I cracked an eyelid open. "Mmm."

"Are you in pain?"

He rocked in slowly again, and I squeezed my eyes tighter.

"A little, but I'm okay."

And I was. I was *more* than okay. I understood why he kept asking, and in a way, it made me want him more. He was so gentle, so reverent, like being the first man to touch me was the highest privilege he'd had his entire life.

Just like with his fingers, every new thrust opened me more, the pain fading slowly until it was just the sensation of being full. More than anything, I felt overwhelmed with pleasure — like there truly was just *too much* of it. It was everywhere — on his lips when they kissed me, flowing from his hands where they touched me, in the air around us. I'd never experienced anything like it, and I never wanted it to end. It was all consuming, the indulgence that came from him being inside me. I never understood before, I never *could* have comprehended it until I'd experienced it for myself.

I would never be the same again.

Emery's lips fused with mine again as he found a rhythm between my thighs, and I tried desperately to hold onto every sensation, every memory of my first time. I listened to the song playing, the roughness of the artist's voice, the sultry notes from his guitar. I tasted Emery's lips, his tongue, felt the weight of him on top of me, inside of me. I cataloged each and every moment, saving them for later, forever.

"You have no idea how hard it is for me to take this easy," he groaned in my ear, another thrust hitting even deeper as I gasped from the feel of it.

His words sent another zing of pleasure jolting through me, and I kissed him harder, pulling him closer. "It's okay, if you want to... if you need to go harder. I can take it."

Emery kissed my collarbone with another growl, his eyes lifting to meet mine. "I have no doubt, but tonight I'm taking it slow. Tonight," he repeated, his eyes dark. "I want to give you part of the fairytale, even if it's just this."

His words almost hurt, they were tinged with such sadness, such a lack of faith in himself. I wrapped my arms around his neck again, pulling him into me, my lips seeking his.

And in my heart, I knew the odds were against us — that we might be able to start a happy ever after, but our chances of finishing it were slim.

I turned the page, anyway.

The wetter I became, the easier it was for him to slide in and out, and he picked up speed. It was just enough, my moans mixing with his, our skin slick as we touched and felt and burned. Every time he rocked inside, he'd brush me where his mouth was before, on that sensitive space above my opening, and I'd cry out his name. It was such an incredible feeling, such a pleasurable sensation, and before I could stop myself, I came again, this orgasm a little duller but still enough to make me gasp his name over and over as my body shook beneath his.

"Fuck," Emery cried as the last waves washed over me, and with another groan of his own, he came right behind me, his fingers leaving bruises on my hips as he rocked into me one last time. He held me there, his body pulsing above mine as my orgasm receded, and as soon as it passed, my legs fell to the side again and he collapsed, both of us spent.

He wrapped his arms all the way around me and rolled until I was lying on him, his breaths hot in my ear as our slick chests rose and fell together. He kissed my lips, my cheeks, my forehead before pulling me flush against him. My legs ached as he softened inside me, my entire body feeling like it just survived a car wreck and a baptism at the same time.

When our breaths evened out, Emery gently rolled me until I was at his side, discarding the condom in the trashcan beside the bed before pulling me into him again. I rested my head on his chest, fingers grazing the skin where his ribs were, evoking chills with every touch.

"Is it always like that?" I finally asked, my voice a raw, sated whisper.

Finally, Emery laughed, the sound of it loud and booming against my ear on his chest.

"Never," he answered, fingers brushing through the tangled strands of my curls.

He swallowed then, as if that answer scared him as much as it excited me, and then he repeated it. Softer. Slower.

"Never."

## Chapter 17
### Las Vegas, Nevada

In my dreams, I replayed the night over and over again. I lived inside that moment, frozen in time, suspended on that unstoppable linear trajectory for as long as time would allow me to be. When the sun finally warmed my cheeks through the sheer curtain hanging over the sliding glass door, I squinted against it before blinking a few times, finally ready to let go, to move forward.

It was quiet, save for the soft music that still flowed from the speaker on the bedside table, and I stretched as a yawn broke through the sleepy haze I was still in. My toes reached for the edge of the bed while my hands hit the headboard, my mind taking note of my body.

I was sore in all the right places, aching in a new way as I rolled toward the wall. Emery was still there, his head on the pillow, eyes cast up toward the ceiling, and Kalo sleeping in a little ball by his feet. I leaned up on one elbow to get a better view.

"Good morning."

Emery shifted, his head rolling just a little to the side as he met my gaze. "Morning."

Another yawn took me under as I nodded toward my sleeping ball of fluff. "I need to take her out, she hasn't been since before I left last night."

"Already done."

As if Kalo sensed me talking about her, she popped her head up, looking back at me as I reached for her. She licked my hand once, letting me rub behind her ear before she laid down again and I turned my attention back to Emery.

"Thank you."

A lazy smirk curled on his lips, one arm reaching up and over my head until it rested on my pillow behind me.

"Come here."

I scooted closer, head finding his chest as I wrapped one arm around his middle. He tucked me into him, pulling the comforter over us again before his hand rested on my waist.

"I have to tell you something."

"Okay," I whispered as confidently as I could, but the blood drained from my face. Those words set me on high alert as soon as they left his lips, my heart already beating overtime, brain shouting every anxious thought I'd ever had about us loud in my ears.

*This is where it ends.*

*He thinks it was a mistake.*

*You were awful, he'll never touch you again.*

*He doesn't care about you.*

Emery didn't speak right away, just held me there, his fingers brushing against my skin. I watched the breaths enter and leave his chest, waiting, letting his gentle touches soothe me as much as they could in that moment.

"It's hard for me to say this out loud, because other than my family and my therapist, no one really knows."

My heart jumped into my throat at the mention of his therapist. Marni. I knew her name when I shouldn't have, and I swallowed down the guilt.

"I battle with depression," he finally said, and his chest deflated with the words. "God, I hate calling it that. I hate admitting this to you, because it sounds pathetic and weak, but I think it's important."

"It doesn't sound weak," I said, my voice low, guilt still churning low in my gut. If I hadn't pried into his private thoughts, this would be a big moment for him — this admission — and maybe an even bigger one for me. But I'd cheapened it.

"It does to me, but I'm trying to embrace it more." He paused a moment, his fingers moving to run gently through my hair. "I wanted to tell you, though, because sometimes I'm okay, and sometimes I'm not. And honestly, I don't really have an answer for why some days differ from others. All I know is that there are days when I laugh and joke and drink and make the most of the hours I have, and then there are others where…"

His voice trailed off, and I squeezed him a little tighter, encouraging him to finish.

"Where even getting out of bed sounds like a task so impossible, I might die in the process."

My eyes were still on his chest, but I felt him swallow, and I let his words sit between us for a while before adding my own.

"I'm glad you told me."

"I had to," he said quickly. "Because I told you last night that I would try, Cooper, but you have to understand that sometimes trying for me isn't going to be enough for you. Sometimes trying, for me, is just..." One hand waved in the air above us. "Existing."

I frowned, because I knew more than he thought about what that sentence meant, about his bad days. I'd even mentioned them last night, right before he put his hands on me. I told him to let me in on the bad days, days I wasn't supposed to even know about. I wondered if I'd struck a chord with him then, by using the same language he did.

And then I felt sick. Because if that was true, it meant I connected with him in what he thought was a genuine way, when really, I'd cheated.

"Is that why you asked me what made me happy when we met?" I asked after a moment. It was something I hadn't read yet, something I didn't even know if he'd written about at all, so I took the opportunity to ask for his answer instead of finding it of my own accord. "Because it was a day where nothing made you feel that way?"

He chuckled, and I latched onto that sound, to the promise behind it.

"No, that's just what I ask people. I feel like the first thing everyone asks when you meet is, 'What do you do?' I've always hated that, like a job defines us. So, I ask what makes people happy." His shoulders lifted a little. "That tells me more about a person than what they do to make money."

I smiled at that, leaning up on my elbow again so I could see him. "So, you were okay the day we met?"

His eyes were still on the ceiling, but he smiled. "Yeah. That was a good day."

"And today?"

Emery let out a long breath, finally meeting my gaze as his fingers pulled one of my curls taut before letting it bounce back into place. "Today's a good day, too."

His warmth permeated my skin in that moment, and I felt him, all of him, from where his hand touched my waist to where his eyes searched my own.

I didn't know how long it would last — his smile, his mood, us — but I knew I had that day. And I'd take it.

"Well, then," I said, rolling until I straddled him, the sheet getting caught between us as I leaned forward and pressed my lips to his. "Let's make the most of it, shall we?"

Emery ordered us room service and we ate breakfast in bed before making our way downstairs to the casino to gamble. Well, Emery gambled — I just stood behind him and rubbed his shoulders while he told everyone at the tables that I was his lucky penny. A little before noon, we packed up the car, Kalo in tow, and we were back on the road with our next stop being Laguna Beach.

It was a perfect day, temperature hanging somewhere in the mid seventies with not a single cloud in the sky. We drove with the top down and I chuckled at the fact that as soon as we'd found that fall weather I'd been dreaming of, we'd left it again. I wondered what it would feel like once we started driving the Pacific Coast Highway, once we reached the tip of California and crossed into the Pacific Northwest.

"We should make it in time for the sunset," I said, plugging our destination into my phone to check our estimated time of arrival. "Have you ever seen it on the west coast?"

"I have," Emery answered, flipping his visor down to unclip his sunglasses before sliding them over his eyes. "My family used to vacation in Santa Barbara when I was younger."

"You and your parents?"

He nodded. "Yep. Three peas in a pod."

I smiled, unwrapping the dog treat the concierge had given me for Kalo on our way out of the casino. I handed it back to her, rubbing her head before turning back to Emery. "I'm an only child, too."

At that his expression flattened, and he shifted, his left hand taking the place of the right on the top of the steering wheel.

"I actually had a brother."

My heart sank at the word. *Had* — past tense. I racked my brain for any mention of a brother in his journal, but came up empty.

"He... he passed?"

Emery sniffed. "Yeah. It was before I was born, though. My mom was about four months pregnant with me when it happened, so I don't really have any kind of connection to him. They talk about him, my parents, but it just feels like they're talking about some family friend I don't know or something."

"How old was he?"

"Almost five."

A jolt hit my heart again, and I pressed my fingertips into my chest, massaging the muscle.

"That must have been really hard for you," I said as we cleared the city, leaving the busy Vegas strip in our rearview. "Seeing pictures of him and hearing your parents talk about him, but not knowing him yourself."

Emery's brows pulled inward, as if he'd never thought about it before. "It was, actually."

He said it not like a confession, but like a realization, like it was the first time he'd even considered it at all.

"They loved him, you know? And we would celebrate his birthday, and I'd listen to them tell stories about him, but I never *knew* him. I felt bad because I couldn't cry or miss him, only the *idea* of him, of a brother." Emery was quiet a moment, the sun directly over us casting shadows under his eyes. "Sometimes I feel like I disappoint my parents, like maybe they wish they had him here instead of me."

"I don't think they wish that at all," I said, reaching over for his hand. I entwined my fingers with his, feeling the warmth of his rough skin on mine. "But I understand why you would feel that sometimes. And if it makes you feel any better, I know without a shadow of a doubt that my parents wish I wasn't here."

Emery was still frowning, his wheels turning, but he squeezed my hand in return. "That's not true."

"It is," I argued. "Trust me — they've told me, more than a few times, actually. It's stupid, because they never wanted me, but they never wanted anyone *else* to have me either — not child protective services or my best friend's family or anyone else. It's like they did just enough to get by as what they considered decent parents, just enough to keep me in their household. But they resented me, they think I stole their life away."

"Right. Because you asked to be born," Emery said, lips flat.

I chuckled. "Well, if they were here, they'd probably argue that I did." Shrugging, I used my free hand to pull my hair over one shoulder. "But it's fine. Lily's family was all I ever needed. And Tammy, of course. I don't think I would have made it without them."

"Lily," Emery mused. "That's your best friend, right? The one who gave you that ring," he said, nodding to the silver infinity loop still housed on my middle finger.

"Yeah. She's crazy, and loud, and sarcastic. She's also probably the only reason I never got bullied in high school. No one ever messed with Lily."

"Does she know you left?"

I laughed. "Well, I shared my location with her in case you killed me, so yeah."

"You're not supposed to tell me that. Now if I kill you, I know to take your phone before I hide the body."

"You wouldn't kill me now," I said confidently, leaning over the console to plant a kiss on his cheek. "Not now that I've hooked you with how adorable I am."

"It'd be like murdering a kitten."

"Exactly. You're not *that* much of a monster, Emery Reed. Even if you think you are."

He eyed me from the driver seat with a smirk, lifting my hand entwined with his to his lips and kissing my fingers. Without another word, he turned up the volume on the radio, and we settled in for the four hour drive to the coast.

# Chapter 18

Laguna Beach, California

We made it.

The glowing edge of the sun had just barely touched the waterline when my bare foot hit the sand on Laguna Beach. I carried my sneakers on the tips of my fingers, walking straight past the Laguna Beach lifeguard stand with my eyes on the water. Emery followed a ways behind me along with Kalo, her tongue hanging out as she hopped around, flicking sand up with her paws in the process.

I paused when my toes hit the water's edge, a shiver running up my spine when the icy water grazed my skin. I'd pulled on a sweater before we got out of the car and I wrapped it around me tighter, thankful for the shield from the breeze rolling in off the water. With the sun fading, the temperature was dropping fast, but it could have been twenty below zero and I still wouldn't have moved.

It was the most beautiful thing I'd ever seen.

Whispy clouds stretched over the blue sky, their white puffs taking on pink and purple hues as the sun dipped farther away. Its orange glow spanned across the water, reaching all the way to the exact spot where Emery and I stood, its bright light softening more and more with every passing second. There were people all around us, some with their family, some on their own, some snapping pictures, some just sitting, watching. We were all strangers, but we shared that sunset together, that punctuation mark on yet another day, each of us hanging on to the sun's whispered promise that it would return again tomorrow.

"I've seen more in the past week than I've seen in my entire life," I whispered to Emery, and he tucked me under his arm, pressing a kiss into my hair.

"Is it what you expected?"

"It's more." I shook my head. "It's like I can't open my eyes wide enough."

"I love the way you see life," Emery said, his eyes on me instead of the sunset. "It's like nothing has ever disappointed you, like you don't have a reason to believe it ever would."

I glanced up at him, the hue of the sun illuminating the different shades of gold in his eyes. "I've been disappointed before," I argued. "But that doesn't mean I have to expect to be let down again. Every day is a new day, you know? A new chance."

Emery shook his head, knuckles hooking under my chin. "You're something else."

"You already said that to me once," I reminded him, my voice just a breath as my eyes fell to his lips. "I'm not sure if it's a good thing or a bad thing."

He smirked. "Good." And then, just as the last of the sun sank beyond the Pacific, he leaned down, pressing his lips to mine.

A moment. Frozen in time. A boy and a girl. A beach and a kiss. I was beginning to measure my new beginning with those little snapshots of time, filing them away in a mental scrapbook for safe keeping.

"Can I ask you something?" I said, pulling back after a while, a little breathless.

"Whatever you want, Little Penny."

I smiled a little at the nickname, a blush creeping onto my cheeks before the question even left my mouth. "That night you left the concert with Emily... did you..." I swallowed, looking down at where my hands rested in the middle of his chest. "Did you sleep with her?"

Emery was silent, his thumbs rubbing small circles where my sweater gathered at my hips. "No."

A breath of relief rushed out of me, and he chuckled a little. "I'm sorry I had to ask, I know you told me not to be jealous. It's just... I also know what you said about casual sex, and we weren't... well, we weren't like *this*. So I know I don't even have a right to ask. I just..."

"It's fine," he assured me, cutting my rambling short. "She showed me her record collection and then I left her place and wandered around Houston alone, because that's all I wanted to be that night. Alone. Then I grabbed breakfast for us when the sun started coming up and, well, you know the rest."

"Would you have slept with her?"

Emery swallowed, the lump in his throat bobbing with the notion. "Before you, maybe. But not after." Then he lifted my chin again, his lips finding mine. "Never after."

Those words, that kiss, it was the more than I could have asked for from Emery in that moment. It wasn't a promise, but it was a confession, an openness I wasn't accustomed to from him that I wanted more of. I could get drunk on it, that transparency, and I fisted my hands in his shirt, pulling him closer, savoring every drop.

Kalo didn't let us kiss for long before she tugged against the leash still in Emery's hands, making him grin, his mouth still on mine. "I think she's hungry."

"So am I." My stomach growled with my confession, making Emery chuckle.

"I saw some food trucks up there," he said, nodding toward the area where we'd found a parking spot. "I think there's some sort of festival going on."

"You had me at food truck."

It was a busy Friday night on the beach, considering it was the middle of November, with local vendors and street performers gathering crowds in different areas on the boardwalk and grassy area beyond it. Emery and I took Kalo back to the car for her dinner first, before grabbing two giant slices of pizza from one of the trucks and perusing the vendor tables. There was beautiful local art and pottery, homemade soaps and candles, jewelry of all kinds, and t-shirt designers galore.

We wandered past each of them eating our pizza and enjoying the cool evening breeze before we stumbled on a man juggling sticks of fire near the volleyball courts. Kalo moved excitedly between our feet, trying to find the best view as Emery polished off his slice, but my eyes were drawn to a small table near the end of the boardwalk.

The woman manning the table smiled when our eyes met, waving a hand softly to invite me over. She didn't look much older than myself, her skin a creamy white, though it was barely visible through the dark ink that painted her from the neck down. Her hair was jet black and shaved on one side, eyes just as dark, and even from where we stood I could see her ears were gauged open with metal rings.

"What do you say?" I asked, nudging Emery and nodding toward her. There was a cosmic sign hanging from the front of her table that read TAROT CARDS. "Want to see what the universe has in store for the last leg of our trip?"

I peered up at him, and he was already rolling his eyes. "You're joking."

"Nope. Come on, humor me."

He shook his head as I slid my hand into his, already dragging him away from the fire and toward her table. "You owe me for this."

"And what exactly do I owe you?"

At that, a salacious grin spread low on his lips. "I'd tell you, but there are children around."

I laughed, smacking his arm before taking Kalo's leash from his other hand. She hopped around in the sand the entire way up to the table, and once we'd reached it, I bent down to pet her fur and give her one of the treats I'd tucked in my pocket. Once she settled by my feet with it, the woman greeted us.

"Thanks for stopping by my table, I was starting to nod off over here," she said. It was then that I noticed the bull ring pierced through the middle of her nose, the bottom of it grazing her top lip when she smiled. "I'm Melina. What are your names?"

"Aren't you supposed to tell us that?" Emery piped.

I elbowed him, narrowing my eyes before extending a hand for Melina. "I'm Cooper, and this is Emery."

"Nice to meet you," she said, not seeming fazed in the slightest by Emery's comment, though she did narrow her eyes at him before gesturing to the two small, cushioned stools in front of her table. "Take a seat."

I sat in the chair on the left, Emery on the right, and I watched his skepticism grow more as Melina grabbed her deck of cards from the corner of the table.

"You don't look like a psychic," he said, giving her a once-over.

"And you don't look like an asshole, but appearances can be deceiving, can't they?" Melina smiled sarcastically, shuffling the cards between her hands as I stifled a laugh.

Emery lifted a brow at me. "Oh, you think that's funny, huh?" he teased.

"I do. Now be quiet, you're disturbing my chi."

He chuckled, shaking his head like I was ridiculous and bending to pet Kalo on the head.

"So, you two want a card reading, yeah?" Her voice was light on the breeze, yet she held herself in a manner that demanded attention, her posture straight, chin high. If I could only use one term to describe her, it would have been *badass*.

"We would."

"*She* would," Emery corrected. "I'm just here to watch. And occasionally roll my eyes."

"Emery," I scolded.

Melina smiled, her eyes on her cards as she shuffled them before she met my gaze. "It's all good. Let Mr. Macho Pants stay skeptical, if that's what he wants. Receiving a message from the universe is a purposeful thing. If he comes into a reading with a closed mind and heart, he'll receive nothing, and in turn feed his belief that nothing is all that exists."

Emery eyed her then, but said nothing.

"Here," Melina said, handing me the deck. "Shuffle 'em up, buttercup. You can move cards around on the table, shuffle like a normal deck of playing cards, or whatever else feels right. And when you're ready, hand them back to me."

I did as she asked, closing my eyes and feeling the cards in my hands as I moved them around. I focused on centering myself, on opening myself to the possibilities, and then I handed them back to her with a calming breath.

"You practice yoga and meditation," she mused when the deck was back in her hands. "You're very spiritually open, and you identify with your zodiac sign." Melina paused, tilting her head a bit. "You strike me as a very curious person, and a giving one, too. Are you an air sign?"

I nodded. "Aquarius."

"Ah," she said with a smile. "Makes sense."

Emery's attention had been pulled from Kalo and the beach to our table then, and he watched me curiously as Melina laid out the first three cards.

"These first three cards represent your past," she said, spreading them a few centimeters apart. "This first card, The Five of Cups, it represents a great loss you experienced."

A phantom pain numbed my left leg, as if it recognized itself in the card, and I massaged the thigh of it gently as she continued.

"But see how it's reversed? That represents an acceptance of that loss. You were at peace very quickly, which allowed you to move on, and that brings us very symbolically to The Ace of Swords. Mental clarity. It seems that the loss you endured centered your mind to your innermost desires, to what you want most in this life."

*Bastyr.*

Her eyes met mine briefly before her index finger tapped the final card. "The Two of Wands. The Wands are tied to the element of fire, which ties, of course, into determination. This card tells me that you took that loss and that mental clarity and you transformed it into a plan, into a strategy. You made a goal, or perhaps multiple goals, and you've spent a great deal of time in your life actively pursuing those goals over all else."

I thought about the diner, about Bastyr, about how my entire life had been spent in Mobile, Alabama, just planning my way out. I'd saved up, I'd studied, I'd done everything I could on my own to make the journey to Washington.

My eyes found Emery's, and he cocked one eyebrow as if he understood. He leaned in toward Melina, just a little bit, but enough to tell me he was curious.

Melina flipped three more cards, explaining that they represented my present, but when they were all laid out, her brows tugged inward as she studied them. "Interesting."

"What is it?"

She shook her head, tapping the first card. "I'm getting ahead of myself. Let's start here. The Page of Cups symbolizes a sort of messenger in your life, something or someone who brought you clarity in a new way. And since this card is followed immediately by The Fool," she said, moving her finger to the second card. "I sense that this messenger helped you begin a new journey recently, one you're on now. It can be a physical journey or a spiritual one, but either way, you are experiencing new sights, new experiences, and in turn, discovering new truths."

I smiled up at Emery, who was still eyeing the cards skeptically, but he smirked in my direction anyway. "You saying I'm your Page of Cups, Little Penny?"

"I'm saying it's possible."

"Probably more likely that he's a fool," Melina murmured playfully, throwing him a wink.

Emery squeezed my right knee with one hand, sending a wave of chills up that thigh. He followed the line of them, his eyes trailing slow and purposefully up over the bare skin under my shorts, up more over the fabric of my sweater, until his gaze landed on my eyes, smirk still in place.

I flushed, ripping my eyes away and back to Melina, who was studying the last card with concern etched on her face.

"So, this is the card that perplexes me," she said, tapping the final card. "The Seven of Swords. If it were turned the other way, if it were reversed for you and upright for me, then it would make sense — it would mean you were overcoming a challenge, breaking old habits and starting anew. But the way it sits right now, it symbolizes deceit."

The color drained from my face.

"Now, this can be read in many ways, of course," she clarified. "Someone could be being deceitful to you, someone you feel you can trust when actually you can't. Or, it could be that you are partaking in sneaky behavior, acting in a way that you know is wrong for personal gain."

Emery's hand left my knee, the spot where his skin touched me turning ice cold as he stood. "Okay, I think it's time I remove myself from the equation before I start making rude, sarcastic remarks." He smiled as if it were a joke, but his eyes were strained as he bent to kiss my forehead. "I'll take Kalo down by the water, come meet us when you're done?"

I nodded, but my eyes were still glued to the card, to The Seven of Swords. If Emery were paying attention, if he believed, he would have asked me what I was hiding.

And I could never tell him.

So, in a way, I was relieved as he took Kalo and crossed the sand down to the water, and Melina sensed it.

"It's you who's hiding something, isn't it?" she asked, though she didn't wait for my response as she flipped three more cards and spread them out below the present ones. "It's unlike you. You wear your guilt like a scarlet letter."

I just swallowed, eyes scanning the new cards.

"Your future," she said, setting the rest of the deck to the side. "The Lovers."

Her finger tapped the first card, her long, pointy black nail resting there as she lifted her eyes to mine.

"This card can be taken in many ways, and most of us want to believe it means true love, that it symbolizes that fairytale romance we often dream of. However, this card is reverse for you, which shows me that, perhaps as a result of your present deceitfulness, you will quarrel with a loved one over an imbalance — different values, different beliefs."

My focus stayed on the card, but I was all too aware of Emery on the beach, though he was the opposite — blissfully unaware, his shoes in his hands as he kicked through the edge of the water with Kalo barking and nipping at his ankles.

My heart ached.

"This next card, The Nine of Wands, again tied to fire. You will be tested, Cooper," she said, and my eyes flicked to hers then. She seemed to be looking right through me, to my innermost self. "You must come into this test with persistence and determination to gain the outcome you desire, and it will not be easy. You may have to come to terms with a loss you didn't foresee, one you can't imagine, in order to move forward and emerge on the other side of this test."

My heart raced under my ribcage, thoughts dizzying as I wondered what the test could be. My first thought was that it tied to Emery, to our time together. We hadn't discussed what would happen when we reached Washington. In fact, I still didn't even know where he was going, or if he'd stay. Was that my test? Would I have to give him up? Or was it the test of a new life, of Bastyr and a new job and a new home?

"This last card," she said, sliding it just a little closer to me. "Is Death."

My eyes jolted to hers, wide and no doubt showing the fear I felt at the indication, but she laid her hand over mine in reassurance.

"Calm down, it doesn't mean a physical death," she said, her voice low and kind. "But it does symbolize the end of an era, the death of a chapter, and perhaps even the death of who you once were. Something tells me that this test, whatever it is, will change you indefinitely. You're on the brink of a new start, and how you begin this next part of your journey will depend greatly on how you walk into this test, and even more so, how you emerge on the other side of it."

I scanned the cards again, heart in my throat, unable to do or say anything. My hands deftly reached into my back pocket and I pulled out the twenty-dollar bill I'd stuffed in there after purchasing our pizzas. I slid it over the table toward her, still in a daze. "Thank you."

"Hey, don't be scared, okay?" she said, ignoring the cash and squeezing my hand still in hers. She leaned down to catch my eyes. "Without the cards, I can still see your strength, your spirit, your light. Hold onto that, onto the person you are inside, and you'll be okay."

I nodded, a faint smile finding my lips as I squeezed her hand in return before standing. She watched me as I crossed the beach to Emery, and even when he turned to me with a goofy grin, Kalo covered in sand and water by his feet, I felt Melina's eyes on me.

"Well, how does your future look? Are we going to drive off a cliff on the PCH and fall to a terrible death?"

I laughed, but it was dry and short. "Probably," I joked, because it was easier than trying to explain the truth, to tell him the weight I felt on my shoulders after the reading.

I wanted to ask him right then what we would do once we hit our final destination. I wanted to know where we would go from there. But we hadn't even discussed what we were, or what we would be. All I'd asked of him — all I *could* ask of him — was that he try. And in order to let him try, I had to give him room to fail, space to succeed, air to breathe.

I needed to have patience.

But I was finding out very quickly that patience was a virtue I did not possess. At least, not anymore.

We checked into a room right on the beach, our patio overlooking the water, and I took the first shower before joining Emery where he sat outside. The wind whipped his hair as he wrote in his journal by the small porch light, and I took the seat next to him, crossing my prosthetic over my right leg.

"She's all yours."

Emery finished his thought, dropping his journal on the table between us with a thud. "Good. I smell like wet dog and Vegas."

"You should bottle that," I joked, and he ruffled the fur on top of Kalo's head as he squeezed past, heading inside.

When I was alone, I inhaled a deep breath, taking in the salty ocean breeze. There was no moon that night, so the beach was dark, but I could hear the waves rolling in over the rocks and the sand, and I closed my eyes, letting it all wash over me.

I hadn't read Emery's journal since the morning we left Colorado Springs, and even though I knew I should never read another page of it, my hands were in tight fists at my sides to keep me from doing it anyway. Nora had told me to be patient, Melina had told me my actions would catch up to me, and still, I wanted so desperately to know what he was thinking.

We'd had such a good day together, I hadn't bothered asking him what he was thinking or how he was feeling about the night before. There was a line we crossed, one we jumped over willingly, and now that we were on the other side of it, I wasn't sure how to act. It hadn't just been a good day, it had been a *new* kind of good day — one with touches and kisses shared between us. It was a complete one-eighty from the day before, and now that I was finally sitting still, I felt the whiplash. I wondered what would happen next, not just when we got to Seattle, but when we woke up in the morning, too.

Today was a good day, but what about tomorrow?

I peered over my shoulder into the room, but it was empty, and I heard the faint sound of the shower kicking on through the open sliding glass door. My eyes found the journal next.

I reached for it, pulling the leather into my lap and running one thumb along the binding. Kalo whined at my feet, as if she, too, was telling me no, but I couldn't help it. I leaned down to pet her long fur, and then I grabbed hold of the ribbon bookmark and opened to the latest entry.

His familiar handwriting filled only half of the page, and it felt like a welcome home sign. He hadn't gotten much down before I'd come out and told him it was his turn to shower, but even the little that was there comforted me, a small glimpse inside his thoughts.

*I wish I believed in something.*

*I feel stupid even writing that, being that I make fun of anything that isn't science, but in a way, I wish I could believe in something bigger than myself. I don't get on my knees and pray to anyone when I'm scared, and I don't have any big man in the sky who I thank when something good happens. I don't read my horoscope and I don't study Buddhism. I guess you could say I believe in Karma, but really, I mostly just believe that some way or another, we're all bound to get what we have coming to us.*

*Really, I don't believe in anything.*

*We left Vegas today and landed in Laguna Beach for the night, and Cooper had her tarot cards read. The way she watched the woman read her cards... it was like she was hanging on to every word the woman said, looking for hints and clues as to how to make the next step in her life. I wanted to tell her she was the only one in control of it, but I could see it — she believed. And who am I to tell her not to?*

*Tomorrow we'll start driving the Pacific Coast Highway, something I've wanted to do ever since Dad drove me a small leg of it when I was younger. Grams had it on her list of things she wanted me to do, too.*

*I haven't been back to California since about the seventh grade. But this time, I'm not with family. This time, I'm with Cooper.*

*Something changed between us in Vegas.*

That's where the entry ended, and I stared at that last line with a mixture of emotions whirling inside like a tornado. It pained my heart that he didn't believe in anything, that he walked through life feeling completely alone, but selfishly, I cared more about that last scratch from his pen.

What had changed between us?

I mean, I knew what *I* felt had changed, but was it the same as him? I turned back the page to the last entry before the one I'd just read, and it was dated the same day as when I explored the Grand Canyon by myself.

*I kissed her.*

*I'm a selfish fucking idiot and I kissed her.*

*She'd never been really kissed, and we were standing there, looking at the mountains and the stars, and I couldn't stop staring at her perfect lips and thinking what a shame it was that they'd never been kissed. I was thinking about how her lips would feel against mine, wondering if she would sigh and lean into the touch or blush and shy away. And instead of doing the right thing and keeping those thoughts in my mind, instead of letting it go, I kissed her.*

*And now I'm fucked.*

*Glen and I took a hike the next morning, when I was still high off her lips, off the way her hands shook as she touched me in the tent all night long. God, I wanted to do so much more to her. I had to fist my hands in her hair to keep them from wandering anywhere else. I knew if I would have started, if I would have touched her, really touched her, I wouldn't have been able to stop.*

*But Glen got in my head yesterday morning. He told me he could sense that Cooper was a good girl, a strong girl, and he preached about how I needed to treat her right. He thought we were married thanks to a joke we were playing, but I wasn't laughing anymore, not when he was telling me that nothing in the world matched up to a strong woman's love.*

*Love.*

*Just hearing him say it nearly made me throw up. I can't imagine ever being in love, ever being loved by someone else, and it was then that I realized that is exactly what Cooper wants. She wants someone who will hold her hand and kiss her sweetly. She wants someone who will ask her to spend the rest of her life with them, for better or for worse.*

*I'm not that person.*

*So, I did what I do best. I shut her out, shut the world out, and had what was possibly the worst day of my life sitting beside her in the car. I knew she wanted to know what I was thinking, and I also knew I'd never tell her. She's the sun and I'm a black hole. I want to swallow her up and lose myself in her, but if I do, I'll destroy her.*

*Maybe a small part of me thought she was what Grams was talking about, that maybe she could be what changed it all for me. But the truth is, I know I won't find what Grams thought I would, not until I reach our last dot on the map.*

*Only then will I find peace.*

I swallowed, eyes scanning the last of the entry with a newfound panic. *What does that mean? What did his grandma want him to find?*

I knew it had to be in there, so I didn't even let myself focus on what he'd written about me or about love before I was flipping back through the pages, searching for the mention of his grandma. The first entry I found was him remembering the one and only time she kayaked with the family in Santa Barbara before she was too old, too fragile to do it anymore. I was only halfway down that page when Emery's voice called from the room.

"I know we just ate pizza like two hours ago," he started, and I jumped, slamming the journal shut and placing it where I'd found it on the table. Kalo popped up and ran inside while I fidgeted with my hair, trying to seem natural. Emery rounded the edge of the sliding glass door, leaning his head out. "But I'm kind of hungry. I was thinking about ordering Chinese to be delivered. The Chinese food on this coast is incredible. You in?"

I forced a smile, heart still in my throat. "I never say no to sweet and sour chicken."

"Or beef jerky."

"Are you judging me for my love of dried meat?"

He shrugged. "Just saying, I've got more empty packages of Jack Links in the back of my car than they have full ones at the nearest gas station."

I laughed, picking up one of the cardboard coasters on the table and flicking it at him. "Smart ass."

"Be right back."

Emery dipped inside, and I listened as he placed an order on the phone before joining me on the porch again.

His journal sat between us like it had a pulse.

For a while we just sat there, our eyes on the blacked-out beach, the sound of the waves the only one existing between us. I didn't even notice him move until the porch light above us went dark, too, and Emery bent to his knees in front of me, positioning himself between my thighs.

"How do you feel?" he asked as my eyes adjusted, just the bridge of his nose coming into focus at first. Though the moon was nonexistent, the stars still fought to shine through the clouds, and the lights from the hotels around us glowed to the left and the right of our balcony.

"I feel amazing."

"No," he said, his hands finding each of my thighs. He slid them up marginally, thumbs brushing the hot skin between them. "I mean, how do you *feel*. Are you sore?"

A tingle zipped its way up my legs from the point of contact where his thumb rested, like a shot of lightning injected straight into my nervous system.

"A little tender," I admitted, my voice breathy and low.

His hands slid up higher, the cool breeze from the water rushing over the warm skin he left behind, leaving me covered in goosebumps. "I figured." He paused, his fingers hooking in the band of my sleep shorts, and I lifted my hips before he could even tug on them. "I know you're not ready to have me inside you again, not yet, but I can't wait any longer to touch you," he said, my shorts already halfway off as he pulled them down another inch. "Can I touch you, Cooper?"

A breathy *yes* left my lips as my shorts hit my ankles, and Emery yanked them the rest of the way off, discarding them on the concrete base of the balcony. His eyes were barely visible in the dark, but I knew they were hot on me as he hooked his thumbs in the waistline of my panties next, sliding them off without breaking eye contact.

His hands wrapped around the backs of my thighs and gripped my hips, pulling until I hung off the wicker chair, the cushion moving with me. Then he ran one hand down my abdomen, his palm cupping me as one finger slipped between my lips.

"Fucking hell," he groaned, the pad of his finger skating down to my opening before running back up to my clit. "I make you so wet. It kills me."

I couldn't respond, could barely breathe as he tested me, just the tip of his finger entering me as I arched into him. I cried out, more tender than I realized, but wanting him nonetheless.

A groan rumbled low in his throat, his finger curling just a bit before he withdrew it. "Yeah, you definitely need a night to rest," he said, but he was already kissing my thighs, his mouth on a direct track for my core. "Maybe this will speed the healing time."

His tongue flattened against that most sensitive part of me, that little button that seemed to be the detonator for my orgasms the night before, and he ran it long and hot over the bundle of nerves. I gasped, hands reaching back to grip the frame of the chair as my legs tensed around him. It didn't matter that I'd had his mouth on me the night before, that I already knew how it felt — I knew right then I'd never get enough of it, no matter how much he gave me.

He moved until my good leg was draped over his shoulder, the other spread wide, and his tongue lashed me again, swirling and flicking before he sucked the detonator between his teeth with a hiss. That's the best name I knew to give it, that little spot he touched, that tiny ball of sensitivity that sparked an electric wave each time he brushed it. And he was an expert, knowing just how long to touch me there before it became too much, before he would pull back and flatten his tongue again.

My orgasm mounted even quicker than the night before, blood rushing to my core in a rising tide with every lick. I squeezed my eyes shut, writhing under his mouth, hips grinding up and reaching. But Emery took his time, and just when I was on the edge of release, he pulled back, blowing softly on the swollen skin.

I collapsed, legs falling to the side as the orgasm I was so close to left as quickly as it had come, but the rest didn't last for long before Emery's mouth was on me again. It was shocking, the sensation of being so close and then cut off, only to have it rush back with a vengeance as soon as he touched me again.

"Oh, God," I whispered, and Emery sucked harder, his hands gripping my thighs.

"Tell me," he said, words vibrating through me.

"I think..."

"Say it."

My head spun, thoughts fleeting as the rush moved over me, and then all senses went numb before buzzing back to life at once.

"I'm coming," I breathed, my cheeks flushing with heat at the admission, and it was those words and the slip of Emery's middle finger inside me that sent me over the edge. He kept his finger inside, curling it over and over, deeper and deeper, his mouth crushing onto mine and absorbing my moans as I fell apart at the touch.

Overwhelmed.

That was the only way I knew how to describe how I felt.

I didn't know what it was like to be touched like that, to be devoured, to be tasted like candy and worshipped like a goddess. Even after I was sated, Emery still ran his hands over every inch of my body, feeling and caressing, soothing and teasing, kissing his way back down.

Leaning up on my elbows, I gazed down at him just as he pressed a final, sweet kiss to my inner thigh. He helped me sit upright, my arms around his neck, and I kissed him with intent.

"I want to do that to you," I said against his lips, my hands already trailing their way down his ribs. He was still kneeling between my legs, his own spread in a V, and when I ran my palm over the bulge in his sweatpants, he shifted forward, rocking into the touch with a groan. "But I need your help. I've never..."

I swallowed, not needing to finish the sentence. We both knew there were plenty of things I hadn't experienced yet, but I wanted to with him. I needed to.

"If you wrap these perfect lips around me," he husked, sucking my bottom one between his teeth. "I might actually fucking die."

"It wouldn't be the worst way to go."

He smiled against my mouth, kissing me hard before using the arms of the chair to stand and pulling me with him. He lifted me easily, cradling my prosthetic at one side while I gripped the other with my good leg, our lips still fused together as he carried me inside. When we were by the foot of his bed, he dropped me back to the floor easily, his eyes somehow darker now that we were in the light again.

His hands trailed down my arms, the backs of his fingertips tickling my skin until they found my hands. I gripped his tight, using him for balance as I kissed him one last time before lowering to my knees, my eyes on his.

Emery swallowed when I hit the ground in front of him, already sliding his sweatpants down his legs. He was commando underneath them, and he sprang forward, hard and ready.

It was the first time I'd seen him — really seen him, or any guy for that matter. The night before, he was inside me, but I hadn't seen him strip down, hadn't seen the curve of the tip or the vein that ran hard and long down the length of him. I hadn't watched as he entered me, inch by blissful inch, all of that disappearing within me. He'd encompassed me, wrapped himself around me, and I'd focused on his eyes, his lips, the two lines between his eyebrows.

Now that I saw him fully, I understood why I was sore.

I looked up at him, my hands braced on my knees as I waited for instruction.

"God," he breathed, shaking his head as he gazed down at me. "Just seeing you like that... I can't..."

His words faded and I bit my lip, scooting a little closer, one hand tentatively reaching out, but I paused.

"Touch it."

It was just a whisper, a plea, and when I wrapped my hand around the middle of him, he groaned, thrusting into my grip. It was what I imagined the first hit of a powerful drug to feel like, the first rush of heat and high. Being the one to elicit that sound from him made me want to stay on my knees forever.

Following the rhythm of his hips, I worked him with one hand, fist tightening slightly over the tip of him before working down to his base. Then, Emery reached for my chin, his fingers trailing the skin there before they ran across my lower lip. I kept my eyes on him, looking for approval as I leaned forward and touched my lips to his crown.

"Christ," he cursed, flexing forward more. "Yes, like that. Take me in your mouth."

It was strange, that I felt so much power. I was on my knees in front of him, smaller in every way, but power radiated through me at the sight of him bending to my touch, succumbing to the feel of me.

I still held him firmly with one hand, the other bracing on his thigh as I leaned forward more, my lips parting. I took him in a little, just enough for my lips to cover the tip of him. Just that contact elicited another groan from Emery, and when I opened my mouth, sliding him inside me slowly with one hand still at his base, he shuddered.

"Fuck," he growled, his hands reaching for my hair. He gathered it at the back of my head before letting it fall again. It was like he wanted to grip it but thought better, pulling his hands up to run through his own strands, instead. "I thought going easy last night was hard, I have zero self-control right now."

I swirled my tongue along his base, sucking him before letting go with a pop and connecting with his eyes again. "Show me. Help me suck your cock, Emery."

It wasn't like me to say the words, but they felt right, they felt sexy and powerful as they rolled off my lips. I didn't even blush, just gazed up at him as I lowered my mouth again, taking him inside.

Emery groaned, one hand finding the back of my head and the other wrapping around my wrist as he guided me.

"Use your hand where your mouth doesn't reach," he said, twisting my wrist a little, showing me how to move it in time with my mouth. When I pulled my mouth off and ran my hand over the wet tip of him, spreading my saliva all the way down to his base before I bent forward and took him inside my mouth again, he cursed. "Yes, *God*, yes. Like that."

His hips pushed forward, slow at first before he picked up speed, and when he held my head in place and rocked into my mouth hard, I gagged.

"Goddamn, that was so fucking sexy," he breathed, head rolling back again. I couldn't understand how, my eyes watering a little from the feel of him in my throat, but Emery was only staring down at me like I was the one he came to worship and he was somehow on the other side of it, a lucky fool to be standing in front of a goddess on her knees.

I moaned, the sound vibrating through him as I took him as deep as I could. I held him there, letting him rock into my throat until I couldn't breathe, my eyes watering more as I pulled back with a gasp.

"Fuuuuck." He dragged the word out, his thighs tense, hand twisting in my hair. He was close.

It was the sexiest thing I'd ever experienced, to have him on the brink of ecstasy at my touch. He gently grabbed my elbow, the one tied to the hand on his thigh, and I understood what he wanted without him even saying it. I pulled that hand to join the first, working them both in time with my mouth. Another moan ripped through him, his hips flexing, the power I felt surging.

I used my hands to cover every inch of him, the parts I couldn't reach, and when I could, I took him deep again. I didn't know it was possible, but he was growing even harder in my grasp, the length of him stiff and firm. When I glanced back up at him, his eyes locked with mine for a split second before he squeezed them shut on a curse.

"I'm coming," he groaned, and I didn't know what I was supposed to do. I thought of pulling back, of finishing him with my hands, but he never pulled back when I was finishing. If anything, he gave me more. So, I did the same, and Emery guided one of my hands under him to where his balls rested. I cupped them, a little unsure, and when I rolled them, he moaned my name and rocked into my hands, my mouth, holding me there with another grunt as he came.

I loved it, the final rush of power, the way he lost control of himself in that moment as he caught his release. I tasted him inside me, a new taste that reminded me of my own on his lips the night before. And when he finished, all of his muscles relaxing as he looked back down at me, the sensitive tip of him slipping from my lips, I did what felt right.

I swallowed.

And Emery collapsed.

"Jesus Christ," he said, almost a laugh as his back hit the bed. I wiped at the corners of my mouth and crawled up to lie next to him, resting my head on his heaving chest as he pulled me closer. "You killed me. I knew it."

I chuckled, blushing now that the moment was over and burying my face in his chest. My mascara stained his chest, wet from my eyes watering, and I wiped it away with one thumb.

"You liked that," he mused, tilting my chin up so he could look in my eyes. "It turned you on, being on your knees for me."

"Yes," I breathed, and he pressed his mouth to mine, kissing me with a stiff inhale, his hands sliding down to my ass and grabbing hard. He didn't say another word, just kissed me until exhaustion took over, our eyes fluttering shut, bodies heavy and sated.

I don't know how long we stayed like that before a knock sounded at the door, and Emery peeled me off of him long enough to answer. It was our Chinese food, but he just placed it inside the mini fridge, crawling back into bed with me and pulling the comforter over us both. I felt his hand move down my thigh, clicking the button on my leg until it popped so he could slide it off. He peeled the socks and liner off next, reaching over me to let them all drop gently to the ground, and then he wrapped his arms around me and tugged me closer.

"Goodnight, Little Penny."

And it was. It was a very, *very* good night.

# Chapter 19

## Laguna Beach, California

"Okay, well... erm..." Tammy fumbled through her thoughts as I sat back against the headboard, fighting back a laugh. "I feel like I should... okay, Cooper, when you engage in these kinds of... activities... with someone, you should be... uh... *safe* about it."

"Tammy" I tried, but she kept going.

"There are condoms, of course, and you can also look into birth control."

"You don't have to give me *the talk*," I told her, laughing. "Surprisingly, that was one thing my mother did manage to do. She was drunk, but still, she gave it."

Tammy sighed in relief. "Oh, thank God, I'm sweating like a pig over here. Example forty-two of why it's a blessing I never had kids of my own."

I chuckled, amused at the difference in conversations between her and Lily that morning. Lily had asked for every detail, *especially* after I'd told her about how Emery had shown me how to go down on him, but Tammy was stuck in that weird zone between motherly figure and friend. It was actually quite comical listening to her try to stumble through it.

"So, now that we got that out of the way, how are you?"

She launched right into telling me about the new guy she was dating, thankful for the change in conversation after I'd confessed to her that I lost my virginity. It was almost nine in the morning, and I knew we needed to get going soon, but when I woke up an hour earlier, Emery had been gone — Kalo, too.

So, I practiced yoga, waking up a little less sore than the morning before, stretching through the aches still present in my thighs. I'd smiled the whole time, flashing back to the two nights before. I'd just had him and I already wanted more. I knew I'd never get enough, and when I laid back in Savasana trying to clear my mind, my thoughts continually drifted to him — his smile, his hands, his lips, his touch.

Tammy asked where we were heading next, and I was detailing our plans to go up the PCH when the door opened and Kalo flew through it, bounding onto the bed where I sat. She licked my face as I laughed, my eyes finding Emery's as he dropped a paper bag from a bakery on the desk. I smiled, cheeks flushing from thoughts of the night before, but Emery didn't return the grin. He barely looked at me before he retreated into the bathroom, locking the door behind him.

My stomach dropped.

"*Please,* be careful, Cooper. That road is winding and there are a lot of tourists on it. Keep your eyes on the road and keep the music down, too."

"We'll be fine," I promised her. "Lots of stops along the way. But Emery just got back, so I'm going to get off here and start packing up."

"Okay," she said softly. "I miss you, kiddo. You'll let me know when you make it to Seattle? Like I said, I can fly up and help you hunt for apartments. Just say the word."

"Thank you, I just might take you up on that," I answered, wondering again what would happen when that final destination was reached. "Love you."

"Love you, too."

I dropped my phone on the bed once the call ended, rubbing Kalo's fluffy head between my hands before hopping up and shoving my toiletries into my bag. I'd been so distracted by Emery's hands on me the night before that I'd almost forgotten what I read in his journal, but now that he was locked in the bathroom with signs of a bad day written all over him, it was all I could think of.

*But the truth is I know I won't find what Grams thought I would, not until I reach our last dot on the map. Only then will I find peace.*

It didn't make any more sense to me in the daylight than it did when I read it in the darkness, but it still made me feel just as sick. I wanted to read more, to find out what I'd missed, put the puzzle together, but the bathroom door swung open before I had the chance.

Emery's eyes were ringed with purple, his hair stretching out in every which way as he ran a hand through it again. He hadn't slept, I knew without asking, and today was a bad day, I knew without him saying a word.

"Hey," I said tentatively, crossing the space between us. I slipped my hands around his waist, resting my head on his chest, but his arms didn't move to pull me in.

"You about ready?"

I nodded against his t-shirt, inhaling the clean scent of the hotel soap still present from his shower the night before. "I'm ready when you are." I paused. "It's a bad day, isn't it?"

My voice was low, barely a whisper, and Emery sighed as his hands wrapped around my upper arms. He peeled me off him, crossing to where his bag was on the bed and shoving the last of his belongings inside it before throwing it over his shoulder. "I walked Kalo, and there's breakfast in that bag. We should head out, I think the early traffic on the PCH should be clearing soon, so hopefully it won't be as crowded."

"Emery."

"Where are we stopping today? Santa Barbara and Pismo Beach?"

I shook my head, eyes on the carpet. He was avoiding me. It was almost worse than when he didn't talk to me at all. I thought of the night before, wondering if I'd done something wrong. Maybe I wasn't as good as he thought I would be. Maybe he realized he made a mistake. Maybe he couldn't try, not like he thought he could.

But when those thoughts washed through me, I silenced them with a calming breath.

*It's not about me.*

I knew that, even if it was hard to understand, hard to accept. He wasn't upset with me, he wasn't avoiding me or doing anything on purpose to upset me. It was a bad day, a day when he couldn't give me much, but he asked me for it to be enough, anyway.

Emery wrapped Kalo's leash around his fist and headed for the door, slinging my bag over his other shoulder, but my hand found his bicep as he passed, stopping him.

"Wait," I said softly, eyes trailing up slowly. He was focused on the door, gaze straight ahead. I opened my mouth to say something else, to ask him to talk to me, to ask him what he was thinking, but all my thoughts died before they left my lips as words.

His nostrils flared, eyes falling to the floor like he was ashamed as he let out his own long breath.

"This isn't easy for me, okay? I told you I would try, and I am, but I don't like to talk about everything. I don't have anything to say. I'm tired, and honestly, I didn't even want to get up this morning, but I did. I'm trying. But I need you to just give me a little space today, okay?"

He didn't mean to say the words harshly, but they came out that way, and my eyes watered a little as I dropped my hand from his forearm. "Okay."

It was all I could manage and still respect what he'd asked of me. It was harder than I thought, giving him what he needed.

He sighed, pinching the bridge of his nose, then he grabbed my hands in his own. "It's not you. The past two nights have been..." his voice trailed off when I lifted my chin. "I don't have the words, okay? But it's not you. Just... please, give me today. I'll tell you what's going on up here," he said, tapping his temple. "When I can. When I figure it out myself. But right now, I just need you to understand."

My heart ached with the urge to help him, to hold him, to sort through his thoughts together, but I wasn't invited.

As much as that stung, even him telling me this much was a step for us, and I held onto that as I nodded.

"Okay."

We loaded up the car in silence, putting the top down as yet another gorgeous California day greeted us. I let my hand ride the breeze as we drove, popping in a CD a local rock band had given us on the pier the night before. Their vibe was a mixture of grunge and reggae, and I bobbed along to the beat, trying my best not to think about what was going through Emery's mind as he drove beside me.

We planned to drive up the Pacific Coast Highway in about three days, give or take, and our first stop would be Santa Barbara. It was breathtaking, driving the coast, the waves rolling in and crashing against the rigid edges of the coast below us as we followed the winding road through the hills and valleys. Somewhere along the way, Emery's hand found my thigh, and it rested there as we drove, a silent promise that even though he wasn't talking that day, he was still there. He was still with me.

When we passed a sign that said we were about sixty miles away from Santa Barbara, an idea sprouted in my mind, and I reached forward to turn the music down.

"You know, I've never been kayaking before," I said, and Emery turned to me then, his brows bent above his sunglasses. "What do you say we change that?"

It was sneaky.

I knew it even before I suggested it, and after Emery agreed to go, I went right back to letting him be silent and in his head. I knew taking him kayaking would make him think of his childhood, of good times with his family, and I hoped it would open him up for the evening. It wasn't fair to play off emotions I wasn't supposed to know about, like winning a game by stealing the other team's playbook, but I didn't feel guilty.

Because it worked.

We spent our afternoon in Santa Barbara, kayaking through the incredible sea caves and hiking on one of the islands. I didn't try to talk to Emery the entire time, and most of it I spent away from him, exploring on my own. Kalo rode in his kayak since I was new to it, and he hiked with her on the island while I did the wildlife tour with our guide. After we were done, we packed up the car and got back on the road, and still, I didn't bother Emery.

He was in his head, wheels turning as fast as the ones we rode on up the coast, and when we stopped for the night in Pismo Beach, he let me take the first shower, reaching inside his bag for his journal and immediately retreating out onto our balcony.

I took my time showering, washing my stump first before sending some of the pictures from my kayaking adventure to Tammy and Lily. Then I ran the shower, balancing on my good leg and lathering up with the premium soaps the hotel offered. I even used their blow dryer to dry my hair straight and long down my back, putting in contacts for only the second time since we began our trip and applying a bit of mascara. I was tan from the day in the sun, so I didn't need much else.

Emery was still outside when I came out of the shower, and I pulled out my dress from Vegas. Antonio had showed me alternate ways to wear it, one of them being as a top, and I followed his directions, tucking it into shorts and tying the left end of it in a knot that revealed just a sliver of my stomach. When my leg was back on, I slipped into the ballet flats I'd bought in Vegas and stepped out onto the balcony.

"I'm going out for a nice dinner tonight," I said, but Emery was still writing frantically in his journal. The sun had almost disappeared already, just a sliver of it beyond the horizon as I stepped closer to him, leaning against the railing right in front of him. "Would you like to join me?"

He went to shake his head, eyes flicking up to me for just a moment before they were back on his journal, but then his pen paused, hovering above the pages as he lifted his eyes again.

They trailed slowly up my legs, catching on the point where my dress-turned-top showed my midriff before they climbed the rest of the way up to my face. The breeze blew in from the beach behind me then, sending my hair up in a whirlwind, and I tucked it behind my ears, waiting.

Emery stood, his journal falling into the chair he'd just sat in with the pen rolling to the ground. His hands reached for me first, finding my waist and sliding around until they clasped together at my lower back, and he moved until every inch of us was fit together in a seam. His nose brushed mine, eyes closing, and I lifted my chin until our lips met.

It was like that kiss brought him back to life, back to me, and he groaned into it, his hands fisting at my back and pulling me closer. *I need you*, that kiss told me, and I deepened it, letting him know I needed him, too. Dusk settled on the beach as he pressed his forehead to mine, quiet slipping between us.

"Thank you," he whispered, leaning back until our eyes connected. "It was a bad day, and you let me have it. And more than that — you told me without words that you were here. I don't..." He shook his head. "I don't know that I deserved that, but you gave it anyway."

"We're both just trying, remember?" I said with a shrug. "That's all we can do."

Emery nodded, a smirk finding his lips as his eyes roamed my body again. "And yes, I'd love to take you to dinner tonight. Give me a second to get changed."

He regretfully let me go, stealing a few more kisses before I shoved him inside, the journal already calling to me before Emery had even taken his last step off the balcony. I picked it up, bending to retrieve the pen from the ground, but instead of opening it, I took it inside, tucking it inside his bag without so much as a peek.

Emery smiled that night at dinner. He told me about how his family used to kayak and I pretended I didn't already know. He told me it was one of his favorite memories with his grandma, and I pretended that was new, too. And he thanked me, for the day, for the understanding, though when we got back to the hotel, he slipped back into his mind, picking up his journal to finish the entry he'd started before we left.

I was thankful for the day turning around, but as the night went on, my heart thumped harder in my chest, reminding me with every beat that we were one day closer to Seattle, one day closer to *the end*. We hadn't talked all day, which meant we hadn't talked about us, about what we're doing, about what we'll *do*.

Anxiety washed over me as I watched him write from my side of the bed, my hand absentmindedly petting Kalo as she slept between us. He felt like mine, that lost boy, but he wasn't — we only had the days we shared the road together, the days we traveled on the same journey with the same destination in mind. I didn't know what would happen once we got there, once we were no longer tied together by a common thread.

I was giving myself to a boy who never promised to keep me, pretending I didn't need that affirmation, that I was okay. I could do casual. I could do *try*. But when Emery turned out the light that night, pulling me into him and fitting his chest to my back, his legs curling underneath mine, I knew I'd been lying — to him and to myself.

I wanted his words, his promises, but I knew he couldn't give them to me — not yet. So, I listened to his breaths, felt his hot skin against mine, and told myself it would all be okay. He felt it, too. I knew he did. I just had to trust that, without asking him to say it out loud.

I had to believe.

I only hoped I actually could.

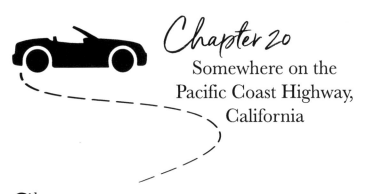

# Chapter 20
## Somewhere on the Pacific Coast Highway, California

Slow.

That was the only way to drive the Pacific Coast Highway.

The small stretch we'd covered the day before was nothing compared to the miles we drove that next day, the road winding up the central coast of California. Sometimes we'd hug the mountainside, high above the coast, the water stretching out to our left while the ridges climbed to our right. Other times we were mere feet from the water, maybe even inches, the salty breeze misting our noses.

I snapped a picture of Emery driving when we passed through Cayucos, the emerald water tinged with turquoise serving as a backdrop, his hair whipping in the wind, sunglasses up, smirk in place. We'd been mostly quiet all day, but it wasn't because it was a bad day. We were quiet because there was so much to see, so much to observe, and we took that stretch of our journey slowly, stopping along the way for food, and sometimes just to sit and stare.

The downside to our quiet drive was that my mind wasn't quiet at all.

All day, I ran through what I would say to Emery when we stopped for the night. I didn't want to tarnish the new openness he had with me by asking for more than he could give, but I knew I needed to hear something... even if I wasn't sure what. It was a delicate balance, wishing for him to give me more when all I'd asked originally was for him to try. Emery was like a firework with the fuse burnt all the way down to the end, momentarily paused, temporarily safe — and I didn't know if he would remain in tact or blow to bits if I took even one step closer.

It was after midnight when Emery reached forward for the music dial, pulling off US Highway 1 and into the Big Sur River Inn. Kalo had been passed out in the back seat for hours, and she let me walk her long enough for her to go to the bathroom before she was over it. Emery checked us in and once we dropped our bags on the bed in the cabin-style room, I let out a long yawn, stretching my arms up over my head.

"Today was amazing," I said, twisting back and forth to work out the soreness in my lower back.

"Day's not over yet. Get naked, I'm taking you somewhere."

I balked, arms falling to my sides. "Um... I think I misheard you."

"You didn't."

Emery smirked, stripping down to his birthday suit before ruffling through one of the paper bags he'd brought back with him after our stop in Cambria. He pulled out two large, white robes, tossing one to me before covering his goods with the other.

I just blinked.

"Hurry up, we have a reservation in thirty minutes."

"We have a reservation at one in the morning?" I questioned, still clutching the robe to my chest. "And you're wearing *that*?"

"As are you. If you recall, you owe me — all thanks to a little wing challenge in Texas. Now," he said, flicking his wind-blown hair out of his face before crossing the room to where I stood. His knuckle found my chin, lifting it until his lips brushed mine as he lowered his voice, his words tickling my skin. "Get naked, or I'll be forced to strip you myself."

I swallowed, his mouth closing over mine so briefly I wasn't sure it even happened before he pulled Kalo's food out and water out. He rubbed her head, grabbed the car keys, and looked back at me with a cocked brow one more time before he was out the door, and I had no choice but to follow.

It was like stumbling upon a secret hideaway, one no one was meant to discover, when we pulled into Esalen. A light bit of fog covered the roads and tumbled up over the wooden sign announcing our arrival, and I let my fingers hang out the window, the cool of the clouds tickling my skin as the guard let us in and pointed us to where we needed to go.

Emery held my hand as we joined the rest of the group, about twenty or so other people who were all fully clothed. I narrowed my eyes at him when we loaded up on the shuttle, but he just squeezed my hand with a mischievous smile.

Everyone was silent as we rode through the lodging areas, and even when we were dropped off at an immaculate co-ed changing area, complete with showers, it seemed no one had words to say. In fact, it was as if silence was the only way to come into Esalen. Emery told me it was a healing resort, a place to meditate and practice self-discovery, but we were just dipping our toes in for the night.

Literally, dipping our toes in. Into the hot springs, to be more precise.

When the guide dropped us off, everyone in the group stripped out of their clothes quietly, each of them taking turns stepping into the shower before heading outside to the various hot spring tubs available. We were on our own, everyone making the night their own experience, and no one seemed to be judging anyone else.

That didn't make it any easier for me to disrobe.

"No one is watching you," Emery assured me, untying his own robe and draping it over one of the wooden benches. He stepped forward and into me, pressing his lips to mine and keeping them there as his hands found the bow tied at the front of my robe. He pulled one end of it, and the robe fell open, only his body blocking my body from the rest of the room. "And it's dark out there, save for the moonlight."

A nervous breath left my lips as he pushed the fabric of my robe down my shoulders, catching it before it hit the floor and laying it next to his. "I kind of want to kill you right now."

Emery chuckled, kissing me again before kneeling below me. "Just trust me."

He placed my hands on his shoulder, helping me balance as he removed my prosthesis and wrapped it in our robes. Then he stood, one arm coming under the bend in my knees, the other supporting my lower back as he cradled me in his arms. He walked us to the showers, waggling his eyebrows as he ran the water over our bare bodies.

"You know what, maybe we should just go back to the room," he mused, running a flat hand over my neck and down to cup my breast with an appreciative groan.

"Nuh-uh," I said, smacking his hand away. "You dragged me out into the cold at one in the morning and got me naked in front of a bunch of strangers. We're not leaving until I get the payout for this torture."

Emery smirked. "I promise, I won't let you go to sleep until you're completely satisfied."

I just rolled my eyes, but a blush crept up my neck as he carried me out of the changing area, the cold night air washing over my hot skin as we walked past the different baths.

Emery settled on one of the smaller tubs, nodding to the only other couple in it as we descended the stairs into the hot water. He let me go when we were all the way in, leading us over to the edge of the tub that hung a bit off the mountain, the water less than one-hundred feet below us. A man took a seat at the edge of our tub, above the water, his hands folding in his lap as he crossed his legs and closed his eyes, settling in for a meditation.

And for the first several minutes, we were both completely speechless.

It was an out-of-body experience, sitting in that hot spring suspended above the Pacific coast, the waves crashing against the rocks below, salt floating on the breeze all the way up to our noses. I existed both in the water with Emery and above it, too — watching as the moonlight painted our skin, listening as the ocean slept, smelling the beached kelp, feeling the hot steam from the bath as it competed with the cool breeze washing in from the west.

The moon was high and bright above us, the stars speckled all around it, almost as if they were close enough to touch. I thought I saw one dive across the sky, burning one last time before it died. Emery's hand grazing my lower hip brought me back into my body, back to the present moment, and I turned to him just as he began to speak.

"My grandma came here in the early seventies," he said, his eyes scanning the waves in the distance. "She said it was a staple in the 'human potential movement.' At the time, my grandma was in what she described to me as the worst depression of her life. It was just after she had my father, and she felt like she was failing as mother and wife both. So, she came here to find clarity."

"She experienced depression, too," I said, though I already knew it from reading his journal. Another confession of his robbed by my curiosity.

Emery nodded. "She did."

He was quiet again after that, lost in his thoughts, and I rested my chin on the cool rock of the tub, watching the white caps of the waves roll under the moonlight. Something about that place, not just the setting, but the sanctuary itself, left me swimming in introspection, and I wanted to share something with Emery, too.

"When I first lost my leg, I didn't even want to try to walk again," I confessed. "Everything just... *hurt,* you know? Not just the actual wound that was healing, but the memory of my leg. It hurt to think of how I took advantage of something so precious, how I never had to think about walking before, and now if I ever wanted to do it again, I'd have to work and work and work, every single day, just to be able to do it half as good as I used to."

Emery's hand squeezed my hip, and I leaned into the touch.

"I'd never felt that, that kind of hopelessness. And then one night, I overheard my parents in the kitchen. They were talking about the accident, about my leg, and my mom said it would be so embarrassing to be in a wheelchair or to have a prosthetic leg. She said it was such a shame, because I was so pretty before. *Before*," I repeated, the word bitter on my tongue. "And that was the first time it occurred to me that the accident had split my life in two — before, and after."

"No offense, but your mom is a bitch."

I laughed, the sound soft, my eyes still on the water. "None taken. But you know, it was what my dad said next that really kicked me in the chest." I swallowed, remembering the sound of his voice as it carried from the kitchen down the hall to my bedroom where they thought I was sleeping. "He said he didn't know how I could even live with myself. He said if he was me, he would just end it all." I couldn't look at Emery when I said the next sentence. "My own father said my life wasn't worth living anymore."

"Jesus," he whispered.

"But you know what? Hearing him say that, it was exactly what I needed. Nothing like hearing someone say you shouldn't live anymore to make you want to do just that to spite them. He lit the fire in me, the one I've had burning ever since. I didn't just learn how to walk, I did it in record time, and then I did yoga, and got a job, and did everything they thought I never would. I lived," I said. "And then I left, just like I promised them I would one day."

We were both quiet again, the weight of what I'd said hanging between us like a lead balloon. Emery's touch at my waist was lighter now, his brows pinched together. I wondered what he was thinking — not just about me, but about himself, about that day when he tried to take his life.

"Is this the place?" I finally asked, my voice thick with uncertainty. "You told me you were driving across the country because you 'had to see something,'" I reminded him. "Is this it?"

"No," he answered quickly. "Well, it's one of the places, I guess, but it's not the final stop."

My stomach rolled, the thoughts I'd been mulling over all day sweeping in on the next breeze to remind me of all the uncertainty I felt when it came to the end of our trip. I let my head fall to the side, cheek on the stones as I traced the edge of the shadows on his face. "When this is all over, this trip... will I ever see you again?"

Emery sucked in a long breath, letting it out slowly, his breath pushing against the steam. "That's an easy question with a complicated answer."

"Is it?" I challenged. "Seems like a pretty simple yes or no kind of answer to me."

He faced me then, his arms moving to wrap around me until my chest was against his, our bodies wet and hot and slick as he molded himself to me. One thigh slipped between my own, brushing against my core, my eyes fluttering shut with the feel of it.

"All I can say right now is that I know where I'm going, but I don't know what I'll find when I get there. And until I figure that out, I can't answer your question," he said, his voice a whisper on the ocean breeze. "It may not make sense to you, but it's all I can give. Is it enough?"

I nodded, swallowing down the nerves and latching onto his words. They weren't a promise for more, but they were an honest plea for understanding, and they were enough.

Emery pressed his forehead to mine, the breaths leaving his chest faster as one hand skated down my back, cupping my ass and lifting me into him. That sensitive part of me rubbed against his thigh and a moan escaped my lips, soft and longing, making him harden against my middle as his hands tightened around me.

"Please, tell me you're not sore anymore," he breathed, rolling his hips into me.

"I'm not sore."

"Thank fuck," he growled, arms moving until I was cradled against his chest once more. He walked us up out of the tub quickly, the cold air piercing our hot skin like needles, his kiss piercing my heart like a knife. "I want you tonight. All of you."

My voice was a breath on the breeze. "Take me."

And with that plea, we were on the road again, driving too fast down the foggy coast back to our hotel.

My back hit the door as soon as it closed behind us, Emery dropping my prosthetic in the corner carefully before his hands pinned me again. They gripped my hips hard, his own grinding against me as I raked my hands through his hair, my lips desperate on his. It was all-encompassing, the way he kissed me, not just with his mouth but with every part of his body. His breaths kissed my neck, his teeth dragging along the sensitive skin as I arched into him, his hands gripping harder, arms trapping, moans cutting deep like the sweetest suicide. I was already gone before he'd even really touched me.

Emery ripped the tie loose at the front of my robe, shoving it back off my shoulders and sucking the swell of my breast as soon as it was unveiled. I gasped, head hitting the door before I gripped him harder, biting the hard muscle of his shoulder as he moved his way back up to kiss behind my ear.

"If I go too hard, tell me to stop," he warned, hips pressing into me against the door so he could free one hand. It hooked under my ass first, gripping hard before sliding down my thigh, snaking up the middle, and one finger entered me quickly and roughly and without mercy.

I cried out, moaning with eyes squeezed shut, legs opening for him. "More."

"That's my girl," he growled, and another finger slid in to join the first, spreading me wider.

His touch wasn't gentle at first, his fingers thrusting in hard, curling at the tips and working in time with his mouth sucking the skin of my neck. I was frantic, arching into him and away from the door, my hands flying from the cool wood to his shoulders to his hair and back again. I couldn't get a grip on anything, least of all my composure. I was lost, spiraling down into nothing, burning from the inside out.

But then Emery inhaled a long breath, the air filling his lungs before it touched my lips with his exhale, and he slowed. His fingers worked in a smoother rhythm, his kisses longer and softer. The crease of his brows told me he was fighting against the urge to go faster, harder, and when his touch turned more gentle, I sighed into his mouth.

Being touched by Emery was my new favorite state of being. When his hands were on my thighs, when his lips were on my neck, when his eyes were on my body like figure skaters, looping and gliding from top to bottom, inch over inch. It was an excavation, a slow and purposeful discovery, each and every time.

Slowly and carefully, Emery withdrew his fingers, my body shaking violently at the loss of heat as he picked me up again, carrying me across our room with his mouth fused to mine. My back hit the bed, the cool comforter puffing up around me as he dropped his hands on either side of my head. The longing in his eyes as he stared down at me, admiring for a moment before he lowered his mouth to mine again, it was enough to undo me. It was enough to make me wish to stay in that moment, in that room with him, forever.

He pushed back to standing long enough to make quick work of his own robe, the white fabric falling to the floor at his feet as I traced the lines of his abdomen. Emery was so hard, every inch of him, from the lines on his forehead to the muscles of his thighs. Lean and toned, strong and tall — he was all man.

His eyes were hot on mine as he knelt, kissing his way down my flat stomach. A soft shudder of a breath left my lips and my eyes fluttered closed at the contact, at the feel of his wet lips on my skin. He dragged his tongue up the inside of my thigh, tugging me forward off the edge of the bed just enough for him to maneuver his way under me, and then his mouth was where I ached for him most.

I moaned, hands gripping the comforter as he ran his tongue flat over me before sucking my bud. He gripped my thighs in both hands, spreading me wide as he buried his face in me, and it was all I could do to just keep breathing. I should have felt embarrassed, exposed for him like that, my most sensitive and private parts of my body on full display in ways never seen before. But I only felt desired. I only felt wanted in a way a goddess is wanted by a man, the way freedom is wanted by a prisoner, the way rain is wanted by a drought-ridden crop.

My legs shook on either side of his face, trembling at his touch, and just when my orgasm started to build, Emery pulled back, the sensation leaving me in a rush as every tensed muscle released at once.

"Oh, God," I breathed, shaking at the loss, and Emery smirked as he towered over me again. Bending forward, he snaked one arm under the arch in my back, lifting and moving me back up the bed until my head hit the pillows and his weight settled between my thighs. For a long moment he watched me again, his hands in my hair, eyes searching mine.

"I don't deserve to touch you like this," he whispered, fingers brushing my hair behind one ear.

It broke me, the way his face cracked under the weight of his words, the words he believed to be true. But I knew they weren't. I knew he was meant to touch me, that he was the *only* one who had ever deserved to. So I leaned up, telling him with a kiss that he was wrong, assuring him with a roll of my hips that I wanted him, too — perhaps even more than he wanted me.

He reached forward for his wallet on the nightstand, never breaking our kiss, and then there was a faint rip of the condom wrapper and a pressure at my center. His hands moved from my hair to my shoulders, fingers curling around them, his biceps encompassing me as he flexed forward.

And then we both sighed, our foreheads pressed together, breaths meeting between us in a current of longing.

He filled me completely, my thighs squeezing his hips at the sensation as he withdrew and rocked forward again. It was as new as the first time, as foreign and exciting and overwhelming. Electricity filled me from the inside out, buzzing my nervous system to life, igniting the air around us with a shock. When he picked up speed, finding a rhythm, I felt the fire catching where his body rolled against mine with each thrust.

"Yes," I breathed as he pulled back, the whole of him sliding out until just the tip was left before he rolled forward again. "More."

"If I give you any more, you'll break," he panted, kissing my collarbone, his hands still curled under my shoulders. He pulled me down, his own hips rocking forward again, the flex filling me deeper.

But I wanted more.

Pressing my hands into his chest, I leaned and rolled until he submitted to me, taking my place on the bed as I straddled him. Emery's eyes widened when I sat upright, his hands falling to rest where my thighs and hips met in a crease. His hard body was beneath me then, sprawled out against the white sheets, and I bent down to kiss him before I used one hand to slide him back inside me.

We both moaned with the new position, and though I knew my bad leg would make it a little challenging, I wanted this — I wanted to bring him the pleasure he was bringing me. I moved slow, adjusting to the new way he filled me, and when I finally slid all the way down, Emery squeezed his eyes shut on a curse.

"Oh, my God," I breathed, sitting there for a moment before lifting again. "It's so... you're so deep this way." I whimpered when I slid over him again, the way he hit me inside like never before, a depth I'd never experienced.

"Fuck," Emery groaned, flexing his hips into me. "I love when you talk like that. Tell me what you're feeling."

"Everything," I sighed, thighs burning a little as I moved over him. "I feel everything."

Emery's hands fell to the bed, letting me take control, and I threaded my fingers with his on either side of us before moving them to my hips again. He held my slight frame in his hands, less shaky than the first night he touched me, and I bent to whisper against his lips.

"Help me ride you."

He growled, the sound low and throaty as I pushed up off the bed, sitting all the way down on him. His grip tightened, and with the help of his hands, I lifted until only the tip of him was still inside me before sliding down again. With his help, I could move faster, his hips thrusting forward to hit deeper, and my orgasm built with the speed of a Ferrari flying down an unmarked highway.

"Cooper," Emery husked, and I peered at him through heavy lids. "I want you to touch yourself."

His eyes fell to my chest, and I hesitantly pulled my hands from where they gripped his wrists, fingertips gliding up my rib cage. When I paused, unsure, Emery tightened his grip on my hips and pulled me down again, hips flexing.

"Touch yourself for me."

Chills broke over my skin as I obeyed, and when my fingers rolled my nipples between them, that same electricity I'd felt buzz to life earlier shocked my system. Every nerve awakened, and I moaned out his name, a prayer answered before I'd even known to ask.

Emery sat upright, moving until his back was against the headboard and our chests were pressed together again. His mouth found mine in a frenzy, his hands still helping me ride him, our bodies connected at every point from hip to lips. He rocked into me slow and steady, a new friction building between us, and I moaned into his mouth with every new thrust.

That night, Emery didn't kiss me like we had forever. He kissed me like it was our last night on Earth, like he had mere moments to fill me, to touch me, to take all he could before we both faded into nonexistence. His teeth sank into my bottom lip, his hands moving to cup my ass as he lifted me to his tip, sliding me back down slowly, every centimeter stretching me more. Then again, faster, harder, his teeth releasing my lip as he moved to kiss my shoulder, the swell of my breast, the hollow point of my throat.

He was all strength and longing, holding the weight of me as he filled me again and again. The friction of his tight abdomen against my center sent a spark of pleasure through me, the heat popping and fizzing with each brush. I rolled into him, each wave reaching farther, climax tickling my fingertips, it was so close. When he groaned in my ear, his entire body surrounding mine, I clenched tight around him until stars invaded my vision and all my muscles tightened and released at once, my orgasm rocking through me like a tsunami. I clutched his shoulders, his name on repeat from my lips like I was speaking in tongues as I moaned out my release.

Emery kissed me hard, his arms wrapping around me tighter as he thrust in twice more, each time hitting me deeper before he held me in place, pulsing out his own release with a longing groan. His hands bruised my hips, holding me there as he emptied, his body shaking, eyes squeezed shut. When they finally fluttered open again, his body stilling, I collapsed into him with a shudder, giving him all of my weight, all of me.

For a while we just breathed, we just existed, two bare bodies wrapped up in each other like tangled wires. The air still buzzed and sparked, and I leaned up enough to look into his sated eyes, my fingertips running through the damp strands of his hair, feeling each one from root to tip before letting it fall and repeating the motion.

Emery watched me, his eyes flicking between mine before falling to my lips where he placed a tender kiss. My heart was so full, swelling with words unsaid, with feelings never experienced. He just held me closer, tighter, like even one centimeter of space between us was too much.

It was like a dream, my body numb and mind distant as we rolled, Emery pulling me under the covers with him and curling into me. He held me, his breaths on the back of my neck, arms wrapped around me like a sweater. But this time, and for the first time, my dreams weren't better than my reality. Emery was real, the way I felt was real, and every ounce of fatigue I had washed out of me at that realization.

I was wide awake, and I never wanted to sleepwalk through life again.

# Chapter 21
## Big Sur, California

It was still dark when Emery woke me the next morning, his large hand rubbing circles on my lower back. I arched into the touch, body sore and aching and incredibly satisfied. My toes curled as I rolled over, reaching for my glasses on the bedside table when I saw he was already dressed and sitting on the edge of the bed.

"Time is it?" I mumbled, rubbing the sleep from my eyes under my lenses. "Is Kalo okay?"

"She's fine," he said on a chuckle. "But there's something I want to show you before we get back on the road."

Emery was quiet as I dressed, taking my hand when I was ready and grabbing my yoga mat and a long towel on our way out the door. I cocked a brow, curiosity piqued, but he just squeezed my hand.

I watched the dawn break behind the mountains, the sky softly lightening to a cerulean blue as we drove. We weren't on the road long before Emery pulled off to the side, parking and grabbing my mat from the back seat.

The waves were calm below us as we hiked down a bit, finding a plateau where Emery laid out my mat, taking the towel and spreading it out a few feet to the left. When he turned to me, I swore the sky lightened more in that moment, the golden hues of the morning racing to match that of his eyes.

"Usually when I have a bad day, people push me," he said, swallowing. "My parents, my therapist. No one ever understands that I can't talk about it when I don't have anything to say. Even Grams, she wanted me to write, and for the longest time I couldn't. I've finally gotten to the point where I *can* write, but even that is hard sometimes because honestly..." his voice trailed off as he tucked his hands into the pockets of his athletic shorts. "Honestly, I don't see what the point is."

I frowned, stepping into him and wrapping my arms around his waist, my head falling to his chest. He sighed, hugging me in return, his chin propped on my head.

"I can't tell you how much it meant to me that you didn't leave, didn't get mad, didn't look at me like I was broken or sad or like you pitied me. I gave you nothing, but you understood." He pulled back, the sun rising a bit in his eyes as they found mine. "You're the first person to do that. You're the first person to make me feel alive, Cooper. In a long time." He shrugged. "Maybe ever."

My heart swelled at the same time guilt seeped low into my stomach. I had left him alone, let him have his bad day, all the while using ammo from his journal to break down his walls a little more. It was an unfair battle, one he didn't even know I was fighting.

"I'd like to practice with you," he said, nodding toward my mat. "If that's okay. I know yoga is important to you, and I know it helped you get through the hardest time of your life. I thought maybe it could help me, too."

It was a resurrection, the way my heart stopped in that moment and kicked back to life with a new beat under my chest. To someone driving by, it would have seemed so insignificant — Emery's towel spread beside my mat, the two of us enjoying a morning yoga session before getting back on the road. But I knew it was more, I knew it meant he was healing, and I was a part of it.

We started in a seated position, our hands at heart center, faces turned to the west as the ocean mist drifted up the rocks to greet us. The sun rose behind us, the water sparkling a deep blue under its shine, our backs warming as it rose higher. With every new stretch, every new breath, I felt our connection grow stronger.

Emery Reed wasn't a stranger anymore.

Looking back, it doesn't surprise me that I didn't see the storm rolling in from the east, the clouds billowing up higher and higher behind the mountains. All I could see was the sunshine, all I could feel was his heart beating, and mine matching the rhythm, falling into sync without so much as a second thought of what would happen next.

We laid down in Savasana and I meditated as if that moment alone was enough to banish any worries I had before. I found a reassurance that wasn't actually present, a promise never spoken.

I thought I couldn't lose him.

But I could, and I would, in a way I never even imagined.

A fter yoga, we ended up staying the rest of the day in Big Sur, eating lunch by the river and hiking the falls. We got up close and personal with the redwood trees, and Kalo found more than a few furry friends as we explored.

The next morning, we took our time driving the rest of the way up the PCH, stopping once we reached Legget before traveling on to Grants Pass the next day. Our afternoons were mostly spent driving or hiking the areas we passed, and our conversations grew deeper with each day. Emery talked more in those few days than he had the entire trip, and I wasn't tempted to read his journal anymore. Hearing the stories of his childhood and his thoughts on life from his own lips instead of those pages was better than I imagined, I only had to give up my need to know what he *wouldn't* tell me — like what would happen when we reached Seattle.

"One day, I was just sitting in my bedroom and I noticed this mug of pens on my desk," he told me when we'd finished our drive up the PCH. We were standing at the northernmost point of it near Leggett, our eyes on the setting sun over the coast. "And I remember being *instantly* annoyed. Why the fuck did I have so many pens?

I needed *one,* maybe two, just in case the first one broke. But I had seventeen. Why?"

I'd laughed, shrugging. "We just collect things over the years, I suppose."

"Exactly. And it wasn't just pens, it was everything. I looked around my room that night at all this... *stuff* that I didn't need. So, I went into the kitchen, grabbed an entire box of trash bags, and locked myself in my room for the rest of the night. I cranked my music, started at one corner, and by three o'clock the next morning I'd bagged up seventy percent of my shit to donate."

I'd nodded, understanding him more than he knew. "I had that same kind of clarity when I was packing up to leave with you. I was standing there in my room trying to figure out what to take with me when I realized I didn't need any of it. There was nothing there that I couldn't leave behind and never think about again. So, I stopped packing."

Emery had slid his hand into mine then, fingers running over my palm before he laced them with my own. "I think when we let go of the materialistic shit we think we need, the stuff we grew up looking for because we thought happiness existed under their price tag, *that's* when we start living a better life. A free, meaningful existence."

"Very Gemini of you," I'd teased, and he'd just lifted my fingers to his lips, kissing them with a playful grin on his lips as the last of the sun dipped away.

That's how easy it was, talking to Emery. Nothing was off limits — politics, beliefs, childhood, future wants and needs. Sometimes we'd talk about something I'd never discussed before and I'd find new beliefs, ones I didn't even know I had. He made me *think* before I answered, before I chimed in with how I felt about whatever topic we had on the table.

Emery pushed me. He challenged me. He opened me up.

The more I learned about him, the more I wanted to know. He told me about his family, about growing up in the affluent neighborhood he called home in South Florida. I asked him about his friends, of which he had few, mainly because, in his own words, *not many people stick around and put up with my shit for long.* It seemed his closest friend had been his grandmother before she passed, so I listened to his stories of growing up with her, of the memories he would have of her forever.

And, for the first time, he talked about his brother. Not just to me, but to anyone — ever. He told me he didn't realize how much he needed to talk about his brother, about the hole left before he'd even been born, until we'd talked about it the day we left Vegas. He was letting me in, more than anyone before me, and I took that gift with more appreciation than I could express.

We talked about me, too — not as much about my past as about what I wanted for my future. Emery sat with me in the business center at our hotel in Leggett helping me fill out applications for apartments and serving jobs near the school. On that same day, I'd received a call from Tammy saying there was a letter at Papa Wyatt's from Bastyr.

I'd gotten in.

We celebrated with a dinner that was way too expensive, one Emery insisted on, and then we spent the night tangled in the sheets, bringing each other pleasure with our hands, our mouths, our bodies. It was my favorite way to spend a night now that I knew what it felt like. It wasn't just sex with Emery — it was passion unleashed. It was every fantasy I'd ever had answered in a language I didn't know, one I was learning to speak with every new touch.

For the first time in the twenty years I'd been alive, I was happy — truly, one-hundred percent happy. I hadn't known happiness like that existed, the kind that fills you from the heart and bleeds into every day. I'd dreamed of leaving Mobile, of attending Bastyr and living in Seattle, of finding a boy who made my heart race, and living in a world where every day was new and exciting and fresh.

Now I was awake, and my life was even better than the dreams.

Emery had been fine the night we spent in Grants Pass, holding me under one arm as we strolled the downtown area where they'd already hung Christmas lights even though Thanksgiving hadn't passed yet. We both sipped on hot chocolate, sharing stories of what the holidays were like for each of us growing up before we retreated back to our room.

But once we were there, Emery grew silent, that storm that had been quieted stirring again behind his golden eyes. I watched them change right in front of me, the bottoms of them lined in black, the tops shadowed by bent brows. I wanted to reach for him, to ask him to talk to me, but I knew he just needed to be alone. So, I turned on the television, lazily rubbing Kalo's belly as he wrote in his journal beside me, working through his thoughts. We both turned in early, and I didn't crowd him as we slept, only reaching one hand forward to press heat into his back and let him know I was there.

He tossed and turned that night, and when we woke the next morning, he declined my offer for breakfast, telling me he was just ready to get on the road. It was cold and gray that day, so we both bundled up, leaving the top up on the car and the heat on low as we cruised up through Oregon.

It was only four hours into Portland, our next planned stop, but Emery drove slower than usual, even stopping at one point at an intersection when we didn't need gas or food. He just got out of the car, walked about ten feet in front of it, and stood there, his hands in his pockets, eyes on the sign that told us how much longer it was until the next city. I took the opportunity to walk Kalo, and then we were back in the car, and if it was even possible, Emery seemed even more distant than before.

My weakness was thrown in my face the last two hours of that car ride, because all it took was another bad day for me to eye his journal, desperate to be inside his head. We were too near to the end of our trip for him to pull back, but I didn't know how to tell him that, to express my own feelings without disrespecting his.

We were about ten miles outside of Portland when the silence became too much. I turned in my seat, arms crossed over my middle, heart picking up speed as I opened my mouth to ask what he was thinking, but the question died in my throat. Something caught my eye on the windshield, and when I leaned forward to inspect it, another flake joined the first.

"Oh, my God," I whispered, rolling down my window and sticking one hand out. The flurries fell harder, one of them landing on my palm before melting away. "Emery! Look!"

I glanced back at him, his eyes still dead as they landed on my hand out the window.

"It's *snowing*," I said, giggling. I wiggled my fingers, hanging my head out the window with my mouth open wide.

Emery didn't smile, just pulled his attention back to the road, steering us between the slower cars until we pulled off the highway and into the parking lot of the hotel we'd call home for the night. It was only three in the afternoon, the sky gray, ground slowly being buried by the snow. He grabbed our bags from the back, slinging one over each shoulder as Kalo tumbled out of the back seat and onto the cold ground.

She paused, nose in the air as she sniffed before trying her paws on the wet ground again. The snow scared her and she jumped back, bending to sniff it next and getting a whiff of powder on her nose. She shook it off as I laughed, then she took off, hopping through the fresh snow as I ran after her.

"It's my first snowfall!" I hollered back at Emery, dipping down to grab a handful before throwing it in the air. I hoped he'd bite, hoped he'd take the chance to let me in, even if just a little. "Come on! Drop the bags, we'll get them in a second."

"I'm tired," he answered, not even looking at me. Kalo stopped short, her tail still wagging as my hands fell to my side. "I'm going to lie down for a while."

"Emery," I pleaded, and he closed his eyes at his name on my lips. I went to say something more, but found I had nothing more to say, so I simply closed my mouth again, asking with my eyes for him to stay.

He opened his eyes again, glancing at me briefly before adjusting the bags on his shoulders and heading inside the lobby without another word. I swallowed back the hurt I felt, trying to understand he couldn't help it, but his coldness stung more than the snow on my bare cheeks.

As I put Kalo's leash on and led her toward the lobby entrance, I couldn't help but remember what Emery had said to me.

He was right.

Everything is quiet when the first snow falls.

I laid in bed with Emery, even though I wasn't tired in the slightest, just listening to the quietness of our hotel room as the snow fell outside. I'd opened the curtains over our window, my eyes catching snowflakes as they drifted down from the sky, eager to join the others already painting the ground.

Kalo slept between us, her body a little furnace that I curled into, and every now and then my eyes would drift to Emery. I watched him sleep, his breath peaceful and calm, though the two lines between his brows were still present, as if he couldn't escape his thoughts even in his dreams.

He stirred around five, moving to lean against the headboard as he rubbed his eyes.

"Hi," I whispered, unsure of which man was waking up beside me.

"Hey."

Emery reached forward to rub behind Kalo's ear, his eyes catching on the winter wonderland unfolding outside our window. I thought maybe he would say something now about it, or ask if I wanted to go outside. I thought maybe he was okay again.

But he only sighed, scrubbing his hands over his face before kicking the covers back.

"I'm going to shower."

I closed my eyes as he closed the door, effectively putting a physical barrier between us where a metaphorical one had already existed all day. When I opened them again, they landed on his journal laying unassumingly on the bedside table, the pages pressed flat onto the wood, leather binding stretched open.

*Don't*, I warned myself, curling into Kalo more. She rolled over, offering me her belly, and I ran my fingers along her silky fur, eyes still glued to the journal.

I wanted so many opposing things in that moment. I wanted to read the journal, to read what he was feeling last night, to find something within the pages to bring him back to me. I wanted to respect his privacy, trust that he would talk to me in time, and spend the evening being there for him in whatever way he needed me to be. Everything I wanted seemed at war with something else I desired equally, and I weighed my options as I heard the shower turn on in the bathroom.

It was, for all intents and purposes, our last night together. At least, our last night *guaranteed* together. Tomorrow we would drive into Seattle, to my new home, and I didn't know if he would stay once we got there. I didn't even know where his final stop was, or what it was that he "needed to see." I only knew it was somewhere in Washington, and that I'd had the time of my life on this journey with him, and now it was ending, and I didn't want to lose him.

I pressed my fingers hard into my temples, massaging the muscle there, my eyes closed as I tried to find the easy answer that eluded me. But there was no easy answer, no simple solution, and as sick as it made me feel reaching a hand out until I felt that leather binding, I couldn't stop myself.

I was an addict, fiending for comfort from his words, chasing the high that came from finding a new layer of him buried in those pages.

Pulling the book into my lap, I ran my hand over the page bookmarked, the entry he was writing last night before bed. Kalo put a paw on the pages with a whine, as if to tell me to reconsider, but I'd already had the first taste. There was no turning back now.

*I remember the first time a girl told me she loved me.*

*It was Melissa Rickman, and we were seniors in high school. She told me she loved me after we'd been dating for a little over a month. I just stared at her before finally asking, "Why?"*

*That night, I talked to my dad about it, and I asked him to tell me how he knew he loved Mom. He'd sat on the edge of my bed with this far off look in his eyes and this goofy ass smile. He told me there was one night where Mom invited him over to her apartment because she wanted to cook a meal for him.*

*But she was an awful cook, he'd told me, which didn't surprise me since she still is. He said watching her try to make a meal for him was the most endearing thing. He* said she was making something so simple, a pasta dish, but the sauce was all over her apron and splatted on her face.

He said at one point, she'd given up, placing her hands on the counter and hanging her head as she started to cry. All she'd wanted was to do something special for him.

Dad said in that moment, he knew he loved her.

It was nothing crazy, nothing she said or did that really stood out, just seeing her standing there with pasta sauce on her face and tears in her eyes. He loved her. It hit him simply and without fuss, and he didn't tell her until a full six months later.

I told Melissa Rickman the next day that I didn't love her, and she broke up with me, which was fine.

I've written about love in this journal before today, always with the firm belief that it didn't really exist. I've always believed it was a fantasy, something we cling to as humans to make this world a little less lonely. Because it is fucking lonely.

But tonight, I walked with Cooper in downtown Grants Pass, and we were just talking and drinking hot chocolate and looking at Christmas lights when she tripped a little. She spilled hot chocolate on her scarf, and her little face crumpled at the sight of it. She was so devastated by that splash of brown on her otherwise blue scarf, and I found it so fucking adorable that all I could do was laugh and pull her into me and kiss her. I mean physically, there was nothing else I could have done in that moment. I couldn't not kiss her.

And I'm not saying it's love, but it made me think of my dad, and my mom, and that damn pasta sauce.

*I'm not saying it's love, but it was something... different. Foreign. Intense.*

I smiled, biting my lip as I traced those words with my fingertips before moving on.

*I haven't said a word to her since that moment, because as soon as her lips left mine, I remembered that Seattle is just seven hours away. I remembered that our trip is ending soon... mine in a very different way than hers.*

*I've deceived her. I've hidden the truth from her, afraid of how she might take it, of how it might break her, of how it might break me, too.*

*But if nothing has changed, if the plan remains the same, I have to tell her soon.*

*Or walk out of her life like a ghost.*

*Which is better — to tell her the truth, or forever let her wonder?*

*That is what plagues me tonight.*

My stomach dropped as I finished the entry, fingers already flying back through the pages to find something more. I'd gone in with the intention of feeling connected to him, of finding reassurance until Emery came back to me. But all I'd found was a new source of anxiety, a new reason to question everything.

*What was he hiding?*

Could he really just leave me, just... *ghost* me, as he'd put it? What was his plan, to tell me he would be back, only to leave me without the intention of ever seeing me again?

Thoughts tumbled over themselves in my mind as I flipped, back and back, looking for something, though I didn't know what. When I flipped past a worn page, one that was dogeared in the right-hand corner just enough to look out of place, I paused. I think I knew right then, in that moment, on that bed as the snow fell quietly outside that I was about to find answers to questions I never meant to ask, answers never meant to be found.

I flipped back to the marked page, eyes glancing at the date before focusing in on the first sentence.

*Grams died today.*

A shiver sped down my spine, from neck to lower back, the snow suddenly seeming like it was falling inside of me instead of outside the window. There were dried tear stains on the pages, blurring some of the ink. He'd cried when he'd written it, or perhaps when he'd read it, or maybe even both.

I couldn't imagine Emery crying at all.

I steeled a breath, blinking my eyes a few times before I continued reading.

*Grams died today.*

*I wrote that sentence three hours ago and then I walked away, because writing it makes it real, and of all the things I wish weren't true, that sentence is at the top of the list.*

*It's like a knife has been jabbed into my throat, the blade rusty and dull, and now I have to somehow learn to breathe with it there. I can't remove it, can't shove it* in farther to finish the job — I just have to exist with an infected wound, with a clogged airway and a constant reminder of the loss of what was.

She's gone. She's never coming back. And I'm still here.

Mom and Dad know I'm not okay. They didn't even want me to go in to see her at the end of it all, when she was literally on the welcome mat of Death's door, but I pushed past them and forced my way in. I had to see her one more time, had to hold her hand while she crossed over.

She didn't even look like Grams on that hospital bed, her body frail and weak, all the machines hooked into her. Her organs were failing her, one by one, for no other reason than that she was tired. Life had been long and she was tired.

Grams asked me for something.

She told me she understood how I felt, which I already knew. She was the only one who ever understood my depression, who ever empathized because she, too, battled with it. She'd been my war buddy, the one I could swap stories with to feel a little less alone. But on that bed, with her hand in mine, she asked me to take a trip.

She wants me to get in my car and take a road trip across the country. She mentioned a few spots she wants me to hit, one of them being an old diner in Mobile, Alabama, where she and Gramps stopped once. She said he ordered the steak and eggs, and being there with him was one of those moments when she loved being alive, when she looked at him and felt it in soul, in her heart, that she was meant to be there with him. Another stop she wants me to make is at a healing institute in California, and there are a few other miscellaneous spots along the way.

She begged me to make that drive, to see the country.

She said if I travel across the United States and don't find a single thing that reaffirms my love for life, if I spend that time alone and find I'm still a victim to the dark thoughts in my head, that she will understand if I choose to no longer bear them.

There's a place she loved in Washington, a place of wonder. She said if I make it there and I still feel the same, that I can end it all. I can find my peace and join her on the other side.

But only she believes that last part.

I know there's no heaven waiting for me, no hell, either. There's just life and the nothingness that exists after we're done here. She wants me to give life one last chance, one last shot to dig its nails into me and latch on, giving me a reason to stay. And I know her, I know she thinks I'll find something. She doesn't think there's even a slight chance I'll actually make it all the way there without changing my mind, otherwise she wouldn't have suggested it at all.

So, tonight, I'll load up the car. And in the morning, I'll go.

But I know the truth.

I know I won't find anything on this trip.

But it was her dying wish, so I'll go. I'll drive and I'll stop at all the places she wants me to. I'll keep my eyes and mind open, and at the end of it all, I'll finally find peace. I'll finally let go.

*Grams told me she wasn't scared with her last breath, and I squeezed her hand, telling her I wasn't either.*

*It isn't death that's scary. It's living without actually living at all, breathing without purpose, existing without essence. Soon, it will all be over, and I won't have to apologize for how I feel, or explain why I feel it. I'll walk into Death's arms willingly with a smile on my face, and that cold embrace will be the warmest I've ever been.*

*I'm not scared.*

*I never have been.*

I covered my trembling lips with one hand, the other still holding the journal as I shook my head in disbelief. Tears were running hot down my face, joining his already on the pages, the snow falling inside of me like a blizzard now. Every part of me was ice, the kind of cold that hurts, and all I could do was stare at that page, at those words, at the truth I was never supposed to find.

"What are you doing?"

My entire body shook at the sound of his voice, my fingers still on my lips as I lifted my eyes to his. He was standing in the bathroom doorway, towel tied at his waist, a menacing scowl branded on his forehead as he glanced at the journal before turning on me again.

Two more tears fell in sync, one hitting my hand as the other hit the page.

"You can't..." I choked, a sob ripping through my throat as I tried to speak over it. "Please, Emery, don't take your life. You can't. Not after..." I shook my head, my emotions strangling me, rendering me speechless as tears flooded my eyes again before pouring down. I'd never felt so desperate in my life, yet so frozen. "Not after this. Not after *us*."

"This is my fucking *journal*," he seethed, crossing the room in three sweeps before he ripped the book from my hands. He slammed it shut, shoving it back in his bag before standing to face me again. "What the hell were you thinking? Why would you ever think it's okay to read that?"

"I was just trying to reach you," I cried, throwing the covers off me and standing. I took a step toward him, but he backed away, holding a hand up to stop me from advancing any farther. "You've been so cold and distant since last night, and we're running out of time. I wanted to know what you were thinking."

"You should have asked."

"And you would have told me?" I challenged, nose flaring as my stomach rolled on itself. I shook from head to toe like a pine tree struck by lightning, the snow falling away, the wood charred and naked beneath it.

"In time, yes."

"Don't lie to me."

It came out as a whisper, my plea almost as silent as the snow falling outside.

"I thought you understood. I thought you were the first person to respect that sometimes I just need time. I was in that shower thinking of how I would tell you, and I came out here with all those words finally making sense, and then I find you with my fucking *journal* in your hands like it's one of your goddamn books. I have never—" He shook his head, hands flying up into the air. "How could you *do* that, Cooper?"

My lips quivered again. "I'm sorry, I just... I was so desperate for you to come back to me. I thought I could find something..."

"What?" He took a step toward me, but I didn't back down. "What could you possibly have hoped you'd find?" His eyes went wide, the words hanging there on his lips. "Wait..."

Emery swallowed, his eyes flicking back and forth as he ran a hand through his hair, glancing back at his journal and slowly finding my gaze again.

"This isn't the first time, is it?"

I blinked, freeing another set of tears, guilt creeping up from my gut in a slow tide.

"Tell me you haven't been reading my journal this entire time," he demanded, his voice cracking as he moved into my space. His chest met mine and I looked away, eyes on the carpet as he towered over me. "Tell me!"

But I couldn't. I wouldn't lie to him any longer.

"Jesus fucking Christ." He blew out a breath of anger, raking his hands through his hair before letting out a frustrated growl. "It was all a lie. It was all a fucking lie. I trusted you," he spat, and when I looked up to meet his eyes again, I wished I hadn't. "I *trusted* you!"

"Please, it wasn't a lie," I pleaded, moving forward and into him. I tried to wrap my arms around his waist but he threw me off, making me lose my balance and fall back onto the bed. "Emery, everything between us is real. I invaded your privacy and I'm sorry, but I never did it to hurt you. I wanted to know you more, to understand you. I loved what I read in there. And I know that doesn't make it okay but those are your deepest, darkest thoughts, and they didn't scare me. They made me want you more."

"They were never meant to be read! Do you not understand that?" He ripped clothes out of his bag, pulling on briefs under his towel before shedding it on the floor and yanking a sweater over his still wet hair. "You played this innocent card with me this entire time and all the while you were betraying me, stabbing me when I didn't even know you had a knife at all."

"Emery, it's not like that." I frantically wiped the tears from my face, standing again, desperate to gain composure and make him see. "I'm sorry, I never should have read it. I wish I could take it all back. But it doesn't change the fact that everything between us is real. It has been since the moment we met and you know it. I *know* you know it."

"Yeah, because you read my fucking journal."

"I did! I did read it, and I know how you feel about me."

When his jeans were on, he yanked the zipper up, turning on me with heat rolling off him in waves of steam. "You know how I felt about who I *thought* you were. I don't fucking know you, Cooper."

His words sliced through me, my heart bleeding out in front of him.

"You know me," I whispered. "You know me more than anyone else. And I know you. And I lo—"

"DON'T," he roared, shoving the last of his belongings in his bag before slinging it over his shoulder. "Don't you dare finish that sentence. You don't love me, you don't know me, and you don't get to *think* either of those things just because you read the thoughts I've written in that book." He swallowed, his voice breaking at the end. "You *lied* to me."

"And you lied to me, too!"

He froze at that, only his chest moving with his heavy breaths, his nose flaring. The same guilt that seeped through me crept across his face then, both of us caught in the sticky goo of truth. We weren't perfect. We didn't mean to hurt each other, and yet it was all we'd done.

I took a step forward, my hand finding his forearm. He didn't flinch, so I wrapped my fingers around his warm skin, praying he'd feel me in that moment.

"We messed up, both of us. But we can start over. Just… let me in, and I promise, I will never lie to you again. We can make it through this. *You* can make it through this." I sniffed, squeezing his arm. "Please, just trust me. Believe me."

His eyes found mine then, the gold shaded with doubt, and his face twisted as he pulled his arm from my grasp. "How can I?"

And there it was, the gust of wind that broke what fragile house we'd built. The blizzard came quick and without warning on the heels of a day of sunshine.

I'd lost him.

"You're close enough to Seattle, I think you can figure it out from here." He ripped his eyes from mine, adjusting his bag on his shoulder as I reached for him again, his name rolling off my tongue over and over again, each time more desperate than the last. "Don't follow me."

He broke our connection, slamming the door closed behind him as I fell to my knees. The most painful scream of my life shredded my vocal chords as I cried out for him one last time, face collapsing into my cold hands when I realized it wasn't enough to bring him back. I crawled to the door, using the handle to climb to my feet, opening it with numb awareness as my heart beat in my ears.

*Thump.*

My bare feet in the snow, Emery shutting the trunk.

*Thump.*

My voice muted by the snow, Emery's hand on the wheel.

*Thump.*

Our eyes connecting, memories striking me like a whip.

*Thump.*

My knees hitting the snow, vision fading to black as the car drives away, taking my bruised and bleeding heart with it.

He left just the same as he'd come, all at once, never expected, a tide that washed me clean before leaving me raw and bare in its wake. He'd asked me that first day what made me happy, but I couldn't answer him. Now that I finally could, he was too far away to hear.

"You," I whispered, the truth of it cracking the last whole piece of my heart, and then everything went dark.

# Chapter 23

## Portland, Oregon

Time.

Such a simple word. Such a complicated concept.

I'd had so much of it, *too* much of it, wasting away in that small town that I couldn't wait to leave. I didn't even notice the ticking of the clock on the wall while I worked at the diner, never considered how many days had passed each time a new birthday rolled around. I didn't even acknowledge time until the day I left that town, until the day I met Emery.

Then, time became a living, breathing, moving thing.

And it was entirely too fast.

I'd tried to hold onto it, to spread it out like jam. I wanted to taste every second, live inside each moment forever and then race to the next to see what waited for me there. Time had started, it had kicked to life with the force of a million years of waiting, shaking off rust and spreading its wings like it was born to do.

But now, that speed that I marveled at was my worst enemy.

Time was ticking by too quickly, and I needed to move — but I didn't know where to go.

I didn't let myself lay in the snow for long before I was blindly crawling to my feet and dragging myself back inside in a zombie state, racking my brain for anything he'd said over the past two weeks that would help me figure out where he was going. He'd turned off his phone, all of my calls and texts ignored, and the sickening possibility that I would really never see him again hit me like a boulder, flattening my heart, steamrolling me to the pavement.

*"I just need to see something."*

*"My grandmother just passed away, and there's a place in Washington that was her favorite in the world. She made me promise I would go see it."*

I squeezed my eyes closed tighter, Kalo whimpering on the bed beside me as I thought through his journal entries, too.

But there was nothing.

No clues, no map, no reassurance that I had any chance in hell of finding him before it was too late.

My fingers were dialing Tammy's number before I even realized, and when she answered, my chest ripped open with another sob.

"Oh, my God, are you okay?" Her voice was frantic. "Where are you? Did he hurt you? Was there an accident?"

"He's gone," I choked.

"Gone? What do you mean, gone? Did he just *leave* you? That little bastard—"

I shook my head as she continued, willing my breaths to come easier so I could speak. "I messed up. I lied to him and I read his journal and he caught me and everything just... blew up." The wind howled outside with another gust of snow, as if to mimic my words. "He's going to hurt himself, Tammy, and I have to find him. I have to stop him. But I don't know where he went and I don't know what to do and I just..." My voice trailed off, tears pooling in my eyes again. The snow outside blurred into one blinding, white blob. "I have to find him. I have to find him."

"Okay, baby, calm down," she soothed, and I closed my eyes, letting the tears fall hot down my cheeks. "It's going to be okay. We'll figure this out. Take a breath, start from the beginning, tell me what happened."

It was a shortened, panicky version, but I somehow managed to get the words out to tell her everything. I told her about the first few days together, about when I discovered his journal, about how I'd promised myself I wouldn't read it again after Vegas and then caved and did it, anyway. I told her everything that had happened, sparing no details, not even the ones I knew I should be ashamed of. I told her about his depression, about how it was getting better, or so I thought. And, with as much composure as I could muster, I told her about the last entry I read.

Just talking about it broke my heart all over again.

"I don't know what to do," I sobbed when there was nothing more to say. "He's gone, and I don't know where he's going or how to stop him. His phone is off. I can't..."

"Think," she interrupted me. "Think long and hard about the conversations you've had with him. Is there anything you might have missed, any clues?"

"There's nothing," I said desperately. "I've cranked through every moment, every conversation, every journal entry. All I know is it's somewhere in Washington. I thought maybe it was the bridge there in Seattle, the George Washington Memorial bridge, because it's known for suicides but it doesn't make sense. He said it was his

Grandma's favorite place in the world, it can't just be a bridge."

Tammy hummed on the other end of the phone, and I imagined her sitting on her front porch, one foot on the banister as she thought. It was her favorite place to think, our favorite place to be.

"Is there anyone you've met along the way who he might have trusted, someone he might have confided in?"

Emily was the first one to pop into my head, but I had no way to reach her, even if he had told her for some reason where it was he was going. We'd talked to a lot of people along the way, but Emery had barely told me anything about his grandmother — would he really tell a stranger?

Then it hit me.

"Oh my God."

"What?" Tammy asked quickly, hope in her voice as I jumped up from the bed.

"Nora and Glen. We met this older couple in Colorado. We camped with them. We got high with them."

"You what?" she asked, her voice a little more scolding this time.

"We were talking about lists, about places we wanted to go and things we wanted to do in our lives. But I don't remember..." I closed my eyes, pressing my fingers into my temples as I tried to sort through the fog. "Ugh, I don't remember! Everything is a blur."

"Well, you were high. Which we will have a long conversation about after all this is over, by the way," she said, her voice stern. "Can you get a hold of either of them? Do you have their numbers?"

I gasped. "I do! Oh my God, I can't believe I didn't think of this. I have to call Nora. I have to go."

"Wait!" Tammy screamed just before I could end the call. "Listen to me. Call her, and please let me know if you find anything, but *promise* me you will sleep before you try to go anywhere. I'm serious. Emery just left, it's dark, if he said he needs to *see* something, he's not going to do anything tonight. You can't drive the way you are right now."

"I have to get to him."

"I know you do, but promise me you'll be safe. I have your location, I'm going to arrange a rental car for you to pick up *in the morning*. Okay? I'll text you with the details."

I sighed, nodding in agreement even though my heart was set on leaving the second I figured out where he was going. I only prayed Nora would know. "Okay. Thank you, Tammy."

"I love you. It'll be okay," she promised, but I didn't believe her. Nothing would be okay until I saw him again, until I held him, until I made him see.

But would I get the chance?

It turned out my trip had to wait until morning, anyway, because Nora didn't answer my call. I left her a voicemail, begging her to call me as soon as she woke up, no matter what time. Sleep didn't come that night, but I laid in bed, tossing and turning and torturing myself with all the *what ifs*.

My phone rang at four-thirty in the morning, and I woke from the half-sleep stupor I'd fallen into, hands scrambling for my cell.

"Nora."

"Hi, sweetie. Where are you?"

"Portland," I answered, throat raw as I moved to sit up in bed. Kalo stirred beside me, her little eyes heavy. She always picked up on my emotions, and I knew I'd drowned her in anxiety that night.

"Oh my, it's so early there. I was going to wait until after we'd had coffee but your voicemail sounded urgent."

"It was, I'm glad you called. Is Glen there, too? Can you put me on speakerphone?"

There was a shuffling noise, their voices faint in the background as they tried to figure out how to turn it to speaker. I would have giggled if I wasn't so sick.

"Okay, you're on with both of us. Is everything okay?"

"No." My voice broke again, the weight of the situation heavy on my shoulders again. Time was running out. "Emery is gone. It's a long story, one I don't really have the time to tell right now, but I need your help."

"What can we do?" Glen asked, his voice gruff.

"The night we camped out in Colorado Springs, when we made our lists... do you remember anything Emery said about Washington? Did he mention where he was going, or anything about his grandmother?" I shook my head. "I know it sounds strange, but... he's in trouble... he's going to hurt himself, I think..." I shook with another roll of nausea. "I have to find him, but I don't know where he's going. You're my last hope."

There was a pause on the other end, my cracked voice hanging in the space between us.

"Oh sweetie," Nora said softly. "I'm trying to think... I don't recall him saying anything about a place in Washington that night."

300

My heart sank, the world falling down to the floor with it before bouncing back in a new, morphed reality. I heard my heartbeat loud in my ears, felt it kicking under my chest.

I couldn't find him.

It wasn't fair. It was cruel and sick and no matter how desperate I was, no matter how hard I tried to think, it was useless. He was gone, I didn't know where he'd gone, and all connection to him had disappeared right along with his taillights.

I covered my mouth with one hand, eyes squeezing shut.

*He's gone.*

"Okay, thank you," I whispered. "I'm sorry, I didn't mean to worry you, too."

"Palouse Falls."

Glen's voice was weary on the other end, his voice quiet, almost as if he wasn't sure if it was the right thing to say.

"When Emery and I hiked together the morning you two left, he asked me if I'd ever been to Palouse Falls. He never said that's where he was going, but... maybe that's the place. I don't want to get your hopes up, I can't say for sure, but he mentioned it."

"No," I said, swallowing down the panic that had risen moments before. "No, it's better than nothing. It's a clue, it's a start. It's *something*."

"I just don't want to break your heart even more if you go and he isn't there," Glen said. "I know it hurts, but you need to be ready to let him go, Cooper. If you make this drive, if you go to find him and he's not there, you need to be ready."

But I didn't hear him. I *couldn't* hear those words, those foreign sounds and syllables.

I'd never be ready to lose him.

Time was ticking again, mercilessly propelling me forward in a race I never signed up for. It would either throw me into a world without Emery or straight into his arms, and I had no choice but to go with it blindly — knowing both were a possibility, praying only the latter would come true.

It was a five hour drive to Palouse Falls, and though fear prickled at my nerves, a sense of calm washed over me as I loaded Kalo up into the taxi that would take us to pick up the rental car.

He was still alive.

I could feel him, his soul tethered to mine, stretching across the distance. That pull, that string pulled taut was my only comfort.

Time pushed again, hands firm on my back, and I realized then that it wasn't time I was racing at all — it was Death. It was knocking, bone fingers curling around the edges of the door, the wood creaking open as I closed my eyes and repeated one thought like a mantra.

*I will find him.*

*I will find him.*

*I will find him.*

I just hoped I'd find him first.

# Chapter 24

## Palouse Falls, Washington

I watched the morning stretch lazily across the sky in front of me as I drove, the sun rising in a steady glow that painted the sky orange before slowly fading into the softest blue. The gray skies and snowy ground was left behind me, and though the weather stayed cool, there was a ray of hope in that sunshine ahead of me.

It was a struggle until I got out of the snow, actually, because I'd never driven in those conditions before. Apparently, it didn't snow much in Portland, which meant the wonderland I'd seen was a rare one, and it also meant the streets weren't exactly in the best conditions in the early morning *after* the snow had fallen. I'd taken it slow and driven with both hands firmly on the wheel until the roads cleared, the snow on the sides of it growing thinner and thinner until none existed at all. Phantom pains racked my leg, zinging up my thigh, my entire body too tense to function.

Once I was in the clear, a numb awareness fell over me, almost like I blacked out. I hardly noticed anything as I drove, my body falling into the automation of driving while my mind tumbled over the thousands of thoughts I had that morning.

It was like a driving meditation, my focus falling inward, body assuming the responsibilities of the physical world while my mind tried to find peace inside. Glen was in my head, telling me to prepare for the worst — but which would that be? Would it be that I drive to Palouse Falls and Emery isn't there, or that I find him, but it's too late?

On the one hand, if I simply didn't find him, he could potentially be alive. But the worst part is I would never know either way. I would never hear from him again, alive or dead, and that pain of not knowing would haunt me.

But would it haunt me more than knowing with absolute certainty that he was gone from the Earth?

I didn't know.

So, instead of focusing on those possibilities, I rested my faith in my heart center, sending vibes into the universe that I would find him, safe and sound, and that he would listen. Those two things were all I wanted, they were my deepest desire, and I set them as my intention as the miles ticked on, my breathing calming, steadying.

It was after ten in the morning by the time I pulled into the park, the sign welcoming me to Palouse Falls with a simple wooden greeting. I paid my entrance, inquiring about camping, and the attendant gave me directions to find the designated areas. The calm I'd found on the drive over was more subdued now, my heart picking up speed as I drove through the different sites looking for signs of Emery.

Kalo was quiet beside me, her chin resting on her paws, sad eyes glancing at me every now and then before they found focus somewhere else in the car. I just rubbed behind her ear, trying to soothe her, to assure her everything was okay when I knew she knew better.

"I miss him, too," I told her, and she let out a long sigh, nudging into my hand before I pulled it back to the wheel. Then, my breath caught in my throat.

Emery's car was parked just ahead, right next to two tents and a Jeep I didn't recognize. The faint smell of eggs hit my nose as I parked next to his car, leashing Kalo and balancing on shaky legs as I neared the tent laid out in front of his convertible.

It was brand new, that much I could tell, and it was small — just enough for one person. The front of it was unzipped, and my heart hammered in my chest as one hand reached forward, pulling the flap open to peer inside.

Empty.

My stomach dropped as I took in the single sleeping bag, rumpled from a restless night, Emery's bag under the top half of it like a pillow. A pair of his briefs and sweatpants lay at the foot of the sleeping bag in a heap, and the backpack we'd purchased in Colorado for hiking was nowhere to be seen.

Neither was his journal.

I stepped inside the tent with Kalo, eyes scanning his belongings as Kalo sniffed around. Her tail was wagging softly, her optimism returning, though mine remained stunted.

"He left about an hour ago."

I jumped at the voice, hand flying to my heart as I spun on my heels and came face to face with a tall, broad-shouldered man. He was exotic, his wide blue eyes set ablaze next to his deep olive skin, dark hair pulled into a bun at the nape of his neck that almost blended with the thick beard lining his jaw. He was dressed and ready to hike for the day, his backpack already on his shoulders, boots tied up around his thick ankles.

He was watching me like he didn't trust me at first, like I was a thief or a murderer or perhaps something worse. But then his expression softened, his eyes taking in my appearance fully. I imagined what I looked like after a night of no sleep, after a long drive alone, worry creasing my skin like wrinkles.

"Did he say where he was going?"

"He didn't," he said, voice gruff and low. "But there are only a few trails around here, wouldn't be hard to find him, I imagine." The man watched me a moment, hand running over his beard before he tucked it in his pocket. "You're her, aren't you?"

I frowned at the question, shame and guilt coloring my face as I nodded. "You... you talked to him."

"A little," he answered with a shrug. "When he felt like talking, which wasn't much."

My eyes closed at the thought, of him opening up to this stranger. I wondered what he said about me, what he didn't say. I imagined him calling me all sorts of names, *liar* and *betrayer* being at the top of the list, but the calmness I'd gathered from the car ride over resurfaced, reminding me my deepest desire.

*I need to find him, and I need him to listen. That's all.*

The man's sigh brought me back to the present moment, his hands falling to his side as he bent down to the floor of the tent. Kalo ran right to him, and as he petted behind her ears, his eyes found mine.

"When he did talk, it was about you, but it was what he *didn't* say that spoke the loudest. Something tells me he convinced himself he didn't want to be found, but his mannerisms betrayed him. His eyes always watching the road, ears perking up at every car that drove by..." He paused, rubbing Kalo's head. "Every dog that barked."

I swallowed, bending down to his level, one of my hands finding Kalo's soft fur, too, as I pleaded with him. "I need to find him. Please, can you help me?"

He was quiet, seemingly debating his role in our story before he stood. "There are three trails — one to a lower viewpoint of the falls, one to a secluded canyon, and the other to the top of the falls."

"The top," I croaked, voice thick with emotion as I planted a hand hard on my knee and pushed up to stand with him. I knew without a doubt that's where Emery was... or at least, it's where he'd gone. I just hoped he was still there. "How do I get there?"

The man gave me directions, telling me parking would be full and I should just leave my car where it was and hike up. It was a fairly easy hike, he said, and it wouldn't take me too long.

After finally telling me his name, Jeremy handed me a bottle of water and offered to watch Kalo until I returned, and though he was still watching me like he didn't trust me, it was as if he couldn't refrain from helping me, either.

"He's a good guy," he said, his eyes softening. "But he's in a dark place."

"I know."

He nodded. "I'm sure you do, or you wouldn't be here." His hand wrapped once around Kalo's leash, but then his eyes adjusted on something behind me, and he squinted, head tilting. "Is that his bag?"

I turned, all the heat drained from my face, from my limbs, settling into a pool at the pit of my stomach as my eyes found the backpack we'd purchased together in Colorado Springs. It was propped against a stump of wood that looked like it was used for a chair beside the fire, and a sheet of lined paper was rolled and tucked into the handle at the top of it.

Swallowing, I walked with lead feet to the bag, bending to retrieve it from where it rested. It was light, and I untucked the rolled paper first, throat thick at the sight of his handwriting.

*If found, please open.*

I unzipped it quickly, throat collapsing altogether at the sight inside.

Three folded sheets of paper, that's all that existed in that big, black empty space. My fingers numbly turned them over, one by one, eyes catching on the familiar script that outlined the outer edge of each. Each of them had an address scribbled under the name on the outside fold. One read *Dad*, one read *Mom*, and the final one, the one with the address for Papa Wyatt's Diner, read *Little Penny*.

Emotion stung my nose, eyes welling at the sensation as I sniffed against it and shoved the papers back inside, zipping up the bag and tossing it over my shoulders. I couldn't read that letter, *wouldn't* read it — because I knew inside those folded edges was a goodbye I wasn't ready to hear.

"Thank you," was all I could manage before I turned, surviving on what little hope I had left as my feet picked up speed to match my racing heart.

It was an easy hike up to the top of the falls. My leg still ached even with the easy incline, my muscles tense and sore from lack of sleep and the worry that had racked through me all night. The skin where my leg ended and my prosthetic began stung a little, the friction from the hike wearing on it. I needed to rest, but I couldn't — not yet.

I was thankful for the scarf and snow cap I'd purchased in Grants Pass, both of them doing what little they could to keep heat in as the wind picked up the higher I climbed. It swept in from the canyons all around, whipping my hair and striking my cheeks, but when I reached the top, it was eerily calm.

It would have been a breathtaking view, if I could have focused on anything other than the back of the man in front of me. I was distantly aware of the deep, earthy canyons, the rainbow that extended from the bottom of the falls, the ice that gathered at the edges of the earth and floated on the water below, constantly broken and moved by the powerful falls crashing. My breath warmed my nose as little puffs of white left my lips, a shiver breaking from neck to tailbone as emotion consumed me.

*I found him.*

He was a painting, a moment in time captured by an artist's hand as he stood there at the edge of the falls. The sky was blue and clear above him, whisps of white cloud slowly floating by, the wind dancing with his hair.

His back was tall and long, his shoulders broad, hands resting easily in the pockets of his athletic pants. I didn't want to speak for fear of interrupting such a perfect sight, but under the peaceful tranquility of the scenery, a storm raged on inside of him — and I wanted to be his shelter.

"Emery."

He didn't jump, didn't turn, didn't acknowledge that he'd heard me at all, though I knew he had. It was as if he expected me, or maybe as if he'd imagined me, like I was just a dream. I carefully moved forward, making sure each shoe gripped the slippery rock before I took the next step.

"Emery, you have every right to be angry with me. You should be furious, you should *hate* me," I said, voice trembling as I closed in, slowly, inch by inch. "I violated your privacy. I asked you to trust me and open up to me when I couldn't even be patient enough to wait for what I asked for. I don't have any excuses, not any that are good enough, at least. All I can tell you is that I'm sorry, that I never meant to hurt you, and that when I met you, before I even got in your car, I felt a connection to you that I've never felt before in my entire life. It was kismet, it was a soul awakening. It was the first day of my life."

I swallowed, still watching the muscles of his upper back as they ebbed and flowed with his breath.

"We've only spent weeks together, but it feels like a lifetime to me. It feels like every moment before you pulled into that diner parking lot was practice. I practiced breathing, practiced laughing, practiced existing in every moment on the way to you so that when you found me, I'd know how to live."

I was numb to my own words, to my own emotions as I spoke. I hoped I made sense. I hoped I was reaching him. I hoped he was listening, it was all I needed him to do.

"There's a reason you asked me to come with you, Emery. Your grandmother led you to that diner, and when you got there, you found me. You may not believe in the universe or God or fate or any of that, but I know you believed in your grandmother, in the way you connected with her. And maybe I'm reaching, maybe I'm reading too much into something I was never meant to be a part of at all, but that's not how I feel, Emery, and I know that's not how you feel, either."

He dropped his head, the only movement he'd given me since I'd first called his name, and I paused, afraid I'd pushed too far, come too close.

"You asked me that first day we met what made me happy," I reminded him. "And I couldn't answer. I *wasn't* happy. I was breathing, and that was all. But then I got in your car, and I took my first breath, and I *lived*. I saw things I'd never seen before, laughed harder than I knew I could, questioned things I'd believed my entire life and more than anything," I said, catching my breath. "I fell in love with you. I fell in love with every dark shadow, with every scar, every flaw, every smile and every scowl. Your journal had nothing to do with that. I fell in love with *you*."

I choked out a breath, shaking my head.

"And I know that sounds crazy," I admitted on a laugh. "It *is* crazy. I've only known you for weeks, such a small snapshot of a lifetime but it was enough. And I know you're tired," I conceded, the truth digging into my ribs. "I know you've been hurt, you've been misunderstood, you've been poked and prodded and judged. I know you've lived on the outside for so long, in a lonely corner of the world where you've learned to embrace the silence. You've lost and you've hurt, and you feel like you've failed your family and your friends and everyone you've ever touched because you can't give them the answers to why you feel the way you feel."

The water rushed furiously below us, churning up energy, my body buzzing to life from the electric feel of it.

"But whether you meant to or not, you let me into that corner, too. And now I'm here, and we're together, and it's not so dark and cold but if you leave... if you jump, I'll still be here. Please, Emery. Don't leave. Ask me what makes me happy now. Ask me. I'll tell you over and over and over again that it's you. It's *you*. You are loved, you are understood, and you are needed. I don't need you to explain why you feel the way you feel because I already know. I have never judged you, and I never will. Please," I begged again. "Stay. Stay with me. *Live* with me."

My voice was just a whisper at the end, the sound of it mixing with the rush of the water. I'd said all I could say, and yet it somehow didn't feel like enough. I was suspended in space, waiting, tethered to a man who could jump or pull me into him, and I didn't know which he'd do.

The water washing over the edge of the canyon was the only sound as Emery turned, his shoes slipping on the rocks a bit before he steadied himself. A piece of me broke inside when his tired, red eyes landed on mine, the irises glossy, corners edged with stress. He took one, small step toward me, nose flaring as his eyes watered more.

"I wasn't even mad," he said, his voice low and heavy and tinged with regret. "When I saw you reading my journal, I wasn't even mad — I was ashamed. I was embarrassed, like I was standing naked in front of a crowd of strangers. Except it was just you, and you weren't laughing." He was shaking, every inch of him from shoulders to ankles. "I knew you understood, I knew you loved me, and that scared me more than if you'd pointed and laughed and run away."

I chewed my bottom lip, eyes welling with his.

"This was always the plan," he said, exasperated, his hand gesturing to the waterfall behind him before it slapped his thigh in defeat. "I was so sure. I knew peace waited for me here, that I'd finally feel okay, that I'd finally be able to let go. This was supposed to be easy," he choked. "And it is. It's the easiest choice. I can jump, right now, and free fall into nothing. I can choose to never wake up to another bad day, or fight to fall asleep with my thoughts haunting me at night, or look into the eyes of everyone I've disappointed and have no words of reassurance to offer them. I can choose that, right now."

A sob broke through me and I shook my head violently, a whispered *no* unheard under my breath. But then Emery closed the distance between us, his hands flattening against either side of my face, thumbs wiping away the tears.

"Living is hard, it's the more difficult choice, but I can't *not* choose it," he said, his golden eyes sweeping over mine. "My grandmother told me if I took this trip and didn't find anything that made me feel alive, I could join her, I could choose to leave this world and she would understand. But I *can't*," he said, brows bending inward as he leveled his eyes with mine. "Because I found you."

I squeezed my eyes shut, a rush of hot tears staining my cheeks. It was too much, the overwhelming storm of emotions I felt in that moment, and when I opened my eyes again and found his, my hands crawled up his waist, gripping his sweater and pulling him into me like he was my first breath. I needed him that much, as much as I needed to breathe, and he was here.

He was alive.

His hands tilted my face up, his lips crashing into mine like he hated me and loved me all at once, like I'd saved him and executed him at the same time. His fingers twisted into my hair, fisting, his mouth consuming every breath I let go on top of that canyon. He bruised my lips and still I begged for more. I wanted all of him, every burning breath, every tortured touch, every whispered curse. The good, the bad, the unthinkable. I wanted all of it, and I took it with that kiss.

"I'm so sorry, I'm sorry, I'm sorry," I cried against his lips, but he just kissed me with more intention, shaking his head.

"I'm here," he answered, and I cried harder, gripping him like he would fall at any moment, like touching him was the only way to keep him with me.

I didn't have any other words, not after all I'd said. "I'm sorry," I repeated, the three syllables weak and not enough.

"Look at me," he said, pulling back and lifting my chin. "Even before you got here, I knew. I watched the sun rise over these canyons and I knew it wasn't the sun rising on

my last day, because I wanted more sun rises. With you."
His eyes glistened, his irises searching mine. "I wasn't
going to jump, I wasn't going to leave you. I'm sorry I
ever made you feel like I could." Emery kissed me softer,
thumb tracing my lips when his own were gone. "You're
stuck with me now."

Something between a laugh and a sob left my lips and
he kissed me again, sealing that promise with heat, his
arms wrapping all the way around me. The water rushed
just as furiously, but I no longer feared it, no longer heard
it as the treacherous siren of finality. Instead, it filled me
in a slow, steady stream, washing me clean, and I pulled
Emery closer, hoping the waves would reach him, too.

It was like every moment between us existed at the
top of that waterfall, the memories sweeping in from the
canyons and up from the water below. I closed my eyes
and saw his wide smile in the driver seat, his hair blowing
back. I inhaled a breath and smelled the beached kelp
below Esalen, the way it mixed with Emery's natural
scent. When his hands gripped my waist, I saw my hips
bare for the first time under his palms, felt him moving
between my thighs with gentle care, like it was a privilege
and a responsibility both. I heard his laugh, his moans, his
desperate pleas for understanding — and I answered them
with a kiss, opening my eyes to take him in.

His thumbs brushed my jaw, eyes searching mine, and
in that moment, we were alive. We were a boy and a girl,
seemingly so opposite yet more alike than we even knew,
standing together at the end of a journey neither of us ever
saw coming, an adventure we never could have prepared
for.

Except it wasn't the end at all.

It was the first letter, the first word, the first sentence with no punctuation mark in sight. It was a beautiful, messy beginning, an honest truth written in script, in a handwriting with loops and curves only we could decipher.

It was real. It was painful. It was healing.

And most of all, it was ours.

**The End**

C ooper bought me a new journal.

I ran out of space in my first one, the one Grams got me, about two weeks ago. It didn't feel right to get a new one, so I just wrote on blank sleeves of paper and shoved them between the pages of the one already filled. I was perfectly content with that process, but I think the mess of it drove Cooper mad, and so here it is, my new journal.

It's kind of fitting, actually, that today would be the day I write my first entry. One year ago on this day, I was pulling into a small diner in Mobile, Alabama, thinking all I'd be leaving with was a full stomach of steak and eggs.

But I left with her.

One year. One year of time, of places seen and moments lived. Three-hundred and sixty-five mornings waking up next to her. Thousands of minutes and seconds discovering more of who she is, who she was, who we both are now — together.

Looking back on the man I was when I met her is like trying to remember a dream that fled in the morning light. When I was him, he was crystal clear. I understood him. I knew how he worked. Now, he seems pixelated and dark, the memory of him unclear, the man I've become nowhere near the one who once existed.

It feels different, writing in this journal instead of the one Grams gave me. I still remember my first entry, how I didn't want to write at all, didn't want to feel, to think, to explain. But Cooper has opened me up. With her, the nights haven't been so dark, and neither have my thoughts.

With her, I've found purpose.

And a dog, but that was just a bonus.

It wasn't an easy journey, especially starting where we did. I still remember our first month in Seattle together, stumbling through, neither of us knowing how to walk yet but holding tight to each other for balance, anyway. We took each day as it came, enrolling Cooper in school, finding a place to live, and, though I was reluctant, finding me a new therapist, and a new medication — one that didn't make me feel like a zombie. One that helped.

There are still bad days.

But there are less of them now.

About two months into our new reality, I started doing yoga with Cooper. Every morning, sometimes again in the evening, and when she got busier with school, I did it on my own.

And then I studied it.

And meditated.

And before I knew it, I was teaching, running my own class at the studio around the corner from our apartment with a focus on overcoming depression and anxiety. It started with just me and Cooper, but it's grown over time, and now, I meet with anywhere from twenty to *fifty students each week. Even if it's just for that hour that we're on our mats, I know they don't feel so alone.*

*Purpose.*

*When I met Cooper, I thought yoga was bullshit. In all fairness, I thought everything was bullshit. She tells me all the time that I opened her eyes to a new world, to new beliefs, but she did the same for me.*

*Now, I think yoga centers me. Meditation helps quiet my mind. I may not look to the universe for answers the way Cooper does, but I believe now. I believe in the power of being quiet, of being still, of addressing my thoughts instead of hiding from them.*

*And I believe in her, in that girl with the glasses too big for her face, and the way she loves me — completely, with everything that she is, without a single fear of being hurt.*

*Last night, Cooper was studying at our dining room table. It's this small, banged-up thing we picked up from a garage sale when we first moved here. It's nothing special, doesn't match a damn thing either, but I love that table because it's where we eat our breakfast and drink our coffee. It's where we fight and where we makeup, too. It's where she cried the day she found out her mother passed away, and where I held her in my arms, vowing to put the pieces of her broken heart back together again.*

*But last night, sitting at that table, she was just studying. Her hair was in the most tangled braid I've ever seen, hanging over her left shoulder, her pencil eraser chewed down to the metal as she flipped through her textbook and notecards. Her glasses had slipped down the bridge of her nose, her eyes dark and tired above where they rested, and Kalo hadn't left the cozy spot at her feet all night.*

*She was on her third cup of coffee when she spilled a bit of it, droplets splattering the pages of her textbook as she cursed under her breath. And one of those droplets hit her scarf, too — the blue one, the same one she'd worn the night we walked through Grants Pass. It landed right next to the other stain, worn and faded now, almost invisible. But I knew it was there.*

*Cooper wiped at the new mess, frustrated almost to the point of tears, until it hit her.*

*Then, she just looked at me, and I knew her thoughts without her speaking them.*

*And just like the night that first stain was made, I kissed her. It was all I could do. I couldn't not kiss her.*

*One year.*

*Every day of it filled with moments like that, with the two of us holding onto each other for dear life, trying to figure everything out together. A year of discovery, of laughter, and, though the me who existed this time last year would have sworn it wasn't possible, a year of love, too.*

*There's a ring in the drawer next to my side of the bed, buried under my socks, pushed to the far back corner so Cooper doesn't find it. She doesn't know I have it, doesn't know I bought it over the summer, that it's been burning a hole in that drawer ever since. I wanted to give it to her that very night, wanted to drop to my knees in front of our couch where we were watching some stupid movie that neither of us really cared about.*

*But with Cooper, everything needs to be magical — most of all this.*

*I may not be Prince Charming, and what we have is far from a fairytale, but I promised myself that day we walked down the hike from Palouse Falls that I would spend every day of my fucking life working to become the man who deserved her, the man she'd dreamed of, the man I wanted to be.*

*Last night, when I'd finished kissing her breathless, when the new stains on her scarf had dried as one with the other, Cooper asked me what made me happy. My answer was honest and sure.*

*Living, and you.*

*Cooper, if you're reading this, which I'm sure you are, since I'm going to press it face down on our table with a note that says READ THE FIRST ENTRY — YES, I ACTUALLY WANT YOU TO READ IT, then meet me at Pier 57 at the wheel.*

*Because I want you, Cooper. For now. Forever. And though my journal did a great job of telling you how I felt about you one year ago, of giving you the words I couldn't say out loud, it can't do justice for what I feel for you now.*

*This, I have to tell you in person.*

*See you soon, Little Penny.*

*Drive fast.*

# A Note from the Author

I'll start this by saying that, like Emery, I've stared at this blinking cursor for far too long now trying to figure out the right words to say. I've decided the "right words" don't really exist, not for this, so I'm just going to write honestly and from the heart. I hope it's enough.

For some of you, this book will just be another one to add to the shelf of those you've read. The "past" shelf. It will sit with you for only a moment, for the hours you read it, and then it will exist only in a memory and on that shelf of things already experienced.

But, for others, this one will hit home. Some of you will read Emery's story, his thoughts in the pages of his journal, and you'll understand. Some of you will identify with how he feels, and maybe some of you will look at those pages and wonder if that was the way one of your loved ones felt when they were facing their own demons.

This note is for you.

I have fought battles with depression and anxiety — not just my own, but those of close friends and family members, too. I know too well how alone you can feel when you're in the depths of it, when the shadows are so dark they feel like an all-encompassing night. I know how it feels to not find sleep, to fake a happiness that doesn't actually exist.

But, I know what it feels like to be *truly* happy, too.

I know what it feels like to overcome those dark thoughts and feelings, through the help of my friends and family and other resources, and walk on the other side of that foggy existence. There were times when I couldn't see the light, when I didn't think a brighter day existed, but it does.

So, I guess the biggest thing I want you to take from this is that you are not alone — and you will be okay, even if it doesn't feel like it right now.

I think one misconception is that depression only exists for people who have been through a devastating event, or that it's something to be ashamed of, something you have to almost... earn? To be able to say you battle with it. It's a difficult concept to understand, made even more impossible for those who haven't been touched by it personally. How can someone just not get out of bed? How can doing a task as simple as driving to the store to pick up milk be *that* daunting?

The truth is, depression isn't a one-size-fits all. It comes in so many shapes, fits us all in unique ways, and we each feel differently when we're under the veils of it. Sometimes we're okay, sometimes we're not, and the truth of the matter is that in both times — we are human.

There is no easy answer to any of the questions we have when we're right in the middle of our "bad days," but there are people around us. There are friends and family members who love us and want to listen. And if you're in a place where you feel like that's not the case, then I want to share the following with you.

If you want to talk, 1-800-273-8255. Call this number for free and confidential support from the National Suicide Prevention Hotline.

Don't want to talk? Maybe you're like Emery and would rather write, instead. If so, you can text 741741 to be connected to the Crisis Text Line. One of my beta readers tested this to make sure it was legit, and they were immediately connected to a real person.

And, if you don't even want to be connected to another human, maybe you can try answering Emery's question — *what makes you happy?* You don't have to tell anyone, just make a list, short or long, on paper or just in your head, of little or big things that bring you joy in this moment, on this day.

I know these resources are already out there for you to find. Me sharing them with you isn't anything groundbreaking or new. But, if you connected with this story, with these characters, then that means you also connected with me — the writer behind the story. So, from me to you, I care about you — every single one of you — and you are not alone.

Remember when I said I had no idea what to write? Well, it's still true as I wrap up this thought. I'm not an expert, and I don't have all the answers. But I am a human, and I do understand, and I do *truly* wish the best for you in your life, and all the happiness you can possibly experience.

Again, thank you for reading my book, for continuing on long enough to read this note, too. I hope as you file this book away on the "read" shelf, you take a piece of it with you and hold it close to your heart, as I hold all of you close to mine.

# Acknowledgements

I'm starting to get to a point in my career where I can't truly thank everyone I really want to, like all of you — the readers — who I wish I could list by name in here to truly express how grateful I am for you. I mean, seriously, there are MILLIONS of books, hundreds of new ones being published each and every day, and you still picked mine. I am honored, truly, beyond words. Thank you for reading my work.

The first name I do have to list in this one is Sasha Whittington, my very best friend. This one was a doozy, wasn't it? Thank you for opening up to me about your own struggles and for loving me through the hardest parts of this story. You helped me to remain honest, critiqued me when I needed it most, and more than anything, cheered me on when I felt like I couldn't do it anymore. I love you with all my heart, and I know this book wouldn't be what it is without you. Thank you.

Staci Hart might as well be a permanent embossed name in the back of all my books, because there hasn't been a single one she hasn't been a part of since we met. Staci, thank you for being there for me on the hard days, the days when the words wouldn't come and I wanted to give up. You always push me, challenge me to be a better writer, and without you, my words wouldn't shine the way they do. This is my favorite book I've written to date, and you helped make it what it is. Thank you. I love you. MTT.

To Brittainy C. Cherry, thank you for being my person. There is no one in the world who gets me more than you do, who understand the ups and downs of a girl who "feels too much." Although I'm thankful for the role you played in helping me write this story, I'm even more grateful for the universe helping us find each other, because I'm not sure how I survived before our friendship existed. Don't ever leave me.

As always, I have to thank my momma, LaVon Allen. Without your constant love and support, I wouldn't be the woman I am today, and I definitely wouldn't have had the lady balls to quit my full-time job to pursue my dream of writing. I needed all my time and energy to fully dedicate to this work, so thank you for showing me that though taking risks can be scary, it's always worth it.

My beta team was CLUTCH this time around, so I have to give a huge shout out to all of them. There were many changes made from the first draft of this gem, and you all gave me the tough love I needed to make it the best story it could be. Kellee Fabre, Monique Boone, Sarah Green, Kathryn Andrews, Danielle Lagasse, Becca Hensley Mysoor, Ashlei Davison, Tina Lynne, Trish QUEEN MINTNESS, and Sahar Bagheri — stop being so awesome. Just kidding, don't ever stop. I love you. THANK YOU.

Elaine York, thank you for your understanding when I pushed back the date I gave you the final manuscript... twice. You understood more than anyone that this particular baby needed more of my time and attention, and you worked your ass off to still adhere to my deadlines even though I asked yours to be flexible. I couldn't do this without you.

I would also like to thank Flavia Viotti, my incredible agent, for having the same hustle and drive that I do. I appreciate our relationship more than I can say, and I know we're just getting started. The future is bright. ;)

To the magical Lauren Perry of Periwinkle Photography, thank you for yet another stunning photoshoot that made this cover my favorite of all. The feels you captured, the lighting, the STORY — it was more than I could ever ask for. I'm so thankful to have your talent in collaboration with my work, and more than that, to call you a friend. I love you.

I also want to thank Angie McKeon, my little bumblebee, who supports me throughout the ups and downs of not only release months, but all the other months in-between. Thank GOD the book world brought us together. I don't know what I did before I heard your laugh or talked with you for hours on messenger. You are an amazing friend, and I'm glad to have you.

Nina Ginstead and the entire team at Social Butterfly PR, thank you for promoting *On the Way to You* with as much passion as I did. You treat me like a part of the family, and I'm thankful to have you on my team, too.

Last, but never least, thank you to my safe place — Kandiland. A group that started with just me and one other person has grown to almost two thousand members, and yet it still feels just as cozy as the first day. There is no place that can make me smile the way you guys do, and I honestly, TRUTHFULLY, could not do this without your constant love and encouragement. You're the reason I keep going on the hard days. I love you all so much. And a special shout out to Jessica McBee, who keeps the wheels turning in Kandiland when I disappear into the writing cave. You da bomb dot com, baby girl.

Oh, and to Pocket, whose aggressive meowing helped motivate me to write long into the night. Meow meow, purr purr, yes, I'll get you an ice cube.

# More from Kandi Steiner

## A Love Letter to Whiskey
An angsty, emotional romance between two lovers fighting the curse of bad timing.

## Weightless
Young Natalie finds self-love and romance with her personal trainer, along with a slew of secrets that tie them together in ways she never thought possible.

## Revelry
Recently divorced, Wren searches for clarity in a summer cabin outside of Seattle, where she makes an unforgettable connection with the broody, small town recluse next door.

## Black Number Four
A college, Greek-life romance of a hot young poker star and the boy sent to take her down.

### *The Palm South University Serial*
Written like your favorite drama television show, PSU has been called "a mix of Greek meets Gossip Girl with a dash of Friends." Follow six college students as they maneuver the heartbreaks and triumphs of love, life, and friendship.

## PSU Season 1
## PSU Season 2
## PSU Season 3

*The Chaser Series*

## Tag Chaser

She made a bet that she could stop chasing military men, which seemed easy — until her knight in shining armor and latest client at work showed up in Army ACUs.

## Song Chaser

Tanner and Kellee are perfect for each other. They frequent the same bars, love the same music, and have the same desire to rip each other's clothes off. Only problem? Tanner is still in love with his best friend.

## Straight, No Chaser
## Tag Catcher

A bachelor party gone wrong and a "meet the parents" nightmare. Two short stories bringing you more shenanigans from the characters you fell in love with in Tag Chaser and Song Chaser.

# About the Author

Kandi Steiner is a bestselling author and whiskey connoisseur living in Tampa, FL. Best known for writing "emotional rollercoaster" stories, she loves bringing flawed characters to life and writing about real, raw romance — in all its forms. No two Kandi Steiner books are the same, and if you're a lover of angsty, emotional, and inspirational reads, she's your gal.

An alumna of the University of Central Florida, Kandi graduated with a double major in Creative Writing and Advertising/PR with a minor in Women's Studies. She started writing back in the 4th grade after reading the first Harry Potter installment. In 6th grade, she wrote and edited her own newspaper and distributed to her classmates. Eventually, the principal caught on and the newspaper was quickly halted, though Kandi tried fighting for her "freedom of press." She took particular interest in writing romance after college, as she has always been a die hard hopeless romantic, and likes to highlight all the challenges of love as well as the triumphs.

When Kandi isn't writing, you can find her reading books of all kinds, talking with her extremely vocal cat, and spending time with her friends and family. She enjoys live music, traveling, anything heavy in carbs, beach days, movie marathons, craft beer and sweet wine — not necessarily in that order.

CONNECT WITH KANDI:

→ NEWSLETTER: bit.ly/NewsletterKS
→ FACEBOOK: facebook.com/kandisteiner
→ FACEBOOK READER GROUP (Kandiland):
facebook.com/groups/kandischasers
→ INSTAGRAM: Instagram.com/kandisteiner
→ TWITTER: twitter.com/kandisteiner
→ PINTEREST: pinterest.com/kandicoffman
→ WEBSITE: www.kandisteiner.com

Kandi Steiner may be coming to a city near you! Check out her "events" tab to see all the signings she's attending in the near future:

→ www.kandisteiner.com/events

Manufactured by Amazon.ca
Bolton, ON